REVENGE

OF A NOT-SO-PRETTY GIRL

REVENGE
OF A NOT-SO-PRETTY GIRL

....

Carolita Blythe

Delacorte Press

Text copyright © 2013 by Carolita Blythe
Jacket art copyright © 2013 by {Erykah's PhotoGraphy}

Visit us on the Web! randomhouse.com/kids
Educators and librarians, for a variety of teaching tools,
visit us at RHTeachersLibrarians.com

Library of Congress Cataloging-in-Publication Data
Blythe, Carolita.
    Revenge of a not-so-pretty girl / Carolita Blythe. — 1st ed.
        p. cm.
    Summary: Fourteen-year-old Faye, an African American living in 1984 Brooklyn, New York, copes with her mother's abuse by stealing with her friends, but when robbing an elderly woman almost turns to murder, she gains an opportunity to learn new truths about life.
    ISBN 978-0-385-74286-3 (hc) — ISBN 978-0-307-97845-5 (ebook)
ISBN 978-0-375-99081-6 (glb)
    [1. Mothers and daughters—Fiction. 2. Conduct of life—Fiction. 3. Old age—Fiction. 4. Family problems—Fiction. 5. African Americans—Fiction. 6. Catholic schools—Fiction. 7. Schools—Fiction. 8. Brooklyn (New York, N.Y.)—Fiction.] I. Title.
    PZ7.B6278Rev 2013
    [Fic]—dc23
    2012012735

The text of this book is set in 10-point Lino Letter.
Book design by Sarah Hoy

Printed in the United States of America
10 9 8 7 6 5 4 3 2 1

First Edition

For Orville Fraser Blythe

REVENGE

OF A NOT-SO-PRETTY GIRL

I've gotta admit, I'm not all that enthusiastic when my turn on lookout duty comes around again. It's making me start to rethink just how badly I really want to come across this supposed movie actress. The stairwell Caroline and I have been tucked away in is one long hallway and a massive lobby from the front of the building, but I can clearly hear the bitterness in the wind. That thing is howling and hissing and undoubtedly trying to warn me against going outside. Even though spring started three weeks ago, it still feels like we're in the middle of winter. But Caroline's shooting me this "What the hell are you waiting for?" look, so I slowly remove myself from the warmth of our little hiding place and start down the hall. I'm making it a point to take my time, dragging my feet along the shiny marble floor with its pretty diamond design, looking around at all the fancy light fixtures on the walls and the tiny chandeliers hanging from the ceiling, taking in how large all the doors to the apartments are and how solid and real the wood appears to be.

It's funny to think that my building is only about seven blocks away. It might as well be in another galaxy. I think we have fluorescent lights in our hallways, and half the time they're either flickering or completely out. And if I had to take a stab at what our lobby floor was made of, I'd say painted-over cement. But I guess that's how it goes in Brooklyn. You get off at the Parkside Avenue subway stop and turn left, you end up landing on pretty average. That's the direction the people who look most like me head in—the people with brown skin and the people wearing workers' uniforms. The white people who come out of that station always seem to turn right and head in this direction, where there are all these fancy buildings overlooking Prospect Park.

I'm at the edge of the lobby when Gillian suddenly comes flying into view, her eyes wide, her long, bony face smashed up against the glass of the outer lobby doors. I can't tell whether she's mistakenly pushing at the handles, which she should be pulling if she's trying to open the doors, or whether she's being pinned there against her will by the sudden hurricane-force April winds. Based on her look of torture, I'm thinking that, more than likely, she's being wind-pummeled. It's not like she's able to put up much resistance against the elements, considering how skinny she is. I mean, she actually makes me feel like a normal-sized human being. And I've seen the most up-to-date height and weight charts for 1984. I'm nowhere near the average for a fourteen-year-old city-dwelling female.

"Faye, she's coming!" Gillian yells as I rush through the inner set of doors, which immediately close behind me, and into the vestibule to try and help her. But even though Gillian has hardly any meat on her bones, I don't have enough strength to combat both the wind and her motionless body, and I can only get the door open about eight inches. Still, Gillian manages to squeeze a scrawny arm and leg through before getting stuck.

I turn back and glance over at Caroline, who's probably the same weight as me and Gillian combined. It's pretty funny that Caroline and Gillian are cousins, considering that one of them is so round and the other so straight. They kind of resemble the number 10 when they stand side by side. Caroline's still comfortably situated in the stairwell, pulling some of the jawbreakers she told me she'd run out of from her pocket and dropping them into her mouth. I start waving furiously at her and finally get her to notice me.

"The lady's coming," I mouth a few times instead of yelling, since I don't want to risk attracting the neighbors' attention. "And we need help."

Caroline finally heaves herself off the steps.

"What the hell are you two doing?" she grumbles once she reaches us. Only, her mouth is kind of full, so it doesn't come out very clearly. But I guess I would have asked the same thing, with Gillian being all contorted and me trying to yank her inside with one hand and keep the door open with the other.

Some stuck-up girl wearing a fresh-looking sheepskin

jacket passes by, glances our way, and whispers something to her friend and giggles.

"You better mind your own business!" Caroline yells after them as she pulls the door open wide enough for Gillian to slip through. Then she looks at me. "So, where's the movie star?" Caroline gets out before a fit of coughing overtakes her. Her already hyperthyroid eyes bulge out a little more, and she starts pointing to her throat and wheezing, so I ball my hand into a fist and punch her in the back, square between the shoulder blades.

"You shouldn't put so much candy in your mouth at one time," Gillian says.

"Yeah, especially candy you claimed you ran out of," I add.

"Both of you, shut up," Caroline responds. "And why'd you have to punch so hard, Faye? Next time you do that, I'm punching you back."

Great, I think. Next time I save you from choking to death on the fistful of sweets you shoved down your throat, don't thank me, assault me.

"As I was saying, where is she?" Caroline asks with some attitude.

"Just down at the corner," Gillian answers. "Only, the wind got hold of her little 'Ho ho ho, Green Giant' hat, and this man had to run it down for her. I gotta tell you, though, she doesn't look like a movie star to me."

"And how many movie stars have you seen in your life?" Caroline asks.

"Plenty. Diana Ross, Marilyn Monroe—"

"I'm not talking about on TV or at the movies, retarded human being," Caroline snaps. "I'm talking about in real life."

Gillian opens her mouth to answer, but Caroline puts her palm to Gillian's face and Gillian's lips snap shut.

"Look," Caroline continues, "she hasn't been a movie star for a thousand years now, so don't go expecting some glamour-puss. Anyway, remember the plan. Just act like you're looking for an apartment number. She'll probably try to help us out. Then just follow my lead."

I turn to face the intercom, where apartment numbers are typed out next to the last names and first initials of the tenants, but I'm not so focused on that. I'm peeping out the corner of my eye, waiting for a glimpse of the movie star. It'll be my first sighting ever, which is pretty exciting. She might not be famous anymore, but it's not every day you come across a Hollywood actress in Brooklyn.

In my peripheral vision, I catch a blur of green whizzing on by, but I can't tell whether it's human, plant, or animal. A few seconds later, I see that green blur return. With great effort, it attempts to climb the stairs leading to the vestibule where we stand. I notice Caroline and Gillian peeking too, but no one does anything. Finally, I move toward the front door.

"Faye, what are you doing?" Caroline screeches.

"Look at it outside. If we don't help her, she just might not make it in here."

This seems to register with Caroline, and she rushes over to me. Actually, let me qualify that. For most normal people, her movement would be considered a lazy stroll, but for Caroline, it's actually a bit of a jog. Anyway, she gets to the door and pushes it open. Gillian and I go out and flank the lady and help her in.

"Oh, thank you," she says, sounding as if she has just crossed the finish line at the New York City Marathon.

All I can think is, Damn, this woman is old. We're talking Roman Colosseum, *The Autobiography of Miss Jane Pittman* old. Like, when did she make movies, in ancient Egyptian times? And she's so tiny. Then I detect a slight hump on her back, which makes it seem like she has a candy cane for a spine. And her hair's all wispy and white and blown about, like a big ball of cotton candy someone forgot to add the pink coloring to. Her powder-white skin is wrinkly and spotted—kind of reptilian. And her green wool coat looks about four sizes too big.

I move so that I'm standing behind her, and I find myself looking down at her feet—at these little ankle boots she has her gray pants tucked into. And I'm thinking, Not only does this woman look like she was never in a film, she doesn't even look like she could afford to live in this hoity-toity building. In fact, she looks as if she might be homeless.

"So, who are you girls looking for?" she asks as she takes her keys out of her little brown pocketbook and opens up the second set of lobby doors. Her voice is small and faint.

"Um. Cheryl. On the third floor," Caroline says.

Gillian and I exchange looks. Caroline does have a friend who lives in the building—the same friend who happened to tell Caroline about this old lady once being a movie star—but that girl's name is Janet, and she lives on the fifth floor.

"I don't know a Cheryl. She's a young girl like you all? What's her last name? Maybe I know her family."

"Oh, I don't even know. She goes to my school. I know where her apartment is, but I can't remember the number," Caroline says.

I gotta admit, I've always been in awe of how quickly Caroline can come up with things. It's a true art.

"Well, come on in," the old woman says once the door is open. She holds it out to us with one hand as she grabs her grocery bag with the other.

Caroline doesn't move at first, and I can tell she's nervous. And Caroline's never nervous. The old lady turns toward her, and Caroline steps forward and kind of wrenches the bag from the old lady.

"I can carry it for you," Caroline says. "Where do you live?"

It takes the lady a few seconds to respond, as if she's thinking over whether to answer Caroline or not.

"End of the hall, near the stairs," she finally says. "That's very nice of you to help."

Caroline's gotta be the gutsiest person I've ever known. I watch as she walks alongside the old woman, whose little boots squeak against the lobby's marble floors. They pass a big fake fireplace with a mantel that must be eight feet high, then continue down the hall we just came from. Gillian and I follow a few feet behind them but stop once we reach the elevator. That was the plan. Hang back at the edge of the lobby and wait for Caroline to make her way into the old lady's apartment. Once she's had a chance to check things out, she'll signal us. So I just stand there, looking up once more at the tiny glass chandeliers. With any luck, this will all go very quickly.

2

The old lady's door opens and she disappears inside.
Then Caroline disappears. And now there's an empty hallway, quiet except for the racket being caused by the wind.

I'm pretty sure only a few seconds pass before Caroline
sticks her hand out the door and starts waving it like she's
swatting at flies, but it feels like hours. Gillian and I just
look at each other; then we run down to the apartment.
The squeak of my sneakers against the floor sounds as loud
as a train coming to a quick stop on metal rails. Caroline
closes the door the minute we're in, and I see the old woman
propped up against the wall like a rickety wooden chair.
The groceries are all scattered on the floor, and Caroline's
got hold of the lady's pocketbook.

"What did you do?" I ask her as I stare at the old woman.

"Is she dead?" Gillian asks, her mouth slack, like she's
got no control over her jaw.

"She ain't dead!" Caroline yells in frustration. "How's she
gonna be dead if she's still halfway standing? And I didn't

do *anything.* Just pushed her so she'd move away from the door, and she went falling into the wall in slow motion, like the Bionic Woman or something."

I see the lady trying to straighten up, only it's taking way more energy and effort than it should. Her little old feet in her *Little House on the Prairie* ankle boots are slipping and sliding around.

We're standing in her hallway, and on the walls are three colorful paintings of three really depressed-looking people. But they look a bit cartoonlike. There's a bathroom to the right side of us and a really big kitchen straight ahead. There's a radiator in the hall—one of those long pole types that stretches from floor to ceiling. It spits and whistles a little. I can't tell if the apartment is really hot or if it's just my nerves. To the left is the living room.

Caroline walks over to the lady and stands in front of her. She's not a very good-looking girl from a straight-on angle, so I'm just imagining what she must look like if you have to look up at her, like the old lady has to from her bent position.

"Well, at least let's put her in a chair or something," I say as I look toward the kitchen.

As we move her down the hall, I start thinking of how fabulous this is going to be. According to Caroline's friend, this woman keeps all her money under her mattress and in the pockets of the clothes in her closets. Now, we're not planning on taking every penny of her savings. That would just be wrong. But even if we only score a thousand bucks each, we'll be set for a good long while. I mean, the only time I ever see anything in the way of an allowance is on the few occasions Daddy shows up after lucking out with some musical gigs. And then it's usually only ten or twenty bucks. Mama would never part with her hard-earned dollars. As she delights in telling me, she pays the rent, light bill, gas, and telephone. She works so I can have food in my belly and clothes on my back, so why the hell should she have to give me extra cash so I can flutter about at leisure, having the time of my life? Oh, and let's not forget her number-one philosophy—which she totally plagiarized: *The greatest gifts in life are free.*

Just to set the record straight, we don't normally go after the life savings of old, decrepit people. We're not completely heartless. We usually have more-deserving targets—pretty, stuck-up girls with loads of extra cash in their pockets. The type who are used to getting whatever they want, whenever they ask for it. The type who are so used to being called beautiful, the word doesn't even have meaning for them anymore. They come in all shades and sizes. And their clothes are always name-brand. Their moms would never think of getting them shoes from the value bin at the Kmart. But what really sets them apart is their foul attitude, which you can sniff out from a mile away. They have a way of looking down their perfect noses at anyone they feel is not worthy of sharing the air with them. They have a way of making us regular girls feel inferior for not winning the gene pool lottery. Torturing them is simply our way of getting a little revenge. Although, I do have to admit that recently it's kind of become more about how much money we can score. It's nice to be able to go to the movies, and to buy records and some cool T-shirts. But with the boatload of cash we'll be getting from this old movie star, we can go back to getting even with these girls first and earning a little extra money second. Heck, after today, it won't even matter if they don't have much cash on them. We'll be like the Brooklyn version of Robin Hood and his Merry Men. Only, instead of giving to the poor, we'll be giving power to the plain and non-outstanding.

Once we get to the kitchen, Caroline continues rummaging through the old lady's purse. She throws a pocket pack of Kleenex on the floor, then some mints. When she comes across a wallet, she pulls out six dollars. Gillian and I begin easing the old lady onto one of the chairs at the table in the center of the large room, but before we can get her down, Caroline is stuffing her giant mitts into the lady's coat pockets. Geez, couldn't she have had the decency to take the coat off first? If a person isn't being a jerk, they should be allowed to have some level of dignity during a mugging. Anyway, the only thing Caroline seems to find there are a couple of pennies. And I can sense her frustration as she undoes the bottom buttons on the old woman's coat and pats her down all NYPD-style.

"Tell us where you hide your money!" Caroline hollers as she throws the pocketbook on the floor. But the lady just shakes her head.

"Don't be acting like you don't got none. I mean, look at all the stuff you have in this place. Nice paintings on the walls, china in that cabinet over there. Tell us where you hide the money."

"What you took from my purse, that's all I have," the old lady says, hardly above a whisper. So Caroline just steps past her, walks out of the kitchen and to the doorway leading into the living room. She stands there surveying the scene for a few seconds, then turns to Gillian and tells her to look through everything in the kitchen. She tells me to hit the living room.

"And, Gillian, keep an eye on her," she says as she walks through the living room and into another hall that has one door on one side and two on the other.

The first thing I notice about the living room is all this big, fussy wooden furniture. Everything looks as if it weighs about four thousand pounds. There's this giant wall-unit thing that has these little pink chandeliers on either side. I can't figure out if it's ugly or not. And the couch is big and purple and plush. I'm thinking if I sit in it, I might just sink right on down to the floor and never make it back up.

"Fay, don't forget to look under those chair pillows!" Caroline yells.

I start with the couch. I tuck my hand behind the cushions, afraid my fingers might touch something fingers have no business touching. But then I realize how clean the place is. There's nothing there. There's nothing in the love seat either. I open the doors of the big wall-unit thing, and there are all these crystal liquor bottles, but no liquor in them. I close the doors. On the sides of the unit are little animal figurines and some pictures. There's a big black-and-white photo of some fancy-looking woman and man standing in front of a huge car. I pick it up. I'm thinking they're in California, 'cause there are palm trees behind them. And they're wearing old-time clothes and hats and look like something out of one of those old Abbott and Costello movies they put on WPIX on Sunday mornings. The woman is all glamorous, and I wonder if it's the old lady. The thing is, I never think of old people as being pretty or ugly. I just think of them as being old. But then you see pictures of them from when they were young, and it's like you're looking at a whole other person.

Caroline suddenly walks into the living room. She grabs the photograph from me and throws it onto the floor. But the glass doesn't break, on account of the carpet being so thick and fluffy.

"Why you out here looking at pictures? Come inside with me. We have to turn over the mattress in the bedroom."

We struggle trying to flip the thing over. And I'm starting to sweat, being all packed into my scarf and coat and hat like I am. We finally get the mattress off the box spring, but there's nothing there. There's nothing under the bed either.

I notice some of the chunky, antique-looking brooches and necklaces scattered across the floor.

"Maybe that stuff's worth something," I say.

"Maybe. But it'll be too much of a hassle to sell. And I don't want to risk some cop or somebody tracing it back to us."

She has a point. Cash is cleanest. So we start going through all the clothes in her closet, pulling them off hangers, checking the pockets, and tossing them onto a pile. What's weird is, even though she looks borderline homeless, the old woman has some really nice clothes. Maybe she just doesn't believe in wearing her good wardrobe in wintry conditions.

I go through all her button-down blouses quickly, since there's really nowhere on them to stash any money. The skirts take a little longer because she has like a million of them—tweed ones, wool, cotton—but most don't have pockets. Some have matching suit jackets, but those pockets are mostly empty. Every now and then I come across something and think it could be a wad of cash, but when I pull it out, it's only crumpled-up tissues or an old receipt.

We have to get a chair from the kitchen to reach the ten or so hatboxes stacked on the shelf at the top of the closet. But we don't find anything there either—except for big, flamboyant hats.

I follow Caroline into another room, which has a desk and chair and daybed. There's no money there either. And Caroline begins breathing all hard and looking all crazy. I'm thinking, Maybe she needs a slice of cake or something. Then I look down at my watch to see that it's nearly five-thirty. An hour and a half till Mama gets home, and I haven't even started dinner or washed the dishes I left in the sink this morning.

"Caroline, it's getting kinda late," I say. "I need to get—" But it's as if she doesn't even hear me.

"Gillian!" she yells. "You find anything in there?"

"Um, no," Gillian yells back, only her voice sounds

muffled. Caroline glances at me and walks out of the room. I follow behind her.

The old lady is where we left her, but her coat is now completely unbuttoned, and for the first time, I notice her patchwork quilt sweater and the giant flower brooch with a silver stem and different-colored petals clasped up near the collar. Then my eyes drift down to her hands, which are resting on her lap, and for some reason, this makes me a little sad. See, her fingers are Keebler-elf small and bowed. And there are so many brown spots, her hands don't even seem like they belong to a white person. My eyes make their way back up to her face, and she suddenly lifts her head and stares right at me. And there's a strange look in her pale green eyes. It kind of gives me the creeps, so I turn my back to her and face Gillian, who's standing near the counter, removing ginger snaps from a cookie jar.

"What the hell are you doing?" Caroline yells.

"I don't know. I couldn't find nothing. And all this looking around made me a little hungry. I didn't have lunch today at school, you know."

Caroline just glares at her for a while, then, as if she suddenly remembers the lady is still there, she turns and looks at her. And then she grabs the ginger snaps right out of Gillian's hand. She doesn't say a thing, just sits down across from the lady, laughs her weird forest-creature laugh, then stuffs the three cookies into her mouth, never taking her eyes off the old woman. She stares and she chews. She chews and she stares. There's just this weird silence that continues on forever. I hold my left arm up a little and point to the time with my right hand, but Caroline doesn't even glance my way. And so we stay like that—Gillian at the counter with the opened cookie jar next to her, Caroline sitting across from the lady at the table, and me standing right at the doorway thinking that Mama will be home in an hour and a half.

Then Caroline jumps up. I knew she couldn't sit quietly forever. She runs over to the counter, grabs another cookie, eats it, and throws the cookie jar against the white tiled floor. The crash startles the lady, and I hear this little gasp. Hell, it startles me. What startles me even more is Caroline wasting perfectly good food. There's another glass container on the counter—one that's see-through, and it has either sugar or salt in it. Caroline picks that one up too and throws *that* to the floor. Then she picks up one with oats in it and does the same. One after another, they go crashing to the floor. With each bang, the lady flinches, but she still doesn't move. Near the table, there's a china cabinet. Caroline opens it and takes out these pretty serving plates. I see the lady's eyes open wider. Caroline throws the first plate to the floor, then grabs the second one and brings it up high above her head. The old lady unsteadily pulls herself up and stands on her rickety legs.

"Please stop it. Please."

She shuffles over to the counter, which has this framed black-and-white photo on it. I've seen pictures on fridges and stuff, but never all nicely framed on a kitchen counter. It's another old-time photo, only not as glamorous as the one in the living room. At least, I don't think it is. It's so faded, it's difficult to clearly make out the images in it. But I can tell that there's a woman holding a baby. The old lady bypasses this and instead opens a drawer and pulls out a book, *The Joy of Cooking*. She flips through it, to a page where there are two crisp twenty-dollar bills, then does this about six more times.

Once the old lady is finished, Caroline grabs the book, turns it over, and begins shaking it so hard the cover separates from the spine. When she's finally convinced that there's no more money hidden away in it, she tosses the book onto the counter. She then snatches the bills from the old woman's bony fingers and begins to count out loud.

My eyes shift back to the faded photograph, and I absent-mindedly pick it up. But the old woman suddenly seems to gain some strength, because she lunges at me all Jack be nimble, Jack be quick–like and grabs for the picture.

"That's not yours," she says. She latches on to my wrist. And her hand is really cold and damp. And her fingers look like they belong on the grim reaper. It's just a stupid picture, so why's she getting so up in arms about it? I mean, she didn't act this way when Caroline was destroying her glass containers. So I pull my arm in, toward my chest. Only, she's still holding on. Two seconds before, she could hardly stand up, and now all of a sudden, she's like a member of the Super Friends with her Wonder Twin powers. So I gather all my strength and extend my arm, and she goes flying. I mean, it's as if I shot her out of a cannon. I hear this noise, and the rest of it happens like a slide show. You know, as if I'm slowly clicking on a View-Master.

There's the old lady's head against the edge of the table. There's the broken glass from the stuff Caroline flung to the floor. There's Gillian, with her jaw hanging loose and her mouth open wide. There's Caroline, looking equally dazed. And the slides all stop once the old lady crumples to the floor like a ton of bricks.

3

The seven-block walk from the old lady's apartment back to mine is like a weird dream. It's as if sight is the only one of my senses that's really registering. I can see leaves and pages of the *New York Post* blowing right past me, but I can't seem to hear the whistle of the wind or the rustle of the paper. I can see Gillian's lips moving a little, but I can't make out her words. A snowflake lands on my nose, but I don't wipe it off. I was so cold earlier in the afternoon, with the dampness of the weather cutting through my jeans, through my long johns, and chilling me to the bone, but I don't really feel the nip anymore. I don't really feel anything. I don't feel warm. I don't feel cold. As Prospect Park disappears behind us, people spill out from the Parkside Avenue subway station. I can see them fighting with flyaway scarves, trying to clear wind-blasted hair from their eyes. I see their lips moving too but still hear nothing. Cars roll down the street, but in this strange silence. Not even the Madonna look-alike in her black lace gloves and black leather jacket and black leggings is able to make much of an impression on me. As we turn onto Flatbush and pass the Jamaican bakery I always stop in front of to take in the strong, spicy scents, it's as if I'm congested. It's as if I was the one who conked my cranium against that table, and not the old woman.

I should have thought through the whole situation better. Messing with those stuck-up girls, the only thing you ever have to worry about is maybe a really spirited one connecting a fist to your jaw or something. But you can pretty much manhandle them to your heart's desire without any serious repercussions. Some might fuss or carry on a little, but they're like rubber bands; they just snap back into place. But you can't do that to some old woman. I see those commercials on TV. I know old people are always falling and cracking hips. I know how easily they can just keel over from a heart attack. That's what did away with my granddaddy on Mama's side. And that's what did away with my friend Keisha's grandfather. Why didn't I think about Keisha's grandfather before I decided to go through with this? He got mugged while waiting for the number 2 train down at Borough Hall and had a heart attack and died right there on the platform.

But just as suddenly as my senses went numb, they come rushing back after a swift and solid punch to the arm from Caroline.

"What's the idea?" I shout.

"We've been trying to get your attention for a minute now," Caroline bellows back. "Look. Up the street. It's her."

I look around, but no one stands out to me.

"The girl in the sheepskin," Caroline adds. "The one who laughed at us. She's getting ready to go into that building. Why don't we teach her a little something?"

Two hours ago, this would have been an appealing prospect. But now, I can't seem to wrap my mind around it.

"I gotta get home. My mother—" But before I can finish, Caroline is charging ahead, with Gillian close behind. So I just shrug and follow.

We reach the girl as she's turning onto the building's walkway. Caroline grabs hold of the girl's schoolbag, commanding her to let go, but the girl just ignores her. That's when Caroline's fist lands on the side of her head. But the girl still doesn't let go. Instead, she starts calling us jealous and ugly and tries to spit on us. I can't believe how arrogant she's being in the middle of getting her butt kicked. Why can't she just let this happen? All I want is for this horrible evening to be over.

"Just let go of the stupid bag!" I yell. But she keeps fighting back.

And then something comes over me and I rush at Caroline and the girl, throw every ounce of my little body at them, and tackle the girl to the ground. We land on a muddy area to the side of the walkway and I start smooshing her beautiful, stubborn, snooty face into the ground. I smoosh it and smoosh it until she stops struggling and starts crying. I smoosh it until her pretty yellow sheepskin jacket turns the brown of the mud.

"Wow, Faye, what's gotten into you?" Caroline asks as

she locates the wallet in the girl's schoolbag and fishes fifteen bucks out of it.

"I don't know," I say. And I really don't. "I just need to get home."

Caroline flashes this weird smile my way, then looks back over to the girl.

"Maybe next time you'll think twice before laughing at people," Caroline says, throwing the wallet at the girl and walking off.

I kind of lag behind Caroline and Gillian the rest of the way home. When I reach the walkway of my building, I mumble a quick good-bye and rush inside. In my apartment, I go into autopilot mode, trying not to think about what happened in that old woman's kitchen, trying not to think of that stupid girl in the sheepskin, trying to start dinner and make sure everything is in its place in the fifty-five minutes I have till Mama gets home.

When I hear the key turn in the lock, I quickly check the chicken stewing in the pot and turn off the front burner. Then I dab up the cooking oil that spilled onto the stove. I breathe a sigh of relief. Finished just in time. I glance around the rest of the kitchen. Every dish and utensil has been washed and stacked in the dish rack. And the orange plaid dish towel is folded in two like Mama likes it, and laid neatly on the side of the sink. I cut it way too close today.

I sit at the table, where my schoolbooks are opened to my homework, and scribble *April 11, 1984,* so the page doesn't look so gleaming white and empty. And then I take a few breaths. I swear I can hear my own heartbeat. And my temples are throbbing like crazy. My pulse must be coming at Mach 2. The breaths are supposed to calm me down, but it's not really working. I just keep seeing that old woman fall. And even worse is hearing the sound that fall made.

Suddenly, the door slams and then there are footsteps. Only nine from the front door to the kitchen. Something's wrong. Only nine when there should actually be thirteen. And they're fast and furious. Mama must not have had a particularly good day. Maybe she broke her employers' priceless crystal punch bowl. Maybe she served them something they were allergic to.

I sit quietly and keep my head down, though I can still see the doorway to the kitchen. When Mama gets there, she doesn't linger. She just passes by without looking in.

"Evening, Mama," I say. Only, she doesn't answer. I know she heard me, so I go back to looking at the almost-blank white page in front of me. Her bedroom door slams, and a few seconds later, I hear the theme to *The Edge of Night,* all serious-sounding and dramatic. It's the only soap opera Mama tapes on the regular. Ever since she got that Betamax recorder, it's *The Edge of Night* every afternoon. Sometimes on Fridays and Mondays she'll tape *The Young and the Restless* so she can keep up on the weekend cliffhangers and figure out what Mrs. Chancellor is up to.

It's never good when Mama just locks herself in her room and starts watching her stories. If something bad didn't happen at work, maybe she got into an argument with Daddy over the phone, or maybe somebody on the train pissed her off. I suppose I'll just have to be satisfied with guessing, since it's not like she'll ever tell me.

There's a roach creeping across the counter. I just look at him for a while. He moves really fast, then stops and lingers, as if he's sensing some invisible force. I can see his antennae moving around. But I don't even think about getting up and killing him. I don't think about doing anything that might make any noise and draw attention to me in any way, so I just sigh and think about Michael Jackson. I wonder what he's doing at this very moment. Probably not looking at some nasty roach crawling across his kitchen counter. Probably doesn't even have roaches where he lives. I wonder whether he's all healed from that accident he got into, shooting that Pepsi commercial. Wish I was there to nurse him. But one day I'll marry him, and this will all be a memory. Keisha says I'm nuts for thinking this since every other girl also believes she's going to end up with him. But I'm different. Even if *Thriller* wasn't as popular as it is and if "Billie Jean" hadn't been number one on the radio, I'd still be interested.

Mama's door opens, and I don't hear the television anymore. She walks into the kitchen with her coat and boots still on and a cigarette dangling from her lips. But it's not lit. And just the very end of it is in her mouth. I wonder how it doesn't fall out.

"Faye, go put on your shoes and your coat."

"I haven't finished my homework yet," I say. But then I notice how red her eyes are. They narrow into slits and dart over to me. I realize I shouldn't have said anything, and I swallow really hard. I've seen that look a million times, and I really don't want the pot of hot chicken coming at my head, so I ease away from the table. I walk past her carefully, turning away a little. Now, at least if she hits me, it won't be in the face. But she just pivots away from me toward the stove and turns on one of the burners. She bends to stick her long skinny Virginia Slim into the fire without taking it out of her mouth. The flame shoots up really high, and for a second, I think maybe it lit not only the cigarette, but also her lips and her nose and her eyebrows and anything else that protrudes from her face. But she doesn't scream or make any noise. She just pulls back and takes a drag from her cigarette and blows the smoke out in the shape of a circle.

"I'm ready," I say as I button my coat. And before I can get my hat on, she's walking down the hallway, grabbing an umbrella from the stand near the door, and walking out into the hall. I hurry and do the same, before locking the door behind me.

It's gotten dark outside, and lights flick on in the windows of the apartment buildings surrounding us. The rain is coming down in the form of little ice pellets, which the wind is smacking right into me. My umbrella is not exactly cooperating, as it keeps turning inside out and flying up into the air.

"Where we going?" I ask once we're a couple blocks into our walk. But Mama doesn't answer. I can't tell if she doesn't hear me or if she just feels like ignoring me. It's already been too traumatic a day. Even though the temperature is near freezing, I'm so shaken up inside, I feel as if I have a fever of 103 degrees. And there are so many different crazy thoughts invading my brain all at once. This is definitely one evening I could just as well skip one of Mama's moods.

A woman coming toward us is having as much trouble with the wind as I am. She's trying to control her umbrella, carry her groceries, and keep her skirt from flying up all at the same time. After a sheet of newspaper hits her in the face, she manages to wrestle it off, but then it takes aim at me. I grab at it and find myself staring at the bold black letters of an old headline: 1ST APPLE MACINTOSH COMPUTER GOES ON SALE.

Mama just keeps walking on ahead, oblivious to how the storm is mistreating me, her giant umbrella as strong and as sturdy as ever. I wonder why the wind doesn't take hold of her. If it did, she'd probably be lifted into the air and be flown across Brooklyn like the black Mary Poppins, flying over the Brooklyn Bridge, across the East River, and over to Manhattan. Maybe it would let her down on top of the Empire State Building, like King Kong. And she'd be stuck there and helicopters would have to take aim and shoot her down.

Mama finally slows her pace once she gets to Holy Rosary Church. As she turns down the walkway and pushes the giant wooden door open, I stop in my tracks. I'm seriously wondering, what with my potential-murderer status, whether I'll remain intact if I cross its threshold or burst into a ball of flames.

4

I'm surrounded by Catholics. Not only did Mama enroll me in Sunday school for longer than I care to remember, she's also forced me to receive four of the seven sacraments. I've been baptized, reconciled, communioned, and confirmed. Not that I remember the lessons I was supposed to have taken away or how they're supposed to affect my soul. So that leaves only marriage, holy orders—which I don't have to worry about unless I suddenly become male, lose my mind, and decide to join the priesthood—and last rites, which I also don't have to worry about right now, unless Mama decides to go through with one of her unoriginal sayings and "take me out of this world as easily as she brought me into it." Whatever.

If that isn't bad enough, I attend Bishop Marshall High in Crown Heights, although that part didn't come about because of Mama. See, you have to pay tuition to go there, which completely goes against her financial belief system. Basically, I was just minding my business over at my zoned high school when there was a stabbing not ten feet from me. This was right at the start of my freshman year. Come Thanksgiving, we get a call from my dad saying he's made plans for me to be enrolled at a Catholic high school beginning the following semester. Boy, did Mama ever pop a blood vessel. She couldn't understand him wasting money on high school tuition when it could have been used to help out with so many other things, but he wouldn't hear of it. Truth be told, I think I'm one of those kids the school allows in with only a portion of the tuition paid. Either way, Daddy sends a check directly there each month, so Mama doesn't really have a say.

Anyway, I decide to go ahead and test my evilness factor, so I open the door to the church, step forward, and wait there for a moment. I don't combust. I take that as a good sign.

Just to the side of me is a font filled with holy water. That stuff singes vampires and those from the dark side, so I decide to leave it be. I walk in a little farther. Mama is up front lighting a candle. There are only a couple of other people in the church: an old woman in one of the last pews, praying to her rosary, and a Spanish-looking man with a thick red scarf looped around his neck, sitting alone crying. I see Father Randall over near the confessionals. The man is as old as dirt and nearly as blind as he is deaf. Mama walks up to him and shakes his hand; then she looks over at me, snaps her fingers, and points to one of the pews. What the hell am I, a dog? Normally, I'd be rolling my eyes and mumbling under my breath at being treated like a four-legged creature, but tonight, that's the least of my problems, so I sit obediently and watch as Mama disappears into one of the wooden confessionals with the thick crimson curtain pulled across the front. I wait a few moments, then crumple up the wet newspaper I never got rid of and stuff it into one of the hymnal holders before getting up and easing in closer to the booth. Mama speaks in a low voice, so it's hard to make out very many of her words.

"He's sent the papers again" is about all I'm able to hear, so I move off and go sit in another pew.

I know she's talking about Daddy. Who knows what's set her off now. My mother and father are still married, even though they don't live together, which is pretty weird if you ask me. They've been apart since I was eight, so it's been a hot minute. How are you going to be apart from somebody for six years and still be married to them? Though, when I think of it, Daddy wasn't around much when they were actually together. He was always traveling to some other city or town, playing his bass, trying to earn some money. I always wished I had one of those dads who went into the office at nine every morning and was home by six at night, sitting around the dinner table, telling stories about his horrible boss. I know if Daddy was around, Mama wouldn't be so mean to me. And there would even be laughter and giggles in our house, instead of silence all the time. Maybe then I would have somebody to tell me they loved me. Or call me pretty—even if they were lying just a little.

I guess I can't blame Daddy for leaving. Mama's just plain evil. I'd run from her too, if I could. Actually, I did try to run—twice. Once when I was nine, just after Daddy left. Things were worse then, if you can believe that. I decided to take another shot at it when I was eleven. But I didn't have it planned out that well. First rule of running away: don't do it in the middle of winter while wearing your fuzzy slippers. There's only so far you can get before everything below your knees goes numb. Second rule: go farther than the creepy basement of your building.

Yeah, if Daddy was around, maybe I wouldn't be as rotten as I am. But I don't want to make it sound like I'm the cause of Mama's stress, because I'm not. She's the cause of mine. I think she's the reason I'm so rotten. Then again, maybe it's a case of which came first, the chicken or the egg. And who's the chicken—me or Mama? I guess it doesn't really matter.

Mama steps out of the confessional and motions for me to come over. When I do, she just points to the booth. You've got to be kidding me. It's like the woman is a witch. It's like she senses that I've done some wrongful deed. Mama is from the Caribbean—Dominica. Dominica, not the Dominican Republic. Everyone always mixes the two up, but they're not the same. I went there with her and my uncle Paul when I was eight. The water was so clear, I could see all the way down to the sea bottom and to the little fish kissing away at my ankles. Anyway, Dominica is one of those little teeny islands they never put the names of on maps, like Nevis and Montserrat. Most people have never heard of those either—most people who aren't from the Caribbean or don't have any ties to it.

I used to hear stories about how Mama's grandmother, my great-grandma, would work her magic across the island. How she would look into a person's eyes and tell his past and his future. I never really believed it, but I'm starting to wonder. Maybe Mama has the power of sensing but isn't powerful enough to change anything, so she has to rely on religion for that. Maybe she thinks my wrongdoings are the cause of the misfortune in her life and that ridding me of my sins will lead to a cure for all her issues. I don't know. Although, if ever there was a time I needed to confess and have a priest say that no matter how serious my crime, with two Hail Marys it will all be forgiven, this is it. But how do you say to someone, "I think I might have killed some old person . . . oops?"

As I walk into the booth, I see Mama heading back over to the candles. And I'm thinking, Light as many as you like, lady. It's not going to help any with Daddy coming back.

"When was the last time you confessed?" Father Randall asks before I'm even fully seated on the small bench. I can see bits of his white skin and white hair through the patterned wooden panel between us.

"I don't know," I say. "I think with Father Hoppe a little while ago." It's a lie. I haven't confessed since my confirmation. Only, Father Randall is so old, I figure I can tell him anything and he won't dispute it.

"You do not confess your sins weekly?"

"No."

"You've done nothing you'd like to ask God's forgiveness for?"

I pause here for a really long time. My temples are beginning to throb again, but I can't seem to form the words to verbalize what I've done, so I just sit quietly.

"You haven't sworn, thought ill of another?" he asks.

"Are those really sins? I mean, seriously, who hasn't done that?" I mumble. Man, the smart-ass really comes out in me when I'm freaking out.

"What?" he says louder than I think is necessary. I'd forgotten about his auditory issues, so I lean forward and repeat myself, minus all the sass.

"Just because others do, does that make it right?" he responds.

I shrug and get quiet again.

"Each day we walk through the darkened forest of life. In the time since you've confessed, there's been nothing you'd like to get off your chest?"

I inch the curtain back a little and peep outside the booth, just to make sure Mama isn't involved in any of her snooping tactics—tactics I learned from her. But she's on the other side of the church. Just as I turn away from her, I glimpse the area just above the altar, where a giant Jesus hangs on the cross. Crucifixes really creep me out.

I allow the thick velvet curtain to close and shield me from that image. Suddenly, I get an idea.

"Will God really forgive me for anything?" I lean forward and ask.

"Of course. You are his child."

"And anything I tell you, you can't tell my mother, right?"

"It's between you, me, and God."

"You can't tell the cops, right?" I try not to sound too hopeful.

"You, me, and God," Father Randall says again.

"Well, what would God think if I told him I stole money from someone who was super old?"

"Why did you steal this money? Were you hungry? Were you in a bind?"

"No."

"Then why?"

"Because I wanted to."

"Why?"

"'Cause . . ."

Silence.

"Because it was something to do." I suddenly realize I haven't actually seen a dime of that money. I was so on another planet about everything that happened, I didn't even get my share from Caroline.

"But the money isn't the bad part," I continue.

"Stealing is not the bad part?"

"No, this is kind of a two-broken-commandments sin."

"What's the second one?"

"Well, what if . . . someone . . . accidentally maybe pushed another someone, and that other someone fell and sorta hurt themselves?"

"Accidents happen. This person who was injured, did the other person call in medical help for them?"

"Uh, no."

"Why not?"

"I don't know. 'Cause no one thought of it at the time.

Anyway, I don't think that part even matters anymore. I guess. Because the person who was injured . . . what if they were not exactly injured anymore?"

"I don't follow."

"Yeah, I know." I take a really deep breath before continuing. "Let's say the person was more kinda . . . dead . . . than injured?"

There is the longest silence, and I start wondering if he just didn't hear me. Then I start wondering whether he did, and I've made my second big mistake of the day. I would do anything to be able to take my words back.

"Are you saying you may have killed someone?" Father Randall finally asks.

I'm trying to swallow, but my mouth has become cobwebs-across-the-tongue dry. What have I done?

"No. Definitely not." I try and backtrack. "That's not what I'm saying at all. No, no, nope. What I'm saying is, well, I'm trying to figure out when a sin is beyond asking forgiveness for."

"So you want to know if murder—"

"No, not murder. An accidental ending of a life. And I never said it was me. Or that it was something that really happened. Anyway, is all this forgivable?"

It's pin-drop quiet for a while again, and I'm wondering if the old priest has snuck away to call the cops. I peep through the slats, where I can still see his shock of white hair.

"All is forgivable if he or *she* who commits that action is repentant. But if a sin is also a crime, part of that repenting involves informing the proper authority, at which point the healing can begin."

"Authority?" I echo.

I no longer feel fever-hot. I now feel as if I've been set on fire.

"It's all good," I say quickly. And I force a ridiculous laugh. "I was just testing you. Trying to figure out what would be the worst sin to commit. It's all good."

And I just about tear the curtain down as I beat it out of that confessional.

* * *

It's raining really hard when I start back home with Mama, and I realize I left my flimsy umbrella back in the church. I try not to walk too close to the curb to avoid the rainwater splashing up as cars whiz by. Mama's moving even faster now, and I've dropped to twenty paces behind her. But she never slows down to check on me or offer me any shelter, which is just fine with me. I'd feel weird and claustrophobic having to be all bunched up close to her as we walk the whole way back to our apartment in silence. Besides, she's probably looking for the rain to finish cleansing me of whatever confession did not. But I can't really worry about her. I have my own horrible trials and tribulations to deal with.

KARMA.

Written in big twelve-inch-high white letters on the blackboard. That's the first thing I see when I walk into my religious studies class. The word *karma,* double underlined. And just as frightening is what—or who—I spy to the left of that word: Sister Margaret Theresa Patricia Bernadette. She takes her usual place in front of the class, waiting for everyone to be seated and settled. Her head is held really high, like she's one of those meerkats. You know, like there's a stick poking up out of her back, holding it up. Her hands are clasped in front of her, and her beady little rat eyes dart from left to right, right to left. She doesn't wear a nun's habit. None of the nuns at Bishop Marshall do. Instead, she has on the same long gray skirt, maroon blouse, and gray angora sweater she wears every day. The first button on her shirt is open, and a gold cross with a crucified Jesus hangs just below her neck. I swear, if I see one more crucified Jesus . . . I don't understand why people wear them. It's just so depressing and all. I wouldn't wear any dead person hanging from my neck, no matter how many miracles he might have performed.

I take my loose-leaf binder out and ease my knapsack under my desk. I didn't sleep a wink last night, but I don't feel tired. Just the opposite. It's as if I've eaten two pounds of sugar. I'm filled with all this anxiety, and it's taking everything within me to not start shaking uncontrollably. I take a deep breath, and as I exhale, I notice Keisha mouthing the word "Karma" and "Ooh," and miming a horror-movie scream. For the first time in the past fifteen hours, I can feel a smile working its way onto my face. But just as quickly, my face muscles tighten and I begin to feel the anxiety again.

I'd have to consider Keisha my very best friend, and even though we don't sit together—on account of the Sister seating everyone alphabetically—she's the only thing that makes religion class and Sister Margaret Theresa Patricia Bernadette bearable. She's the only thing that made starting a new high school in the middle of freshman year bearable.

Keisha and I kind of have a bit of history, since we went to junior high together. And even though we weren't great friends there, we were friendly. But then her stepdad bought a brownstone and moved the family to Fort Greene, and she started at Bishop Marshall right off. Mama and I moved too, but just deeper into Flatbush. By the time I got to Bishop Marshall, everyone was already part of one clique or another, and most didn't want to let in a new kid. But not Keisha.

I know best friends are supposed to tell each other

everything, and I wish I could explain to her all the angst I feel inside, but I can't. She could never understand what it's like being me. After all, she has a mom who's interested in every little thing that goes on in her day. She has a mom who hugs her and tells her how much she cares. And though her dad died in a car accident when she was two, she has a stepdad who comes home every night and treats her and her brother, Kevin, like they're his own.

I keep looking as Keisha continues clowning, but I suppose me not laughing causes her to become serious. The next thing I notice is that she's mouthing, "Are you okay?"

I shake my head and force a smile before turning away and looking down at my desk. That's how Keisha is all the time: sensitive and caring and ready to help out. She's always taking in stray animals with broken limbs and making sure everyone is okay. On Saturdays, she even volunteers at this nursing home in Williamsburg with her cousin, so just imagine me telling her I think I might have killed an old woman I was in the process of robbing. She's so sweet and good that sometimes it makes me feel like even more of a bad seed. And I feel like I'm one of those wounded animals she's always trying to rescue. I guess that's mainly why I keep hanging out with Gillian and Caroline. With them, I can be as rotten as I want, and I don't have to feel guilty about it. I don't have to make any apologies.

As Keisha continues to clown around, I try to forget everything that happened in that old lady's Parkside Avenue apartment. I even chuckle a little. But the nun must have some weird laser lock on me, because with all the whispering and fidgeting going on, I'm the one her death stare focuses on.

"Ms. Andrews, may I inquire as to what you find so comedic?" she asks.

Oh, I have a million good ones I could come out with, but I just sigh and mumble, "Nothing, Sister." Then I wait for her to call on us to read our homework. The assignment was about the principle of reincarnation and whether it is represented in Christianity. I'm just hoping she doesn't go alphabetically, because I'll be called first, and honestly, I never got past writing my name and date on that piece of notebook paper last night. That's the problem with having Andrews as a last name—you're always the first one up in front of the firing squad. But maybe she'll do her picking in reverse alphabetical order. That way, Kiara Harding will go before me. And since she always has those A-plus book reports, I'll be able to jot down some good ideas from her. Of course, I'll have to change it around a little so it doesn't sound completely like I'm cheating, though I see nothing wrong with taking advantage of such a situation, if it's done in a creative way.

Everyone finally settles into their seats, and the murmuring dies down. That's when Sister Margaret Theresa Patricia Bernadette walks around to the front of her desk and clears her throat.

"Today, I would like to jump right into the Hindu philosophy of karma. Who has an understanding of what that is?"

Charlene Simpson, an average-looking girl's worst nightmare, is one of the first to raise her hand. What's new? And Sister just beams at her.

"Basically, it's the principle that whatever you put out will come back to you. So, if you do good, good comes to you. If you do bad, bad comes to you."

"As usual, Charlene, you've hit the proverbial nail on its head."

And teacher's pet flashes her hundred-watt, spent-two-thousand-dollars-on-braces-to-get-the-chompers-perfectly-straight smile, then flings her thick, shiny black hair this way and that.

"Yes, this philosophy asserts that for everything you do, there is a direct, balanced consequence that will take place sometime in your life. Does anyone have an example of a karmic experience?"

Sylvester Young shifts his bulk uncomfortably in his too-tiny chair, then raises his hand.

But another kid yells out, "Sylvester ate a tubload of fried chicken. Two hours later, he threw it all up. Now, that's karma."

"Class!" the nun says sternly before the laughter can expand any further.

"No," Sylvester says. "I was gonna say, I helped this little old man who had fallen on a patch of ice a few months ago, and later he gave me a twenty-dollar bill."

"That's one way of looking at it," the Sister says. "Anyone else?"

And it goes around and about like this with everyone highlighting a good deed that was in some way rewarded. It comes back around to Charlene again, who mentions something about rescuing a cat from a tree or stopping a speeding bullet from hitting a baby carriage or preventing the atom bomb from going off, or something as ridiculous as that. Whatever. And the Sister oohs and aahs and drools and slobbers.

"But karma can also be bad," the Sister continues once she's able to tear herself away from Charlene's "awesomeness." "I'm sure some of you have dealt with experiences that led to rude awakenings somewhere down the line."

Okay, I'm really starting to feel queasy. If there is such a thing as karma, the worst consequence must be given for killing someone. I mean, even with the Ten Commandments, isn't "Thou shalt not kill" the mother of them all?

"Okay, bad karma, bad karma. Whom shall I call on . . . Let's see . . . Who would have some experience with bad karma? Faye Andrews!"

If there is a God in heaven, please strike me down. Now! Is "old-person tormenter and potential killer" stamped on my forehead for all to see?

"Why'd you call on me?" I ask. "I wasn't even raising my hand."

"No, but you were looking a bit shifty."

"I don't know what that means," I say. "I was probably looking the way I always look."

"Exactly," the nun says. "Anyway, an example of bad karma. Go."

"I don't have one," I say between clenched teeth.

"Oh, I'm quite sure you have a few."

The thing is, having the mom I do, I have a lot of experience with people saying not-so-nice things to me, either blatantly or in a backhanded way. But I still manage to give them the benefit of the doubt. So I take a few seconds to process the nun's words. Who knows, maybe she didn't mean them the way they came out. But then I look around the class and see some kids giggling, and I see Keisha's "Oh no she didn't" expression, and I know what I heard is actually what that nun said.

Now, I've always been a little suspicious of Sister Margaret Theresa Patricia Bernadette, and it's not just because she has four first names and she makes us call her by all of them. Not just Sister Margaret. Not Sister Margaret Theresa. Not Sister Mags Terry Pat. It has to be Sister *Margaret Theresa Patricia Bernadette*. And even though servants of the Lord are supposed to be caring and compassionate and nonjudgmental, this woman's just plain mean and petty. Case in point: the bizarre beauty contest she had all us girls take part in a few weeks back—which of course Charlene won even though it wasn't supposed to be a test of outward beauty. Something about examining the virtues of prudence, justice, restraint, courage, faith, hope, and charity. Still, Sister was judge and jury, and somehow all the pretty girls ended up on top while the girls like me ended up down at the bottom. I mean, what the hell does beauty have to do with religion class, anyway? I'm completely convinced Sister is Satan's kin.

"An example of bad karma," I say. "Okay. Well, I did cut Mass one time and used my offering money for soda and chips. And now I've been put in a horrible religion class with a crazy, frustrated, mean old nun."

I see Keisha quickly look away. There is mostly silence. But then someone in the back of the class laughs. Satan's daughter does not. Her face just becomes rock hard. She stares at me awhile, like she's trying to figure out whether she should turn me into a pillar of salt like Lot's wife and risk blowing her demonic cover. But instead, she walks back over to the blackboard and stands next to the word *karma* again.

"Let's talk about karma as it relates to Christianity," she says. "Proverbs eleven eighteen. 'The wicked man earns deceptive wages. . . .'" She fixes her eyes on me as she says this, then turns to Charlene as she adds, "'But he who sows righteousness reaps a sure reward.'"

6

The minute school is over, I'm flying through the hallways like a bat out of hell. I hardly even shoot a second glance at Anthony "Curvy" Miller—my future husband in the event that Michael Jackson is unavailable. I dash through the doors and run out into the streets of Crown Heights, trying to make it to the bus stop, almost taking out a Hasidic boy who's not watching where he's going.

"Sorry!" I yell as his black hat goes blowing down the street.

But there's no bus to be found, and I have all this karma crap floating around in my head, and I know there's something I have to do or I'll just burst, so I take to running past the main library and alongside the gated-off Botanic Garden. I glimpse the Ebbets Field apartments as I get to Empire Boulevard, where Flatbush and Ocean Avenues intersect. The smell of cheese and garlic and sauce bursts from Antonio's Pizzeria as someone opens the door to go in. I decide to go down Ocean Avenue, where I take turns fast-walking and running through Prospect Park. A guy strolls toward me holding a giant, mailbox-sized boom box on his shoulder. It's covered with a black plastic garbage bag, to protect it from the weather, I guess. The thing must weigh at least a hundred pounds. I don't know how he doesn't get a cramp in his arm. And I really don't know how he hasn't blown out his eardrums. Or maybe he has, which would explain why the way too loud, way too distorted sound of the Soulsonic Force's "Planet Rock" doesn't seem to bother him one bit. A couple minutes after passing him, I can still hear the music.

It's not until I get to Parkside Avenue that I finally stop to breathe and to watch as the number 16 bus passes me by. Right at the entrance to the park, there's this guy sporting a Run-DMC-looking red tracksuit and fat gold chain under his puffy black parka. He's standing behind a garbage can that has a thick piece of cardboard laid out across it. And on top of the cardboard are these three playing cards. A small group of people, mostly kids my age or a little older, are gathered around. He picks up one card and holds it out so everyone can see what it is—a three of clubs. Then he shows the other two cards. They are not threes of clubs. He turns them back over, puts them down, and shows the three of clubs again. As he turns it back over, he tells everyone to keep their eyes on that card. Then he moves the three cards around, lightning fast. He stops and tells this one little kid to point to which card he thinks is the three of clubs. The kid picks the right card, and everybody else gasps and claps.

"Damn, shorty. You lucky. You need to put some of that

luck to work and double your money. Inflation too high in 'eighty-four, wages too low. All of you need to put some green down. What you got?"

I'm figuring these people know how much of a scam this is. I'm figuring they're just going to turn and walk away. But they don't. Of the seven or so people gathered, at least five put their money down. And all five of them lose their cash.

"Damn, guess luck's gotta run out eventually," the guy says. "But the great thing about luck is, ya never know when it's gonna come back. And y'all look like some lucky people. You think ya got what it takes to make back your money?"

I shake my head and move away from those stupid people. But the farther I move along Parkside, the crazier I begin to feel. I suddenly start sweating. This bad feeling comes over me the closer I get to the familiar beige brick building near the corner of Parkside and Parade Place. I climb the few stairs that lead to the outer door of the lobby, but I don't go inside the vestibule at first. I just peep through it. I can see down the first-floor hallway. The old lady's door is far enough away that I can't really tell whether it's open or closed from where I stand. And I most definitely can't tell whether it's locked or unlocked. I can't tell whether she's still in there, lying dead on the floor. Or whether she woke up and made it to the phone to call a doctor. Or whether somebody from her family came over and found her there and called the cops. Or whether the cops are in there right now.

I have to step away and stand to the side of the doors. I lean against the bricks and take a few deep breaths. Then I close my eyes. Even though it's overcast, a bit of sun sneaks through the clouds and warms my face a little. I decide that I'm just going to have to do this quick. Before I lose my courage. Before I lose my mind. So I enter through the first set of lobby doors and stand there in front of the intercom, waiting for someone to enter or exit; waiting for someone to let me through the second, locked set of doors. Only, the universe is just not cooperating with me, and I have to wait twenty more minutes for someone to leave the building.

Once I'm inside, I walk through the large lobby and past the elevator, but my feet seem to stop moving. I guess they don't want to get me any closer to apartment 1H. It's like I'm in one of those scary movies and my feet are trying to warn me to stay away. So I'm just standing there in the hall, looking like I don't belong, and I have to use every ounce of what little willpower I have to move myself along.

Once I get to the old lady's apartment, I just stand in front of her door, staring. I put my ear to it, hoping I'll hear some noise—maybe the television or the radio. Maybe she's listening to Lawrence Welk records or Frank Sinatra or whatever old white people sit around listening to. I don't really know. I'll take a toilet flush or a blender. Anything. But there's only silence.

I try to look through the peephole, but I can't see anything, just a small stream of light. I take a couple of deep breaths. The brass doorknob is just staring up at me. It's telling me to turn it. We didn't lock the door behind us when we left, so if the knob gives, then I'll know no one has been in or out of the apartment since we were there yesterday. But my hand is shaking so much, I can hardly get it around that doorknob. I swear, it takes like fifteen minutes for me to concentrate long enough to grab hold of it. It's smooth and cold against my palm. And suddenly, I realize I'm having a problem breathing. It's like my breath is being held hostage in my throat and not making it all the way down to my lungs. Thank God I have my inhaler. And my knees are trembling like crazy. I don't really have a remedy for that. Maybe if there was more fat on them, they'd be more stable.

Okay, just turn it a little to the left, I say to myself. Maybe it won't turn at all. But I only apply enough force to make it turn a smidgeon; then it clicks back to its normal place. I remove my hand, shake it out, then put it back on the knob. I take one more deep breath and crank the thing as far as it will go, expecting it to not turn very far. But it does. It goes like in a full circle, and the next thing I know, the door opens a few inches. But I don't have much time to be freaked out, because I hear footsteps on the stairs.

I try to let go of the knob, but now I can't seem to. It's like that guy on those commercials whose hard hat is Krazy Glued to that beam. I can't move my hand. And so I just stand there frozen, like an icicle. My heartbeat is coming as if it's in stereo, making it hard for me to hear anything else. And suddenly, I see these two kids land on the first floor. And there's an older man behind them—their father, maybe. But thank God, they never turn around.

I watch as they walk through the front doors and turn left once they reach the sidewalk. I'm sweating bullets. That door shouldn't have opened. It shouldn't have. That means she's still in there. Probably where we left her. Oh man. I'm just going to have to hypnotize myself into forgetting about this. It's out of my control now, and there's no way I'll be able to eat, sleep, or function if I dwell on it. If I turn on Eyewitness News and see Bill Beutel or Roger Grimsby reporting about the murder of some old lady on Parkside Avenue, I'm just going to have to do the best acting job ever. Give an Oscar-worthy performance.

I yank the door shut and my hand away from the doorknob and take off running. It must be forty-five degrees outside, but I'm sweating and panting like a thirsty little puppy on a hot summer day. I pass the shady card dealer surrounded by a new batch of suckers, and I yell out:

"Are you people stupid? It's a scam. A scam! You can't win." And I keep running down Parkside Avenue like I've lost my mind.

The running continues once I reach my block. I shoot straight past my building, past the next couple of buildings, and past the tiny houses wedged between them. I keep going until I get to the six-story brown brick building near the other end of the street. My hands are shaking so badly I hit the wrong intercom button at first. But I tell myself to breathe, and I focus really hard and manage to press 4B. There's a crackle, then Caroline's voice.

"It's me, Faye!" I yell. "The knob wasn't supposed to turn. The door wasn't supposed to open. She's dead! She's dead! I know she is!"

The intercom buzzes immediately, and I run through the lobby and to the stairs, taking them two at a time as I make it up to Caroline's fourth-floor apartment. The door opens without me even pressing the bell, and Caroline's big fat mitt of a hand comes forward, grabs me by the collar of my coat, and yanks me in.

"You shut it till we get to my room," she whispers, which

means she's actually speaking at normal-person level. "My mom's in the living room sewing. Just shout hi to her as we walk by."

Mrs. Johns is wedged behind the Singer sewing machine she has set up in the corner of the room, along with mounds of clothes and bobbins of thread and pincushions shaped like tomatoes and onions.

I hardly get a "Hi, Mrs. Johns" out before I'm being pushed into Caroline's room, with the door closing behind me.

Gillian's sitting at a desk near the window, staring at me.

"What fool thing did you do?" Caroline asks.

"I went over there."

"Why?"

"I just wanted to make sure she wasn't dead. But the door opened. Don't you think if she was alive she would have gotten up and locked it?"

But Caroline doesn't answer that question. Instead, she just comes at me with another one.

"How stupid are you? Seriously. What if somebody saw you messing around at her door? What if somebody had called the cops on your ass?"

"I didn't think about that. I just wanted to make sure she wasn't dead," I say as I sit on the edge of Caroline's bed. "Maybe we should make a call to someone anonymously."

"To who? If she's dead, what the hell does it matter?" Caroline asks as she leans against her dresser. "I mean, she was like a thousand. And if she's not dead now, she will be in no time. No fault of ours, just the natural order of things.

And we got a lot of money from this. So think about that instead."

"Doesn't it bother you any?" I ask.

"I mean, I don't want to be responsible for some dead old person. But there are worse things in life. Besides, I wasn't the one who pushed her, so it's not on my conscience any."

And my jaw just hits the floor. I can't figure out what to say next. Can't even unscramble all that's going on in my brain, so I get quiet instead. I think of turning my back on Caroline right then and there and never seeing her again. But then I think how she and Gillian were the only ones to stick up for me when I first moved to the neighborhood and those roughneck girls were tormenting me. And they do seem to genuinely like having me as part of their crew. I don't know. I suppose it's better to be accepted by someone, no matter how contrary they can be sometimes, than to not have any friends in the neighborhood at all.

I glance over at Gillian, who still hasn't said a word. She just shifts her eyes from Caroline to me and back to Caroline again.

The tension is momentarily interrupted by a knock on the door. Mrs. Johns comes in with a tray of peanut butter and jelly sandwiches and three glasses of milk.

"Faye, you flew in here like a little bumblebee," she says as she puts the tray down and smothers my face in her giant breasts. "How was school?"

"Fine," I mumble.

She takes a glass of milk and puts it in front of me.

"Um, I can't drink milk, ma'am. Remember . . . ?"

"Oh, that's right. I guess I think if I keep giving it to you, that all might change. Just never knew a child who couldn't drink milk."

"It hurts my stomach."

Mrs. Johns shakes her head. "That's why you're so itty-bitty. Milk fattens you up."

I glance over at Caroline and decide that if that's the case, she should probably never go within ten miles of a cow.

"Well. I'll bring you some Hi-C," she says. "I think we have cherry."

"Cherry's my favorite," I say.

Mrs. Johns manages to find what little cheeks I have and squeeze them. Then she walks out of the room with the tray under her left arm and one glass of milk in her right hand. She's a bit chunky herself, so I guess she had her share of milk back in the day, but this doesn't seem to cause her any worries. Not a day goes by that she's not wearing her high heels. Her nails and hair are always done up. And she's always wearing these great outfits. Since she's the neighborhood seamstress, maybe she makes them herself. But what I really love is how she fusses over me and makes me feel present. Sometimes I wonder if Caroline wasn't actually adopted, or spawned from jackals, like Damien in *The Omen*. That would explain how she got a mom as sweet as Mrs. Johns and I got Mama. Then again, I could be Gillian. Gillian's mom died when she was five, and her dad, who is Mrs. Johns's brother, didn't know how to take care of her, so he just gave her away to Mr. and Mrs. Johns.

No one says a word as we wait for Caroline's mom to

return with the juice. My heart is beating as fast as a drum. I can't shake the image of that old lady falling backward and cracking her skull against the table. *Thunk!* Then nothing. Like when you open a jar of peaches for the first time.

"All right," Mrs. Johns says as she comes back into the room. "One cherry Hi-C for the girl who can't drink milk. You all enjoy your snacks and do your homework."

I start chewing on the peanut butter and jelly sandwich, but I can't seem to come up with enough saliva to make it go down. Even a swig of the Hi-C doesn't help much. I'm just so consumed with the thought that I've killed some old lady who lived through the Second World War, maybe even the first one. She might even have made it through a dangerous childbirth or a car or bus accident. And here I am, some kid who should have been helping her to cross the street or pick up her medication from the pharmacy. Instead, I could possibly be the thing that has ended her life.

"Well, if you don't care whether or not she's alive, at least give me my share of the money," I say. I just want to get away from Caroline and get home and start on dinner.

"What you gonna get with yours?" she asks me as she heads toward her closet.

If this question had come even two days ago, I would have been so excited. I mean, I had it all planned out. The Gloria Vanderbilt jeans Mama refuses to buy for me cost forty-five bucks. The Michael Jackson "Beat It" jacket costs fifteen dollars, and the tape recorder I could use to tape songs off the radio costs nineteen ninety-nine. I probably could have gotten it all with the money I've been saving up, but with my share of the almost three hundred dollars, I'll have enough for four jackets—one in every color. But suddenly, the jacket doesn't seem all that important.

"Dunno. Have to think about it," I mumble.

Caroline turns to her cousin. "What about you, Gillian?"

Gillian just shrugs and taps her fingers against the desk. But then the tapping comes to a sudden stop.

"What if she really is dead?" Gillian asks.

"Shut up," I hear from Caroline.

"For real. I mean, she was all mashed up against the wall when we first walked in, but she got up. She was moving. She was okay. But after Faye pushed her—"

"I didn't push her." I try not to yell. "She was holding on to my arm. Her fingers were all cold and bony, and I was just trying to get her off."

"But what if somebody does find her and they call the cops and the cops find our fingerprints? Then what? What if they come after us and they put us in jail? You can't go to the movies if you're in jail. You can't hang out at Coney Island or go shopping—"

"Gillian, stop it," I say.

"Gillian, me and you, we're not about to go to jail," Caroline says. "Once again, we didn't do nothing. If anything, it would be Faye. She's the one who pushed that woman down."

"We all went in there together," I remind them, my breath coming faster and faster. "I never even knew this woman existed. You're the one who came up with this brilliant idea of messing with her after your friend Janet told you about her being a movie star. And by the way, we still don't even know if that's true. I mean, just two hundred and eighty dollars? When she was supposed to be some big-time actress?"

I feel my heart racing and my eyes burning. My words are getting all caught in my throat, and they're not coming out the way I want them to, so I just sit there and stare at Caroline, who has this weird grin on her face. And for the first time, I notice how ugly she is. I'm no Miss Universe, but I don't look like an otherworldly being either. I mean, she really does look like she could have doubled for E.T. in that Steven Spielberg movie—if E.T. was put on a McDonald's-only diet. And I want to just take her big fat face and smoosh it into the bed. Maybe I could beat her. I do move a lot faster than her. Maybe I could get in a couple of good licks before she even realizes what's going on.

"We all went in there," Caroline babbles on. "But we didn't all knock that little old woman over, that's all I'm saying."

"But we'd all be in trouble."

"Trouble for stealing some money and trouble for killing somebody's grandma are two completely different kinds of trouble," E.T.'s sister says. Then she just stares at me with her big, bulging eyes. "I don't know why you're looking so shocked."

"I have to go. Just give me my money," I say quietly.

Caroline takes some cash out of a brown Adidas shoe box, starts dividing it up, and hands a few bills over to me. I don't have to count it to realize how little there is. And all of a sudden, my head starts to get real hot. I'm staring at two twenties.

"Where's the rest?" I ask.

"Rest of what?"

"The money."

"There is no rest. You get forty. Same for Gillian."

"That means you're taking two hundred dollars for yourself."

"That's right. I came up with the plan. I did most of the work."

"We did just as much work as you. More, even. We were the ones who ended up standing out in the cold on lookout. Us. Me and Gillian. Skin and bones. You got all that extra padding and you never once went outside the building."

"'Cause I had to make sure Janet didn't see me."

"You told us Janet works at Burger King till eight on weekdays. And I could be in a lot of trouble. I'll probably need the most cash—for bail or something. This is the most money we've ever gotten from anybody, even more than from that snotty girl who was going to Woolworth's with her grandmother's money. We all did the same work, so we should get an equal share."

"Please. You wouldn't have done squat if I hadn't been there with you. You would have zero dollars now instead of forty. Do you understand just how much forty dollars is? You ain't never made that much money ever. So why you giving me grief?"

"This isn't fair," I say. "This isn't fair. Gillian, you know it isn't fair."

I don't know why I even say anything to Gillian, because she just starts shaking her head and shrugging like she's about to blast off into the stratosphere. My head is spinning and this weird, volcanic churning is taking place in the pit of my stomach. I'm seeing the old lady all crumpled against the floor in her kitchen. I'm seeing me sitting in the back of a police car. I'm seeing my classmates all looking on in shock as Sister Margaret Theresa Patricia Bernadette mouths, "Karma." And I can hear Mama saying she's not surprised, that she never thought I would ever amount to anything.

And suddenly, my head feels like it's going to explode. Without thinking, I find myself running for Caroline's closet and grabbing that Adidas shoe box. But before I can make my escape, Caroline snatches me up and body-slams me onto the bed.

I'm trying to yell, maybe have Mrs. Johns come rescue me, but my nose and mouth are being pushed into the bed and only a few muffled groans trickle out. I can make out Gillian standing in front of us, shaking her head even more furiously and spazzing out. Eventually, I realize the only thing struggling is going to get me is suffocated, so I stop. That, and the fact that I run out of energy. But then Caroline starts shaking me. And I'm telling her to stop, but she doesn't. And the volcano that seems to have taken the place of my stomach is growing larger. It feels like someone lit a fire in there and it's about to come raging out. But Caroline doesn't listen to me. She just keeps shaking me and laughing her forest-creature laugh. And the more she laughs, the more my stomach quivers. And then the churning that started in my belly begins rising up into my chest and my throat. Before I can even try to pull away from her, it's too late. There's a chunky lava river of peanut butter and jelly and bread and cherry-red Hi-C and the pizza we had for lunch at school flowing all over Caroline Johns. She lets out this loud, deranged scream.

"You gonna be sorry you did that!" she yells as she grabs at my hair, which I had parted down the middle and done in two braids. I can feel a few strands being pulled out, but I somehow manage to slip from her grasp.

"You already stole my money! What else can you do?" I yell back as I flee from her room, her building, her whole sick, twisted little world.

As I walk back to my apartment, not even the cold air outside can calm me.

8

Maybe I shouldn't have called Sister Margaret Theresa Patricia Bernadette "crazy, frustrated, and mean," because I'm now convinced that she has cast some kind of karmic spell on me: torment an old woman and ye shall inherit your own tormenters. Or maybe my crazy grandfather on Mama's side was right about God not liking ugly.

It's only been a day since everything happened with that old lady, but not one thing has gone right since then. And this has to be the worst, by far—me stumbling in on a robber.

I shouldn't have entered our apartment in the first place, but I was so distracted after discovering the little gift Caroline had left in my hair. Bubble gum! Everyone knows you don't mess with a black girl's hair. As I put my key into the first lock, I was focused on getting to the closest mirror. I was focused on the door to the old lady's apartment opening, on whether she had moved from that kitchen floor or whether she was still lying there, all cold and beyond this world. I was focused on everything except what was directly in front of me. Didn't even notice that the first lock didn't turn. But when the second one didn't either, I realized it was because it was already open. I thought maybe Mama had come home early and was doing laundry or emptying the garbage and had forgotten to lock the door behind her. I was scared because I had left the house a mess this morning, and I knew Mama would be mad about it. But if I had to choose between a homicidal robber and my pissed-off mama, I would choose my pissed-off mama . . . I think.

By the time I realized something was wrong, I had come too far into the apartment. I had walked past the small hall leading to the bathroom, but I didn't look in that direction. It wasn't until I got to Mama's bedroom door that things began to sink in. See, Mama always locks her door when she leaves in the morning. Guess she thinks I have nothing better to do than snoop through her stuff. But today her door was wide open, and the inside frame where the lock should have been was busted.

Now I'm huddled in the broom closet in the kitchen, scared for my life. I hear these footsteps, but they only last for a few seconds before there's silence again. This is the worst part, I think—the silence. Because we have a really long hallway leading to the front door, and those five or six footsteps are not nearly enough to lead that robber out of the apartment. And although I picked up the butcher knife before jumping into the broom closet, I'm not too confident. Even if I could surprise him and maybe get a whack at him or something, the way my hands are shaking, I'm not so sure I'd do him any harm.

I shut my eyes and make a promise to God that if he lets me live, I will try my best to be a better person. I won't say things under my breath to Mama, and I'll even try not to wish I had a different mother altogether. If he lets me live, I will figure something out to make up for what I did to that old woman. I don't know what, but something.

I've never been so scared. I open my eyes and try not to breathe, but that only lasts about thirty seconds. I wonder how long the greatest breath holder in the world could hold his breath. Probably should have paid attention in science class that day. I think Mr. Glenn said the human brain can go without oxygen for four minutes. Something like that. But suppose the robber takes longer than four minutes to leave the apartment? I wouldn't want to pass out with him still in the house and then fall out of the closet right in front of him. But maybe that wouldn't be such a bad thing. I'd probably scare him half to death, and maybe he'd drop his gun or knife or shogun sword or whatever weapon he had and just run on out.

The sound of the wooden beads that hang from the living room doorway knocking together snaps me out of my thoughts. It's not loud enough for him to have walked through them, but it's loud enough for him to have brushed past. And the living room is almost directly across from the kitchen. And now my breath won't come the way it should, and I realize my inhaler is in my schoolbag and my schoolbag is on the kitchen counter. I don't have really bad asthma, so I hardly ever have to use it, but every now and then, I'll have an episode. And this situation definitely qualifies as one of those every-now-and-thens. But if this robber is standing where I think he is, he has full view of the kitchen. And if he has full view of the kitchen, I'm sure he can see my bag. Oh man.

With my winter coat and knit hat on, and with the radiators humming with steam, I'm starting to get overheated. I can feel a bead of sweat drip into my left eye. And another. But the broom closet is so narrow I just barely fit into it, so I don't dare try and take the coat off. I don't dare move an inch. And I'm wondering if this was how that old lady felt when we were in her home. Was her heart beating the way mine is now? Did everything she had ever done in her life come rushing forward, *Speed Racer* fast? Every good thing? Every bad thing?

And so I try to go to my calm place. I try to think of Michael Jackson again and the words to "Billie Jean," but all that comes to mind are the ones to "Thriller."

It's close to midnight and something evil's lurking in the dark. . . .

Man, that's not the right song for this moment. I have to force myself to stop thinking. And suddenly, there are another three or four footsteps, and they sound as if they're close to the doorway to the kitchen. They stop. Again. And I grasp the knife handle even tighter. Maybe he's coming to steal my schoolbag, or to check all the cupboards to see if anyone is hiding in there. So I try to be as still as possible. And I wait.

Silence. The longer this goes on, the harder it is for me to control my shaking. And I begin to wonder if he can hear my knees knocking.

There's the sound of movement again, but this time, the steps seem to be getting farther away. I wait for the sound of a door slam, but it never comes. And then that unnerving silence returns. I try to count to twenty, try to will my lungs lighter, but between the heat and the sweat and the fear and the narrow closet, I freak out and barrel through the door.

I start running, not remembering to grab my schoolbag or my inhaler. I run past Mama's ransacked room. I brush against the wooden beads that hang from the living room doorway. I don't look in the direction of the bathroom, where the robber was. I don't hesitate going down the long, dark hallway that leads out of the apartment, the one with closets on both sides. Closets where a robber could lie in wait and then spring out all Jason Voorhees from *Friday the 13th*–like and pull me in with him. Nope. I just zoom by as fast as humanly possible, never letting go of that butcher knife, my knees buckling and knocking their way out the door.

I stay at Widow Mason's apartment until my uncle Paul shows up. Two policemen arrive about twenty minutes later, and Mama maybe fifteen minutes after that. She interrogates me even more than the cops do. Once my statement is taken and the cops leave, Uncle Paul hangs around for a while. But I'm not the one he ends up having to try to calm down—it's Mama. Once she stops running around like a lunatic, double- and triple-checking what might have been taken, Uncle Paul heads home, and it's just her and me.

9

"*How do you forget* to lock the door when you leave the apartment? It's not like you have grown folks' worries, like you have to go hustle to cook for white folks to make ends meet. Rich white folks who are so stingy, they won't even allow you to take home a little of the leftovers they always end up throwing out anyway. You don't have to figure out how to juggle the bills so everything doesn't get cut off," Mama says as she surveys the damage to my hair. It's only been an hour since everyone took off, but I feel as if Mama and I are the last two people left on earth.

I sit on a tall stool in front of the bathroom mirror, which is just above the sink. Mama stands behind me with a cigarette hanging from the left side of her mouth. I'm not so sure the ashes aren't falling onto my head. As she studies my hair, I study her: how long and graceful her neck is; how with her creamy brown skin, wavy hair pulled back into a bun, and high cheekbones standing out the way they do, she looks kind of like Queen Nefertiti.

"You don't have a damned thing to worry about," she barks out, still managing to look beautiful with her face all contorted. Just not fair.

"Where was your head, girl? What were you thinking about? Why are you always doing everything wrong?"

I don't say anything 'cause I can't figure out how I did what I did either. Mama stops going through my hair and starts staring at me. And I can't figure out whether she's trying to think of some other nasty thing to say, whether she's going to shoot some super-villain death rays from her pupils or just haul off and backhand me. But even if she doesn't do anything now, it'll come later. She'll just stash it away in her "Ways to Torture Faye" brain file. And when I least expect it, when I've had the last bit of lemonade she intended to drink, or I don't finish making dinner on time, or I spill a couple of drops of milk on the counter, she'll get me.

Mama opens up the drawer below the sink. I don't see what she takes out, but then I hear these clipping sounds.

"He took my jewelry. That's the only thing I had worth a damn in here. He took my good sapphire earrings and the matching bracelet your father gave me. He took that gold chain Mina Singh brought me back from Trinidad. He took all my valuables. Because you didn't lock the door." The clipping stops.

"Or did *you* take it? Like you did last summer, to show off to your friends. You know I don't like you touching my things. I don't like you playing around with my clothes, my shoes, my jewelry."

"I didn't take anything," I plead.

"Yeah, maybe that's what happened. You wanted to get at my jewelry, so you broke my door open and decided to stage this little robbery thing. Because I don't think you could actually be stupid enough to not lock the front door."

And now the clipping comes faster and more furiously. Then this pink blob surrounded by all these black strands lands in the sink. And then more black strands come down as the clipping noise continues.

"Mama, what are you doing?"

"That gum was right in the middle of your head. Can't just cut that out and leave the rest."

"Don't cut off all my hair!" I scream.

"You should have thought of that before you let some girl get in your head and do something like that to you. You should have thought about that before you let somebody come in here and take my property. . . . And don't you try jerking your head away, because then you can't blame me for where these scissors might land."

And so I just close my eyes and scrunch my face up tight. I really don't want any tears to fall. I try to steady my breathing, so I think of *The Wizard of Oz*—when Dorothy, the Scarecrow, the Tin Man, and the Cowardly Lion are running through that field of poppies. Only, I'm Dorothy and Michael Jackson is the Scarecrow, just like in *The Wiz*. But the other two characters are the actual ones from the original movie. And I think of how pretty everything looks and how calm. I think about us all falling asleep, and even though it's the Wicked Witch's doing, how peaceful and happy this pretty field of flowers makes us.

I hear this loud "Hmm," and I realize Mama's no longer cutting. She's looking me over. I guess she's satisfied, because she puts the scissors down and walks out of the bathroom.

"You clean things up in there, and then come clean this mess of an apartment," she calls out over her shoulder.

I gather enough courage to look down into the white sink, which is now coated with the curly black patches of what was once my hair. Then I gather enough courage to look up into the mirror and see this sad little face that seems so unimportant without anything framing it.

And suddenly, I can't help but wonder what would have happened if that robber hadn't run the other way. What would have happened if he had come into the kitchen and my rubber arms couldn't hold that knife straight enough to defend myself? Would anybody really care? Maybe Daddy. Maybe Keisha. Maybe Uncle Paul. He's the only one I've ever heard tell Mama she needs to lighten up on me. But who else, really? Not so sure Caroline and Gillian would. And I already know how Mama feels—that the only purpose I serve is to take up space and use up her energy and her hard-earned money. Maybe if I had died, I would have turned into one of those angels in heaven. That would be pretty cool, since you never see any black ones. Only little white ones. I mean, what's the deal? Is heaven segregated? That's hard to believe, especially since Dr. Martin Luther King is up there. But maybe it's just taking him a while to get heaven in order. If I'd died, I could have helped integrate it, just like those nine students did to that school down in Arkansas way back when. See? I remember one thing at least from class. But then again, maybe I didn't die because I wouldn't be going to heaven. Maybe I didn't die because I'm being given a chance to redeem myself.

The next morning, I walk the block and a half down Clarkson Avenue to the B41 bus stop on Flatbush Avenue, like I do every morning before school. Only, I don't stop there to wait with the other kids. I decide to take a detour onto Parkside Avenue. People headed to work are filing into the subway station. I move past them and over to Ocean Avenue, where the southern boundary of the park is. Then I move on to a building that's become way too familiar over the past couple of days. This time, I don't hesitate when I get to apartment 1H. It's not that I've gained any extra courage over the last sixteen hours, it's just that I can't go through all the suspense again. If the knob doesn't turn this time, then fine, I'll know somebody's been in there. If it does, well, I guess I'll just have to deal with that. So I fix my hand right on that knob and I crank it. It turns. All the way around.

I'm hoping I won't see anything there on the floor. I'm hoping that the old lady has just been absentminded and forgotten to lock her door. I'm hoping she might be out running errands and buying some support panty hose and Geritol.

I push the door open and slowly step inside. Once again, I find myself standing on the shiny wooden floor of the old lady's hallway. Her shopping bag and all the stuff that was in it are still scattered about, and she's still lying there on the kitchen floor, just as she was when we left her a day and a half ago. Only thing is, she's not on her back anymore. She's leaned up against her side, the legs of the table holding her in that position. So I guess she wasn't dead then, but I'm sure she is now. I mean, what old person can survive on a hard kitchen floor like that? Then I get a thought. If she moved, then I didn't really kill her. Maybe she tried to get up, but the blow to her head made her dizzy and she fell and hit her head again and that second blow was the one that did her in.

I close the door behind me and take a couple of steps forward. Where I'm standing in the hall is dark, but the ceiling light is still on in the kitchen. And it's making a little buzzing sound. I never noticed that when we were in there before, but it wasn't as quiet then, what with Caroline huffing and puffing, and Gillian babbling to herself like an insane person, and my heart beating as loud as it was.

The dishes Caroline threw down are still broken and spread across the floor. I'm kind of trying to avoid looking at the old lady, so I just stand there closing and opening my eyes. Maybe if I do it often enough, one time when I open them she won't be there anymore. I'll open them and

I won't be standing in the warm hallway listening to the steam coming up out of the radiator. Maybe I'll be standing outside her front door and the knob won't turn. I'll hear a television blaring, and I can just head off to school, where my main worries will be that crazy religious studies Nazi, pretty and perfect Charlene Simpson flirting with yummy Curvy Miller, and me unveiling my new, unflattering hairdon't.

I try to take a few more steps forward, but it's as if I've landed in quicksand and I'm being sucked under. The thing is, I realize I don't really know if this old lady is dead. I mean, I think she is. She looks like she is. Her face is all ashy-looking and her eyes are closed and she's just not moving. But it's not like I have much experience with dead people. The only real dead person I've ever seen was my grandfather. They had an open casket and it creeped me out for an entire year. He didn't even look like my granddad. He looked all waxy and fake, like the plastic fruit some people keep in a bowl on their dining room table.

The old lady doesn't look waxy from where I'm standing, so maybe she isn't dead. I drop my book bag down on the floor and force my legs to move. I step on this one floorboard and it squeaks something awful. I don't remember it making any noise the last time I was in here, but maybe we all managed not to step on it. Maybe we did step on it, but we were so caught up in our criminal caper we didn't even notice. Anyway, I pass the bathroom and keep going. But I feel all hot and bothered, because if she is dead, I did it. I mean, even if she did try to get up and fell down again and hit her head a second time, technically, I'd still be responsible because I put her in the position to fall again in the first place.

I never meant to kill anybody. I truly believe that taking some old person's money isn't the most horrible thing in the world, especially if they've got a lot of it. I mean, they probably won't live long enough to use it all anyway, so why let it go to waste? But killing somebody, even if they are old, that's horrible. And I know I cut Mass all the time, sitting in the stairwell of my building eating apple Now and Laters and flipping through *Right On!* magazines I buy with my offering money, but I'm pretty up on all ten commandments. Between Sunday school and religion class at Bishop Marshall and that ninety-two-hour-long movie with Charlton Heston that comes on ABC every Easter, I'm all too familiar with "Thou shalt not kill." I'm familiar with "Thou shalt not bear false witness against thy neighbor," "Honor thy father and thy mother," and "Keep the Sabbath day holy," but to be honest, most of the commandments aren't really that serious. I mean, if you lie or if you party on Sunday or if you call your mother something under your breath 'cause she has horrible mood swings and she deserves it, I don't see what's so wrong with that. That's not going to change the world that much. If you break the other commandments, there's a good possibility that nobody but you and God will know about it and no harm will be done. But "Thou shalt not kill," that's the biggie. You can't make that one better. You can't undo it. You can't say sorry and make it go away. That's it. Somebody's life might be over, and I'm going to have to live with that forever. I don't think I'll ever be able to look at another old person again.

The closer I get to her, the more dead she looks. She has all these little wrinkles around her lips, like she was sucking on a lemon or something. And her skin is really white, but I can't tell if she's looking waxy. Who knows— maybe only black people look waxy when they die. Maybe white people look chalky. So I get closer to her and I just stand there for a second. There's a broken glass near her face. I don't remember that. Broken plates. A broken cookie jar. But Caroline never threw any glasses. And the door to the fridge is open a little bit. I don't remember that from before either. And there are two puddles of liquid. One above her head—that one looks pretty clear. But there's one around her legs, and it smells really strong. I'm thinking, Dead people don't pee. But maybe this all happened while she was still alive. Maybe if I had come in to check on her before, I might have been able to anonymously call the ambulance and they would have been able to help her. I can't tell if her heart's still beating or anything, 'cause she's not moving, and she's kind of wrapped up in her green coat.

I don't really want to touch her, but I tell myself the quicker I do this, the quicker I'll be able to maybe wipe down all the stuff we've touched—you know, get rid of the fingerprints and all—and the quicker I'll be able to leave this place and try to forget what happened. I kneel down without looking at her, and I put the side of my face close to her nose. I don't feel anything. No air. No breath. Nothing. I'm getting really freaked out. So I stand, turn around, and start moving away. That's when I hear this weird strangled gasp. I turn back to find myself looking down into her pale green eyes.

I thought nothing could freak me out worse than the movie *The Exorcist,* but looking into the face of the old lady's ghost has got that beat, hands down. And now I'm petrified it might try to strangle me or get inside me and possess me all Linda Blair–like.

I try to back up, only I trip over my own two terrified feet and stumble to the ground. I can't seem to handle walking, so I start on this backward crawl toward the door. But I'm still facing the old lady's ghost and the old lady's ghost eyes, which look as if they have a film over them, like somebody pulled a not-so-clear Saran Wrap window shade down across them.

I'm still on my hands and knees when I get to the old lady's front door, but I manage to figure out how to get my legs to straighten up. I pull on the knob, but it doesn't open. Then I remember I locked it behind me. So I try to unlock it, all while trying to stop my hands from shaking like leaves. I finally manage to pull the door open when I hear this hoarse voice say, "P-please." And now I'm shaking even more because maybe it's not the old lady's ghost. Maybe she's really alive. And suddenly, I'm not so sure which is worse. If I leave, she won't be able to tell on me and I'll be able to get away. Maybe no one will find her and I won't get in trouble. But if I leave and no one comes to find her, she might really die. But then again, I thought she was dead before, so would it be so wrong to just keep on acting as if she were? I really don't know what to do. Maybe God is trying to test me. But I'm not quite sure how this divine forgiveness works. I probably shouldn't have played hooky from Mass so much.

"Please," she says again. And I turn around a little, but I don't walk back to the kitchen.

"Help me."

She's lying there so helpless, and then I realize something. Maybe she doesn't even remember me. I mean, old people are always confusing stuff. My grandfather used to mix up all his grandkids, even the boys and girls. He'd call me Andre sometimes and call my cousin Andre Lisa. So who knows.

"Please, help me. Help me get up," she says as I inch toward her. "My back . . ."

Once I reach her, I bend and put her right arm around my neck and try to pull her up, but I guess old people weigh more than they look like they do. She's no bigger than a Smurf, but I can hardly even budge her. I have to put one leg on either side of her and lean against a chair, which pushes against the table. And my right foot is in that puddle of pee, but there's not really much of anything I can do about that. The table slides all the way over to the china cabinet in the corner of the room before it stops, and I'm finally able to get some leverage and pull her up a bit.

"The bedroom," she says. And it takes like forever for me to help her to her room. I'm breathing so hard and sweating. I mean, the apartment is really warm. I don't think the radiator has stopped sizzling since I've been here, and my coat is still zipped up over my uniform pants, vest, and blazer. Then there's my knit cap and scarf.

The bedroom is a wreck, with the mattress halfway off the box spring, the fancy red velvety bedspread and sheets on one side of the room, and the drawers from the long, wide dresser piled on the floor with all their stuff scattered about. I guess I didn't realize how much of a mess we'd made.

I have to rest the old lady in an armchair near the dresser and readjust the mattress on the box spring, then put the sheets back on the bed. Once that's done, I'm really sweating buckets, but I don't want this woman catching a glimpse of my uniform or the Bishop Marshall crest, which is stitched into the left breast pocket of my blazer. I've watched enough of those cop shows to know that you should never reveal any identifying symbols. I go back over to the old lady and pull her coat off. Then I put her arm back around my neck and hoist with all my might since she's not really able to help any. I drag her over to the bed, which we both fall onto. I'm practically lying on top of her, but I'm breathing so hard and I'm so spent, I can't really move. And so we lie there for

I don't know how long. This is about as awkward a moment as I've ever had, but there's nothing I can do about it. And I can hear her breath coming in harsh, interrupted spurts.

"Some water, please," she says, her puckered lips all white and peeling. I run to the kitchen and take a glass from the china cabinet, but I have to be careful of all the broken glass and stuff on the floor. The water from the faucet gushes brown when I first turn it on, so I let it run a little while before filling up the glass. When I get back to the bedroom, I have to take the pillows off the floor to help prop her up a little. She makes these slurping noises as she drinks, and she holds the glass as if it's the most precious jewel ever. I just stand there with my hands in my coat pockets, listening to the slurping. I'm trying to figure out how to make my exit.

"Maybe I can call a doctor for you," I say. "Maybe you should go to the hospital."

She just shakes her head. "I don't much like hospitals," she says.

"But maybe you're really hurt." I'm feeling a little better now because she doesn't seem to remember me.

"No hospital," she says again. "I've lived a lifetime. If I'm going to die, I'm going to do it in my own bed, in my own home." She finishes the water, so I walk over to take the glass from her and rest it on her nightstand.

"Look at me," she says. "Bathed in my own urine. What a life." And I look away because I know she wouldn't be in this position if it wasn't for me.

"In that dresser there," she continues. Only, she doesn't point or anything. Just looks toward it. I guess she notices that the drawers are all on the floor. She adjusts her eyes downward.

"I have some sleepwear. . . ."

I walk over and skim the piles of stuff on the floor. I pick up this ruffly flannel nightie, then walk over to the bed, put it down, and back away. She picks it up and tries to raise herself off the pillows, but for all the breathing and grunting going on, she doesn't get very far.

"I don't know if I can do this by myself," she says. I don't know what she expects me to do. "If you can just help me get this sweater off."

Okay, I can do that. I unclasp her colorful flower brooch, careful not to poke her accidentally in the neck with the pin part as I pull it away from the sweater. Then I tell her to raise her arms, and I just yank the sweater up. Only, from all the groaning and moaning she's doing, I'm not so sure I'm not breaking one of her arms.

"You okay?" I ask. She nods. I figure my job is done, so I start backing up.

"I'm going to need a little more help," she says.

I glance at the white button-down shirt she has tucked into her gray slacks, wondering exactly what form of help she's looking to get from me.

"The shirt," she says.

So I walk back and start unbuttoning it. And as soon as I get it open, I see all this wrinkled chicken-looking skin dotted with spots. And there's this mole just below her collarbone, and it's got like three long white hairs growing out of it. Good Lord! I just shake my head, suck in a breath, and lean her to the right side so I can pull her arm out of the left sleeve. Then I lean her to the left side and do the same with her right sleeve. Even though she's skinny, the skin on her arms is all saggy and loose, like it's not really attached to the bone. And she's wearing this beige bra, but I'm not sure what purpose it serves, 'cause I'm standing there looking at these two really old, deflated balloons. Suddenly, I don't feel so bad anymore about not having any breasts at all, because when I get older, there'll be nothing to sag.

I fold the shirt in two and lay it at the foot of the bed.

"And now for the trousers," she says. I guess I shift my eyes a little, 'cause she then says, "I'm not proud to have to ask for help taking off my own clothes. I'm not proud to have a young girl looking at this body, but what choice do I have?"

Honestly, I don't want to have to help this little old woman get naked. I'd rather scoop my own eyeballs out with a rusty spoon. I try to think about things logically. If I help her, then I will have gone above and beyond anything that could be expected of me, and all my recent bad luck will be reversed. So I just count to ten really fast, take a big breath, and go back over to the bed. I'm trying to figure out the fastest way to do this. I take off her boots. Then I have to roll her over some so I can get to the zipper at the back of her pants. Then I slide it down and have to hold my breath for a second, on account of the smell of old pee. This is getting worse by the minute.

I get her pants all the way down her legs and pull from around her ankles. And I thought her arms were rubbery-looking. She's wearing these big nylon panties, but I can see her hipbones poking out from her sides. They look awfully sharp, like if I was to accidentally rub my hands across them, my palms would be sliced to pieces. She takes the ruffled nightie and slowly gets it over her head, then her arms. I help pull it down over her chest and her hips. But then she starts tugging at those oversized nylon panties.

"Can you help me with—"

"Nope, can't help you with that." I cut her off before she can finish getting the sentence out. She was about to utter words my ears don't need to hear.

"Okay," she says quietly, then starts panting and breathing hard as she struggles to get the pee-stained panties off. Good baby Jesus! I'm realizing that it's probably more uncomfortable to watch her than to just go over and help, so I turn my back, lift her nightgown, and without really looking, I pull the panties down her legs and drop them on the floor. She just lies there, breathing a little easier.

"Thank you," she says. I nod, and then there's silence. She's breathing more regular-sounding now, so I'm thinking I should probably make my move. Only thing is, I can't seem to figure out what to say to excuse myself. And the silence goes on and on.

"I'll get you some food," I finally blurt out as I run out of the room. I turn down the hall toward the front door, where her groceries are scattered. After picking them up, I head back to the kitchen. I really don't know what to give this woman to eat, so I gather a little of everything: some bread, a jar of jam, a couple of pears, a box of wheat germ, and a jug of water. But as I reach for a tray, I catch my reflection in the china cabinet. I forgot for a moment that Mama sheared me like a sheep. Even my maroon knit hat can't hide my complete lack of hair. I force my eyes away from that cruel image and head back toward the old lady's room, where I lay the tray of food on the nightstand closest to her side of the bed.

"Thanks," she says softly.

"That's cool," I say. "Okay, bye!" I try to make a mad dash, but her voice stops me.

"How did you get in here?"

"What?" I ask. I heard her. But I'm not as skilled as Caroline when it comes to lying, so I have to buy some time to come up with a good story.

"I asked how you got in here."

"Oh. Well, this friend I go to school with lives in this building. I was waiting for her to come down so we could ride the bus together, and I was kinda bored. Well, you know, sometimes I play around with doorknobs. I always try them. It's something weird I always do. But they never open. But then I tried yours and it opened, so . . . I mean, I wouldn't have come in or nothing, but I saw you lying on the floor." I stop talking and shake my head a little. The thing is, when you have to make up a lie on the spot, you can never tell whether it's a good one or not—at least, I can't. She just gazes at me for a while with her squinty, cloudy, Saran Wrap–covered green eyes. I mean, she's really looking at me, and I'm getting very nervous. I start twisting my scarf around my neck like it's a noose.

"So, how come you were on the floor?" I ask.

"Because some bad little girls pushed their way into my apartment so they could take my money."

"Really?" I say. Only, I don't know how convincing I sound. "That's a terrible thing to do to somebody."

"I'm glad you know that."

"Okay. Um, when did this happen?"

"A couple of days ago, I believe."

"Oh," I say. Man, I thought old people didn't remember anything. "Well, I have to go. Your telephone is right there. Maybe you can call somebody to come look after you. Your family . . ."

She makes this weird grunting sound and turns away a little.

"I don't have any," she says softly.

"Oh, okay. Then maybe your friends. Everyone has friends. Some people have lots. Me, I only have three, although two of them, I've been rethinking lately. Don't even know if you'd consider them true friends. So I guess I really only have one definite friend and two possibles." I realize I'm rambling, so I stop. "You do have friends, don't you?"

"Most have passed on."

"Well, that sucks," I say. And then there's the silence again.

"Maybe you could come back sometime," the old lady finally says in hardly more than a whisper. "If you can find the time."

"O-k-kay?" I stammer out, because I know full well there is no way in hell I'm ever coming back. "How about I get your phone number. You know, in case I can't quite, uh, get . . . down here."

She looks at me for a while, and I do my best not to look away. They said on this TV show once that looking away from someone is a sure signal that you're not being on the up-and-up.

"Top drawer of the night table, there's a pen and paper."

After I take down her number, I notice her still staring at me all weird.

"Well, okay, got your information. And there's the phone right nearby, so when I call, you don't have to move very far for it. Or, in case you think of a friend, maybe, who isn't dead." I stop myself when I realize how stupid I sound. "I mean, in case you think of somebody to call. Well, I really need to get a move on. My friend's probably taken off without me."

I don't wait for her to say anything else. I just crumple up the piece of paper and stuff it into my pocket, then shoot out of the room and down the hall. I don't even come to a full stop as I scoop up my schoolbag and flee that apartment.

Maybe God doesn't hate me after all. The old lady's not dead, so there's no possibility of me being brought up on criminal charges or facing eternal damnation—not for murder, at least. There's probably a long list of other things I could be found guilty of. Anyway, now I can wash my hands clean of this incident. Personally, I think I went above and beyond what was necessary. I brought her food and drink, and talked to her a bit. And I looked at her naked body. Touched it, even. So if you ask me, I've more than done my penance. Disaster averted.

I settle in to wait for the bus for school in front of a large poster advertising Easter candies in the window of a half-price discount store. I try to keep my focus front and center on the cars passing by and the people dodging in and out of traffic to make it across the street, but eventually I give in to the urge to turn and look at my reflection. I slowly ease my knit cap back. One good thing dealing with the possibility of a murder does, it allows you to forget that you look like a hairless cat. But with my mind now free and clear to concentrate on other things, I'm forced to deal with my suddenly changed appearance. There's not even enough hair to cornrow, so I have to settle for a tiny Afro—and that style hasn't been in since the end of the last decade.

I think about not going to school, but then I'd just have to deal with it on Monday, since Tuesday begins our Easter break. But then what do I do the following week, and the week after that? I can't possibly avoid school each and every day until the end of the school year in June, although it's a thought. I mean, it's only two and a half months away, Or maybe I should just take it one week at a time. Survive through Monday; then I have nearly a week off to figure out some sort of camouflage for this thing on top of my head.

As the B41 pulls up, I look at my reflection again. I notice how big my ears look without any hair to offset them. Like satellites. Then I pull my knit cap so far down over my head my eyes are almost covered, too.

Three people get off, and the bus driver keeps the doors open for me, but I don't advance any. He calls out to me and I just stare at him. Finally, I take a deep breath and move forward. Might as well get it over with.

* * *

"Faye, you weren't in first period," Keisha says as she eases over to my locker and stands directly in my line of vision. It's all for the best. There's only so much I can take of Charlene Simpson giggling and throwing her hair back and casting her spell over Curvy Miller.

"Got here right near the end, so it didn't make any sense to go in," I explain.

"What happened? Did you oversleep?" she asks as she walks around to the locker on the other side of me, freeing up my line of vision to Curvy and Charlene just as his right arm coils around her waist like a muscular chocolate-brown snake. I look at Charlene for a moment. She twists her body a bit and balances on one leg, and all I can see is this round little curve of a butt. It's just not fair. Even in our shapeless gray uniform pants, she looks good. My slacks always look as if they're fighting to stay up on my hips, and barely winning at that. And forget it when the weather warms up and we have to wear the pleated skirts. Honestly, unless I'm wearing my undershirt, you can't really tell that any progress has been made in the mammary department. I can only hope that one day something will curve, swell up on me, or indent. To think I'm less than six years away from being twenty and still pretty much waiting for puberty to kick in—how terribly wrong is that?

My line of vision is interrupted again as Keisha crosses back over to the other side of me, and she follows my gaze.

"Like I told you before, Faye, if you really want to have some time with your boyfriend without Charlene around, you should start hanging out at my place after school. Even though they're on different teams, Curvy and my brother have become really close playing baseball. And since he lives nearby, he's always hanging out at our house when they don't have practice or a game, talking about strikeouts and earned run averages . . . and girls, of course."

"No, I'm good," I say quickly. Truth be told, I wouldn't know what to say to Curvy if I got the chance. It's just that he has those dimples to die for, and those great arms, which I suppose he got from throwing that amazing curveball of his.

"So you'd rather stare at him from afar? Why not just speak to him?"

"I've spoken to him," I say a little too defensively.

"'Oops, sorry,' 'Your pen fell on the ground,' and 'Did they run out of orange juice?' is not speaking to someone. I mean, it is, but it's not a conversation. Besides, you could talk to him and find out he's not all that."

I just shrug.

"Anyway, you didn't answer me," Keisha continues. "Did you oversleep this morning?"

"Yeah, something like that."

"You didn't miss much of anything. It was all about East Germany again."

The bell rings, indicating we have about two minutes to get to second period before we're officially marked late. There's a flurry of activity as metal locker doors slam shut and kids secure their books and move off to class. I stare at Curvy as he and Charlene head our way, but he doesn't look in my direction. Not even when his knapsack nearly decapitates me. He just keeps laughing and smiling and succumbing to the spell of perfection.

"Faye, come on. We're gonna be late. You know if Sister Margaret Theresa Patricia Bernadette shuts that door and we're not at our desks, seated, well, that's a whole can of worms I'd rather keep shut and sealed."

"Okay," I say hesitantly. I stuff my coat and scarf into my locker and close the door, all without taking my cap off.

"Why do you still have your hat on?" Keisha asks.

"My head's cold?" I say. Only, not so convincingly.

"Well, you might be able to get away with it in some of your other classes, but that's definitely not going to fly in religious studies." Keisha lowers her voice all serious and steps closer to me. "That crazy old nun will yank it off with that crucifix that's always dangling from her neck, if she has to."

Truth is, my head is overheating and I can feel the perspiration getting trapped in the knit cap. I look over at Keisha's hair, which is all neatly combed and pulled into a ponytail with a red bubble clip. I look around at the Puerto Rican and white girls still milling around in the hall—their hair all long and cascading over their shoulders. I want to keep my cap on for as long as possible, but I know it has to go, so I suck in some air and pull.

"Jesus, Faye. What did you do to your hair?" Keisha says as her eyes light up and grow bigger—almost to the hyperthyroid size of Caroline's.

"I don't know, Keisha. It looks really bad, huh?"

"Well, um. Not *really* bad, but . . . I think it's a little uneven."

"Tell the truth. I look like the long-lost daughter of Mr. T and Grace Jones, don't I?"

"No. I wouldn't say that. Anyway, short hair is in these days. Look at those models in *Jet* and *Ebony*. And what about Annie Lennox of the Eurythmics? You're just being fashion forward."

"Thanks for trying to make me feel better. Even though you're lying. Anyway, I didn't cut it. My mother did."

"Why? Was she mad at you again?"

"She's always mad at me. But Caroline stuck gum in it."

"Why would somebody do that to somebody else?"

"It's a long story."

"I swear, Faye. I don't know how you can say those girls are your friends."

"I told you before, they really helped me out when some of those other kids in the neighborhood weren't so nice, or welcoming."

"Yeah, well, couldn't you have just said thank you to them and moved on? I mean, what do you even talk to them about? What do you all do together?"

I just sigh. I wish I could really tell Keisha what caused the gum-in-hair incident. I wish I could tell her how I redeemed myself by checking on that old lady, how I had to help her get into some clean clothes, and how her old body looked and felt, but I can't.

"I don't want to talk about Caroline and Gillian," I say as I stuff the hat into my locker.

"Well, don't worry about your hair," Keisha says. "It really doesn't look that bad. And the good thing about hair is, it always grows back."

13

It's five-thirty in the morning when I hear Mama's bedroom door creak open. Her slippers drag across the carpet as she makes her way to the bathroom. The sun's not really out yet, but it's not as black as it was when I went to sleep. I can see a little gray peeping through the sides of the window shades. I can even make out my Duran Duran *Rio* and Michael Jackson "Rock with You" posters. My alarm won't be going off until seven, but I've already been awake for a half hour or so, thinking about the decision I came to over the weekend. I will not be going to school. Not today. Not tomorrow, maybe not ever again.

Friday turned out to be worse than I could have imagined. There were all these stares and snickers and giggles. And let's not even discuss Devil Nun, who took one look at me and mumbled, "Karma." I did the only thing that could have been expected of me. I looked right back at her and mumbled, "Fat!"

So there was nothing to do but feign sickness the entire

weekend and keep to my room. I went with abdominal cramps, which are always a good bet because they imply that you need to be near a bathroom at all times. They got me out of church and out of running Mama's stupid little errands.

Unfortunately, Mama does not believe in missing school, so unless I actually mess on myself, there's no way I'll be able to stay home today. But I've got a plan. I'll get up when Mama's leaving, like I always do, and head to the bathroom like I'm about to tidy up. Once she's gone, I'm going to whip up a little breakfast and camp out on the couch in the living room, where I'll spend a glorious day watching TV and doing whatever I please.

Today is actually supposed to be the first day of our Easter break, but on account of the school shutting down for a snow day earlier in the year, we're forced to make it up now. The way I see it, I'm honoring the original school schedule. Come tomorrow, I'm officially on break, and I won't have to worry about my hair for nearly a week.

I turn over, bury my face in my pillow, and drift off as I try to close out the thoughts of the last few horrible days.

"Faye, up, up, up," I hear. Only, the words come to me dreamlike and hazy.

"Faye, get up and get ready for school."

My eyes shoot open and I see Mama standing in her blue-and-white-striped robe in my doorway. I squint at my alarm clock.

"Mama, it's not even six o'clock."

"I don't remember asking you the time," she says. "I just remember telling you to get up and get ready for school."

I have no idea what the heck is going on, so I do as I'm told. I wash up and brush all my hair back, trying to get some type of variety, though it doesn't look particularly attractive this way either. I kind of look like Frederick Douglass, only with a much smaller Afro. After I put on my clothes and suck down some cornflakes, Mama walks into the kitchen dressed for work.

"Come on. Get your schoolbag and put on your coat," she says.

"School's not for another two hours," I say. But the heaviness of her stare convinces me to do as she says.

I stand out in the hall and watch as she locks the door.

"Where are your keys?" she asks.

"My bag."

"Give them here."

Once I hand them over, Mama jingles them a little, then stuffs them into her purse.

"I need those to get back into the apartment," I say. But she doesn't answer. She just starts down the hall toward the elevator. Once inside, she presses the button for the fourth floor instead of the lobby. It's bad enough I'm getting the feeling I haven't shaken this bad karma yet. Then, to make things worse, those menacing words from that Shakespeare play pop into my head: *Something wicked this way comes.*

The elevator jerks to a stop one floor below ours, and Mama gets out. I walk slowly behind her. Very slowly. We pass apartments D4, D3, D2, and then I see her approaching D1. She extends her long, graceful pointer finger and pushes the bell. Oh God! Everyone knows what goes on in apartment D1. I think about making a mad dash. Why didn't I just tell that robber to do with me as he pleased?

"Since you're not responsible enough to be on your own," Mama says as she waits for the door to open, "you'll be coming here each day."

And suddenly, I'm feeling very faint. Is this woman for real? This has got to be the ultimate humiliation.

The door creeps open, and there standing before me is Viola Landish, child-care purveyor, aka babysitter. I mean, who's ever heard of a fourteen-year-old having to go to a babysitter? Aren't fourteen-year-olds supposed to be the ones doing the babysitting?

"It's good to have you here with me, Faye," the sitter says as she clutches a tiny, sleeping baby to her bony chest. She maneuvers it a little, frees up her left hand, and latches on to my forearm for a squeeze. The mortification that has taken over me prevents me from speaking.

"You'll be helping Ms. Viola with whatever she needs help with," Mama adds. And I feel a glimmer of hope.

"So I'm gonna be working?"

"Exactly," Mama says.

"I thought I couldn't start working till I turned fifteen. Okay . . . well, how much am I gonna get paid?"

But instead of an answer, Mama throws her head back and cackles, pivots, and walks back down the hall and into the elevator. I turn to Ms. Viola, who is standing there smiling. Her face is really chubby for someone who doesn't have much meat on her bones. I'm thinking all the fat in her body just happened to have gotten stored north of her neck.

"So how much will I be getting paid?" I ask.

"Well, dear, it's not exactly like that."

Ms. Viola is one of those people whose age you can't really figure. She looks like she could be in her thirties, but she speaks and acts like she's someone's grandmother.

"What's it like, then? If you work, you get paid."

"Well, in this case, your payment is your mother not having to pay me to watch you."

"So I'm not really working. I'm really being babysat."

"Oh no. You're working." And with that, she hands me the baby.

I try to hold it as far from my body as my arms will allow, but she takes him and presses him right against my chest. And he starts crying and squirming and basically alerting me that he dislikes me about as much as I dislike him. And so I just continue to stand there in her hallway with this alien baby attached to me, unsure of what exactly to do with it.

Within the next few minutes, four more kids under the age of three show up. So there you have it. I'm the oldest person there by far, if you don't include the babysitter herself and her lanky son, Gerald, who is fifteen and keeps stealing glances at me and flashing his toothy smile. I've heard a few kids in the building calling him Mr. Ed—you know, as in the talking horse. And to be honest, with his giant, Chiclet-shaped chompers, he does look like he would be right at home grazing in some field. But Ms. Viola and Gerald live here. They don't have to hang around being "sitted," or whatever it is you call it.

I hand off the kid I've been holding to Gerald as he walks

by, and scope out the rest of the apartment. There are two bedrooms and two bathrooms toward the back, but everyone is camped out in the living room. Ms. Viola only has one couch in there, which is pushed up against a wall. There's also a small television set. But those are the only things that suggest any adults ever use that space. The rest of the room is taken up by playpens and toys and a couple of miniature desks. And on the walls are posters of Big Bird and Bert and Ernie and a family of Smurfs. Once I see this layout, I know I have to find a space that's all my own.

I decide to set up camp in the dining room. Outside of the bedrooms, which are off-limits, it looks as if it's the only place in Ms. Viola's apartment that doesn't get much in the way of toddler traffic.

"You're kind of old to be coming to a babysitter," I hear once I'm seated there. I know who it is without even looking up. Gerald has returned and is leaning against the doorway staring down at me. I can't really tell whether he's smiling or whether his lips just refuse to close all the way over his colossal teeth.

"Why do you have to come here?" he asks when I don't respond to him.

"I really don't want to be bothered right now. Got some homework I need to finish up," I say. I need for him to leave so I can come up with an alternate plan of action now that Mama has thrown this monkey wrench my way.

"Well, I'm sure this must suck for you," he says, which is followed by what sounds like a laugh. I give him a sideways glance.

"I'm not laughing at you. It's just, whenever I get nervous, I snicker a little."

"I make you nervous?"

"A little." And then he just stands there for a while. "Look, if you ever need to escape, let me know. I'll come up with some errand and get Mom to allow you to tag along with me. Or if you ever just wanna talk . . ."

"I think I'll be okay," I say. Gerald flashes those teeth at me again before finally lurching away. What a weirdo.

But I'm not allowed any peace, because the moment he's gone, I see Ms. Viola's head poking into the room.

"So glad to have you as my little helper. And as I've always believed, the best way to learn is to dive right in," she says as she extends a diaper my way.

"I don't know how to use that," I bark out as I try to hand the diaper back.

"Oh, it's easy to learn. Baby Owen needs changing, so why don't you come watch? Then maybe you can help me with the other kids."

"Why don't you get your son to help?"

"Gerald? Oh, please, child. You know how boys are. He just shuts himself away in his room doing God only knows what."

"Well, I have homework," I blurt out.

"It's Monday morning," she says. "Didn't you do it over the weekend?"

"I was sick."

"Oh, you're just stalling," she says as she waves me off. "I get the feeling that no matter how sick you might have been, that mother of yours would have seen to it that your homework was completed. Besides, this won't take very long, and you have almost an hour before you have to leave for school."

No amount of sighing and eye rolling will deter the woman. So I end up standing over this changing table with this kid gawking at me. I try not to watch as Ms. Viola unfastens the tabs on the sides of his diaper.

"So, I want you to remove the diaper and take his legs," she says.

"Me? Why?"

"Because you're going to change him."

"I thought you were. You know, to show me how it's done."

"No better way to learn than to be involved . . . now come on."

Has this woman lost her mind? I'm not changing this little mini-humanoid. I'm thinking, since Ms. Viola lives on the fourth floor, maybe I could step out onto the ledge of her window and just jump. But with my luck, I'd probably miss the pavement and land in a rosebush and be perfectly fine, with the exception of my eyeballs, which would be scratched to blindness by the thorns.

"Death by hanging," I mumble as I separate the kid's two fat Michelin Man legs and pull the diaper down. That's when I'm greeted by the foulest stench ever known to man, and I'm faced with a diaper coated in some runny orange-brown glop. I feel my stomach quiver, and I have to make a beeline for the bathroom. It's like the whole peanut butter and Hi-C incident in Caroline's room all over again.

"Don't worry. You see enough of those diapers, it won't even bother you anymore," Ms. Viola tries to reassure me as I rush past her.

It's taken me all of twenty minutes to realize I don't like babies much. Seriously, what came out of that child was in-human. I don't understand why people think they're cute and get all stupid around them, talking that weird baby talk. Talking like an idiot isn't cute. And babies aren't cute. They look like old people, only shrunken down, like little old Yoda dwarf aliens. And they smell funny—milky and sugary sweet and stinky, all at the same time. It's like medicine and lotion and Johnson's Baby Powder and farts all mixed into one.

I've got to get out of this place. I go over my options in my head. No keys means I can't get back into my apartment. I obviously can't stay at the sitter's all day. Go out on the streets, I risk getting picked up by truant officers. And until I can figure out what to do with this hair, I'm not going back to school. Death by slow torture would be better than that.

That leaves only one option.

14

I'm a lot calmer this time around, walking across the shiny lobby floor and down the all-too-familiar hallway with the pretty wooden banisters and sparkly baby chandeliers. Out of habit, I try the doorknob once I get to apartment 1H, but it doesn't give. I never thought I'd be here again, but I really need a place to lie low. Besides, the old lady seemed so desperate for a friend before, I'm sure she'll be grateful to see me. I put my ear to the door, trying to detect whether there are any voices coming from inside, but there's only silence, so I ring the bell. Nothing. I ring the bell again. Still nothing. Finally, I hear some footsteps. It takes just shy of forever, but then I see the peephole open up. She doesn't say anything. I stand there waiting.

"I can see you looking through the peephole," I finally say.

"Who is it?" comes her old-sounding voice.

"It's me. Faye. From the other day."

Again, nothing.

"Faye," I say again. "I found you and helped you up into your bed. . . ."

"What do you want?" the voice says dryly. Okay, not the enthusiasm I expected.

"I just came by to see if you're okay."

Once again, there's no answer.

"Um, and just to see if you might need anything."

Another long silence.

"I need some lemon for my tea," she finally says. "A quart of milk, a few sticks of butter, a loaf of bread. Wheat. And applesauce." That's it. She doesn't open the door. She doesn't say anything else. Then I hear her moving away. I don't really know what to do. The whole point of coming here was to keep off the streets. But what choice do I have? So I go to the market.

When I get back and ring the intercom, it takes at least five minutes for her to answer.

"It's Faye," I say. "I got the stuff you needed from the store." The door buzzes and I walk into the hallway. But when I get to her door, she doesn't open it.

"I have your groceries." I wait and wait and wait.

"Leave them right there at the door," she finally says. "You can go now."

"Okay?" I say as I put the bag down. "Well then, I'm off. You can get it when you're ready." I walk away, making sure to stomp as I do so, but then I tiptoe back until I'm standing right near the door, on the opposite side from where it opens. After about ten minutes, I hear a couple of clicks. The door opens a little, but not all the way. I see this old white hand with brown spots come forward and latch on to the handle of the shopping bag. It pulls the bag in and the door starts to close, only I swoop in and shove my school-bag forward so it can't. The old lady backs up a few steps and I walk in. It's really weird. I'm looking at her and she's looking at me. She has this cane in her left hand, and in her right one she's holding the Key Food bag. Maybe she doesn't remember me. It has been three days since I was last here. And maybe that amount of time to an old person is like three years to a regular person.

"I got you your groceries," I say. "You didn't even say thank you. You didn't even open the door to me. And it cost me five dollars and twenty-eight cents." And as soon as I say that, I feel a little strange. Telling her she owes me this mi-nuscule amount of money when we took nearly three hundred dollars from her. But maybe if I didn't say it, it would seem even more odd.

"I don't have money to pay you with. Some bad little girls broke in and stole it from me," she says. And I can't tell whether she's just saying this or whether there's something behind her words.

"It's okay," I say. "Forget about it." But she doesn't move. She's still in her ruffly nightgown, and she looks even smaller than she did that day we busted into her apartment.

"Maybe you don't remember me. But I'm the one who found you lying on your kitchen floor, barely moving. And I helped get you out of your clothes and into your bed."

"Oh, I remember you."

Okay, it's confirmed. She's definitely making me

uncomfortable. I just stare at her. Only, she doesn't look away—she stares right back with those lizard eyes of hers. And there's so much weight in that stare.

"Are you alone, or do you have any friends today?" she asks.

"What?" is all I can come up with.

"You can take what you want," she says. "But I have no money for you."

"I don't understand what you mean," I fib. Only, I stumble a little over the words.

"Because a body is old doesn't mean a mind has to be too," she says. And she's still staring dead into my eyes.

I decide to give up the innocent act. It's wasting too much energy.

"Aren't you scared of me?" I ask. "I'm young and strong."

"You're not strong," she says. "You're like a scrawny little blade of grass in the wind."

"Well, that's better than being old. Look at you with your cane. You're weak."

"There was a time in my life when I was said to have power, when people cared about the clothes I wore, the food I ate, the places I went, and the people I went there with, when whatever I requested would be gotten for me, no questions asked. And now, today, I could go dancing naked in the streets and no one would even look twice. I've lost all the money I made and all the people I cared most about. So am I scared of a thirteen-year-old girl—"

"Fourteen, if you don't mind."

"And I'll be eighty-one," she says. "And I'm going into my

kitchen. You can go wherever you please." She uses her cane to waddle slowly down the hall. I don't know what to do or what to say, so I just stand there frozen for a minute, looking off at her as she makes it into the kitchen and starts unloading the groceries.

I feel so stupid standing there doing nothing, so I move toward the kitchen. All the broken stuff is still there, but now it sits in one big pile in the center of the floor. I unzip my coat, walk over to the old lady, and try to help her with the groceries. Only, everything I take out and hand to her, she just sorta snatches. What a jerk.

I stand away from her and watch as she opens the loaf of bread and sticks two slices in the toaster. When they pop up, she puts two more slices in. She maneuvers around the pile of broken glass pretty well as she goes into the fridge for a jar of orange marmalade, which she sets down on the table along with the butter I just bought her. She does all this without saying a word to me. Then she gets two dishes and two teacups, puts them down on the table, and sits. She pushes one of the teacups and one of the dishes toward me, then begins spreading butter on her bread. I keep waiting and waiting, but all she does is take a bite of her toast.

"If you're not going to leave, might as well do something with yourself," she says when the next two slices of bread pop up from the toaster.

Once I pull them out, I try handing them to her.

"I've already got what I need," she says. "Besides, I don't know where your hands have been."

I stare daggers at her, but she doesn't seem to notice or care, and I finally just give in. I place the two slices of bread on the plate in front of me and settle onto the wooden dining chair.

"You go to Catholic school?" she asks. I forgot about my uniform.

"So, what of it?"

"It's a little ironic, don't you think?"

"How do you mean?"

"Think about it. You'll get it."

I just ignore her and spread the marmalade across my toast. I'm feeling really weird, but I manage to take a bite. The jam is sweet and tangy at the same time. I put on a little more and steal glimpses of her hands as we eat in silence. I notice how they shake as she puts her teacup down. I wonder if that's how my hands will look when I'm eighty-one, all trembling and fragile, like old paper blowing in the wind. I wonder what would happen if she tried to undo a top that was too tightly screwed onto a jar. Would her bones all crack into pieces and crumble into a mound of powder?

"So you do remember me?" I ask.

She doesn't say anything, just brings the slice of toast back up to her lips with her feeble little hand.

"Did you—did you know who I was when I came in the other day?"

"No, but I wasn't thinking about it. At the time I just needed someone to help me. I was more concerned with that."

"I didn't mean to push you, you know."

She doesn't say anything.

"I'm sorry. And look, I'm here again. I came back to check on you."

"Three days after leaving me helpless and alone. If I was going to die, I would have been dead already."

"Geez, you must be Catholic," I say under my breath. "Like I need any more guilt."

"I guess I just don't understand why such nice little girls would do such things. Is it because you needed the money?"

I shrug. "No . . . I don't know. I guess it's just something to do. And I guess we're not really that nice."

"But you could get into a lot of trouble for it."

"What do you mean? You're gonna tell?"

But she doesn't say anything else.

"You shouldn't say that. 'Cause, like I said, I'm stronger than you. . . ."

"You're scrawny," she says again, but I ignore her.

"And I could still do something to you right now."

But she just stares at me and keeps eating. "So do it."

And I'm thinking maybe this lady is not all there, and everyone knows you're not supposed to look crazy people in the eye, so I turn away. When I finally glance in her direction again, I notice that she's focused on the faded black-and-white photo, which is back up on the counter—the one with some woman holding a baby. The one the old lady attacked me over.

I start looking at the photo, too. The woman in it is standing in the light, but she seems to be casting a shadow over the baby. Maybe she's trying to protect it from the sun. Or maybe it's not a shadow at all but just some kind of smudge over the kid's face. It's hard to tell.

"Why does that picture mean so much to you? Who are the people in it?" I ask.

She doesn't answer.

"So when you were talking about power, is it because you were famous? I mean, I heard you used to be a movie star or a singer or something," I say next.

Still no answer.

"If you have so much money," I try again, "how come you don't live in a mansion? I mean, this apartment's nice and all, but it's still an apartment. In Brooklyn."

When she still doesn't answer, I slam my teacup against the saucer.

"It's fine if you don't want to talk to me. Nothing new. Same treatment I get at home. But I don't get it. You were so desperate for company, you gave me, some random kid, your phone number so I could check in on you. And even today, when you knew who I was, you still gave me toast and seemed to want me to sit here with you. But now that I'm doing that, you don't talk to me. What's with that?"

The old lady looks over at me with those eyes and searches my face; then she stands and leans on her cane.

"I was probably just delirious," she says.

"Fine," I say. "If we're gonna be honest, then you should know that the only reason I'm here now is because I cut school and needed a place to go. Our Easter break starts tomorrow, and I just needed to fill the time."

"Then you can leave, because I'm not about to shelter a truant little child."

"Fine!" I just about yell. "It's no wonder you don't have any friends."

"It's true. And you remember that. Because what you do in life, how you treat people, it always comes back around. You keep it up and one day you'll be my age, and you'll be just like me. With no one there for you. And you'll spend your days going over all the mistakes you ever made. Over all the terrible things you ever did. And all the people you did them to."

And her eyes suddenly look glassy, like she's about to cry or something. I don't know whether to feel sorry for her or to hate her. But I figure she's just a nutty old crone, so I grab my bag and take off. I don't say good-bye; I don't say anything. And as an exclamation point, I put some extra oomph into slamming the door. There's no way I'm going to be like her when I get older. And under no circumstance will I ever waste my time on this woman again.

After leaving that crazy old woman's apartment, I wander around for a while. Thank goodness I stumble onto the Kenmore Theatre, where I'm able to buy one ticket for *Footloose,* then afterward sneak into *Friday the 13th: The Final Chapter.*

When I get back to my building, Caroline and Gillian are in the lobby doing what they do best—loitering. Caroline is slouched against the old musty gray couch in there, the one no sane or hygiene-conscious person ever sits on. I don't know if the thing was always gray, or if it just turned that color from all the dirt and grime it's soaked up. Anyway, she's looking over a supermarket circular, while Gillian is sitting on the equally musty armchair next to the couch doing nothing in particular.

"There she is," Caroline says as I walk through the door. "We were just about to leave. Kept ringing your bell, but there was no answer."

I don't say anything.

"'Cause we haven't seen you since our little disagreement. You know, when you vomited all over me," she says as she stands.

I sense Gillian sizing me up.

"Why the attitude?" Caroline continues.

That's when I decide to slide my hat off my head.

"Oh my God, Faye. You look like a man," Gillian says with a gasp.

"Thanks."

"Oh snap" is all that Caroline can come up with. And I just want to ball up my fist, jerk back, and punch her square in the lip.

"That's all you got?" I ask.

"Faye, I really didn't mean for you to have to get your hair cut off. It's just, you were acting up so much. And you vomited all over me. You didn't even turn away. It's like you were aiming for me with it, and that's pretty nasty. But I never imagined this would happen. Look, we've had a few days to cool off. Why don't we just call it even?" She sticks her big man-hand out. But I don't accept it.

"Look at my hair, Caroline. It's a disaster. And there's nothing I can do about it."

"It does look terrible," Gillian volunteers. Caroline waves her off but doesn't say anything to the contrary.

"Thanks again, Gillian," I say.

"I didn't mean for you to have to get it all cut," Caroline says again. "And we missed hanging out with you this weekend. Seriously. Don't be mad."

She extends her hand even more, and I just look at it. I

wonder what she would say if I told her I'd been back to that Parkside Avenue apartment. I wonder how she'd react if I told her the story of helping the old lady off the floor and into her bed and out of her clothes. I wonder how she'd react if she knew I was over there again today. But I'm not eager to see what her wrath might bring about this time around, so I just give in and accept her handshake.

"So, you wanna go up to the corner store and get some snacks?" she asks. "My treat."

And I'm thinking, You took enough of the money we got from the old lady; that's the least you could do. But I don't say it.

"Nah . . . I've gotta go do something for Mama," I lie. I might have shaken Caroline's hand, but I'm still plenty sore at her.

"All right. Well, come over to our place when you get a chance."

I watch as they head down the walkway and turn left once they reach the sidewalk. I can't figure how Caroline can think we're even. Vomit, yeah, it's gross, but you can wash it away. Hair shaved off, not as easy to overcome.

Just as the elevator door slides open, they disappear from my view. I step in slowly and press the button for the fourth floor. Now I'm faced with the next fun phase of my day—my indentured servitude.

* * *

I guess miracles do happen, because just as I'm being asked to change another foul diaper, Mama calls down to Ms. Viola to have me come home, and it's only six o'clock.

Never thought I'd be happy to hear from Mama, although this early call is making me a little nervous. Mama is never home before seven. That rich family she works for lives on the Upper West Side of Manhattan. She never leaves there earlier than five-thirty, and it's impossible for her to get back to our apartment in only a half hour. I guess I'll find out what's going on soon enough.

It's weird having to ring the bell to an apartment I've been letting myself into since we moved here last year. Actually, I've been letting myself into our apartments since I was nine years old. But I just ring the bell and stand there. I'm waiting for what seems like forever and there's no response, so I ring it again. That's when I hear Mama's footsteps coming down the hall. They're moving fast, almost like they're running. She's probably going to be all ticked off since I rang twice. The locks click open and I hold my breath. But there's Mama standing in her long green satin gown. The one with the halter neck and the big Christmas-present bow on the left side. The same one she wore to her friend Darlene Wilson's wedding. Her hair is all done up and pulled into a big bun with little curls hanging down the sides. She's wearing so much perfume, I have to fight for some breathable air. And her lips are Ringling Bros. and Barnum & Bailey clown red.

"Why are you standing out in the hall like some little lost animal, Faye? Come in. Come in."

The minute I'm inside, she locks the door behind me and actually puts her arm around my shoulder, though I'm not so sure whether she's hugging me or pushing me along. I'm thinking, Either I'm in a whole heap of trouble, or she's finally gone off her rocker—not that she had very far to go.

The apartment smells sweet and spicy, the way it always does when Mama makes oxtail. Only thing is, she never makes it unless it's a pretty special occasion. Actually, she never cooks, period, unless it's a special occasion, which, blame it on temporary insanity, I decide to bring up to her.

"We haven't had oxtail since Aunt Nola's birthday," I say. "What gives?"

"Shut up," she says. Only, she says it in a nice way, if it's even possible to tell someone to shut up nicely.

"I laid out a dress for you. The blue one with the cowl neck you like so much. And your hair, well, I guess it'll have to do. That's about the best it's going to look, I suppose." And she's pushing and pulling and rushing me all at the same time.

"You go on and bathe. I expect you to be seated at the kitchen table in thirty minutes."

"Why do I have to wear a dress?" I ask. "I think I'd be more comfortable in my jeans. And why are you wearing your 'going somewhere special' outfit?"

Her eyebrows arch up like they're about to shoot from her forehead. I'm convinced she's about to yell something. But she doesn't. Instead, she smiles. At least ,she does something with her lips that resembles a smile.

"Just go get yourself together," she says.

After finishing up in the bathroom and dressing, I stand before my bedroom-door mirror, studying my reflection. But just as I'm trying to get the zipper on the back of my dress all the way up, the door comes flying open, crashing into the wall.

"It's six-forty-five," Mama says as she begins fidgeting with her hair. "Why is everybody late? And why aren't you at the table?"

I walk into the kitchen with my dress still halfway open in the back. I guess Mama notices me fiddling with it, because the next thing I know, it's quickly being zipped up. Maybe a little too quickly, because it catches a bit of the skin on the back of my neck. But I don't scream. I don't say a thing. Once she moves away, I have to unzip it a little, and even though I can't see it, I'm pretty sure some of my skin has been ripped off and is caught up in the zipper's teeth.

Just as my butt is about to hit the chair, the downstairs bell sounds. I pop back up to go and answer it.

"No. You sit down," Mama says as she walks out of the kitchen and disappears into the hallway. Twenty seconds later, she's back, but there's no one with her. And I never heard her ask who it was into the intercom.

"Faye, go get the door."

"Isn't that what you went to do?" I ask. Mama shoots me a look. And then she slows down her words, as if she's trying to get through to someone with a learning disability.

"Go . . . stand . . . by the door . . . and wait . . . for the bell . . . to ring. Then open it . . . and let . . . the person . . . in."

I look back at her as I walk from the kitchen. She's patting her hair and looking at her reflection in the toaster oven. Thick black lines are drawn across the tops of her eyelids, which makes her look a little like Cleopatra. And her cheeks are red and shiny. She sits down at the table and crosses her thin legs, then her lips stretch into this weird smile. Some of the circus red lipstick is now on her teeth. I point at it.

"Mama, there's some lipstick—"

"Why are you standing here staring like you're slow or something? To the door," she says with a clenched jaw. I change my mind and don't say a thing.

I don't like the feel of this. Who could she possibly be expecting? If you discount Uncle Paul and Aunt Nola, no one ever visits us. Maybe Mama's gotten wind of my exploits with Caroline and Gillian and has convinced them to come spill the beans. Or maybe she somehow found out what happened in that Parkside Avenue apartment and has set it up for the old lady to come and tell the whole sordid story. Maybe it's that robber from before. Maybe Mama has just decided to get me off her hands once and for all, and the minute I open the door, there'll be a samurai sword to the gut.

My left eyeball is positioned in the peephole even before the bell rings. As the figure approaches the door, it's blown out by the too-stark hallway light. All I can tell is that it's a man. But once he steps closer, I realize just who it is and quickly undo the locks.

"Hey, baby girl. You better come give me a hug," my father says as he bends and wraps his skinny arms around me, bear hug–style.

"What are you doing here? I haven't seen you in months," I say.

"Been getting a lot of gigs. Trying to make that money. Then had to spend a little time down in Florida. But I'll tell you all about that when I take you out on our dinner date."

"Dinner?" I ask. "Just you and me?"

"Faye, dear . . . ," I hear Mama call. I grab Daddy by the hand and lead him down the hall.

"You're looking fancy," he says. "And what did you do? Get one of those new short hairstyles?"

"Something like that," I say as I shake my head. "FYI, I think Mama had something else in mind for dinner. Maybe you should talk to her first."

When we get to the doorway of the kitchen, Mama pops out of her seat like a big green jack-in-the-box. She lifts the hem of her special-occasion dress and flies past me and over to Daddy.

"Faye, give your father a chance to breathe," she says all friendly and charming. "There'll be more than enough time for you all to catch up over dinner, won't there, Charles?"

Daddy looks around the kitchen, and his eyes lock on to the stove.

"Something smells good," he says.

"Yeah, I bought some oxtail the other day and left it out in the fridge, so I figured I should cook it before it spoils. And you know oxtail is not cheap."

"Oh," Daddy says. "See, the thing is, Jeanne, I was thinking Faye and I could just go out. To Faye's favorite. Red Lobster."

"Wait a minute. Wait," Mama says, twisting her curls and acting even weirder than she's been acting all night. "I mean, I have all this food. Everyone's hungry. Why let it go to waste? Come on, sit down."

Daddy doesn't look so sure.

"Then you can tell me about this life change you mentioned over the phone. This big news. And I don't want to have to wait till you two get back from Kings Plaza to hear it. We'll all talk. After we eat."

Before Daddy can say another word, Mama is taking him by the arm and leading him over to the table.

"Now sit," she says. "There'll be no restaurant when we've got perfectly good food right here."

"I don't know, Jeanne. I wanted to do something Faye wanted. Something different."

"Oh, but she loves oxtails," Mama says. "And talk about different. I can't tell the last time we had them. She doesn't want any Red Lobster, right, Faye?" Her lips are smiling when she says this, but her eyes are not.

Daddy looks at me. "Faye, it's up to you, baby. You say Red Lobster and we're out of here."

My lips are ready to form the words *Red Lobster,* but I see Mama shooting me her death rays. I guess it's going to be oxtails.

16

I truly hate my life. Why didn't I just defy Mama's will for once and say what I really mean? Now instead of sitting across from Daddy at the restaurant, enjoying some shrimp scampi and a Shirley Temple, I'm staring at Mama in her ridiculous gown.

"You sure about that?" Daddy asks once I give my half-assed answer. I just nod without any enthusiasm.

"Oxtails you want, oxtails it is," he says before turning to Mama. "By the way, what's with the dress, Jeanne?"

"Oh, this?" And she does this weird fashion-model turn. "I was going through my closet. I have a few beautiful pieces. This one I got when we first got together, remember? Anyway, where do I have to wear them to nowadays? So Faye and I decided we would do like the rich people and play dress-up when we had dinner."

I look up, 'cause unless I'm losing my mind, I don't remember ever having such a discussion. And Mama's not really the type to play anything.

"Hmm," Daddy says. "Hope that giant bow doesn't get in the way of your food."

I giggle, because I figure Daddy thinks this is as ridiculous as I do—Mama getting all dolled up in her ball gown to have dinner in our small Brooklyn apartment, where the roaches outnumber us a million to two.

"I suppose it *is* a nice dress," he says. And Mama smiles her smeared lipstick smile. "You got something on your teeth, Jeanne."

Mama brings her napkin up to her mouth. When she removes it, she smiles again, only with her lips together this time.

Daddy takes off his leather jacket and his orange-and-blue Mets cap. Every time I see him he looks thinner, and he was never all that big to begin with.

"You're growing a beard," I say.

"It's a goatee. You like?"

"It's got some grays in it. Makes you look older."

"Personally, I prefer the word *distinguished*. So, how you doing in school?"

Things start out normal enough, but it doesn't take long for the conversation to take a turn and for Mama to completely go off the deep end. The "change in plans" Daddy needed to talk about comes up way before the end of dinner. Mama starts babbling about how nice it is for the three of us to be eating together, and how like a real family it feels, and on and on and on. And I start noticing just how uncomfortable this seems to be making Daddy. I mean, his eyes are shifting about. He's poking at his food and chewing on the same piece of oxtail for like ten minutes. Finally, he takes his napkin, wipes at the corners of his mouth, and pushes the plate away a little. Then he just sits there, quietly staring at his Seven Natural Wonders of the World placemat.

"Jeanne, maybe we can go into the living room and talk."

"Whatever you have to say, you can say it right here," she says. But Daddy looks at me out of the corner of his eye.

"Maybe we should go into the living room," he says again. And Mama's face clouds over. She actually looks a little scared. She clasps her hands together and sits up really straight. Then she just plops out of her seat like she's lost all control of her muscles, and she's kneeling on the cold linoleum floor in her fancy gown. She grabs Daddy's hands and starts laughing.

"I've changed so much over the last couple of years, Charlie. I'm more secure with myself, I'm happy. I've learned to laugh. You know I don't want to sign those papers. I mean, you've been out there. You see how hard it is. We had something good. Why don't we just give it another shot?"

"I'm going to be based out of Fort Lauderdale from now on, Jeanne. I've met a really great woman. Her name is Melba, and, well . . . we're getting married." And Daddy turns to me. "Baby, I'm getting married again. . . ." Then he turns back to Mama. "I'm really going to need you to sign those papers this time. No putting it off any longer."

"Fort Lauderdale? Florida?" I say. "Why do you have to go there? Couldn't you just get married and stay here in New York? I mean, it's not like I can hop on the forty-four bus and go visit you there. It's not like I can get on the number two train or ask Uncle Paul to give me a ride." I hardly see Daddy now, when we technically live in the same state, so I can just imagine how those visits will dwindle once he's based out of Florida. My stomach sinks. And all of a sudden, the oxtail in my mouth becomes like rubber. I just keep chewing and chewing, but I can't seem to swallow it.

I figured with Daddy traveling around so much for his music, he must have had other girlfriends, but none has been serious enough for him to come and talk to Mama about.

"Jeanne, one of the things I wanted to discuss with you . . . Maybe Faye could come live with me awhile. Give you a chance to maybe do some of the things you've always wanted to."

"Really?" I say. And I almost jump out of my chair. A new life away from Mama? It couldn't get any better than that.

"Live with you?" Mama says softly. "But she's all I got." I'm sure my head snaps around, because I've never heard Mama say anything like that before. She's still kneeling on the floor, and in that one brief moment, she seems so much smaller.

"If not all the time, maybe summers and holidays. Look, I know you're the one who's been holding things down for the past few years now. I know you've shouldered a lot of the burden while I've been out picking at my bass, but I've stumbled on a nice full-time gig at a hotel down there. I'll have some stability. . . ."

Mama begins rising from the floor. Only, it takes a lot of maneuvering, 'cause there's plenty of green dress she has to work with. She walks back over to the table, grabs Daddy's plate, which still has some food on it, and flings it into the sink, breaking it into a hundred pieces.

"Melba? What the hell kind of name is Melba?" Then she grabs his glass and does the same with it. And then the words just start spilling out of her mouth. She's talking so fast and her lipstick is smearing so much, it looks as if somebody has taken the time to paint each of her teeth red.

"You come in here after six years, wanting to be some hero and take my daughter away to Florida to stay with some woman named Melba, show her the good life, what she's missing by living in some cramped little Brooklyn apartment with me. Since you've been gone, you've done what? Given a couple dollars here and a few cents there. Just because you throw money at that Catholic school of hers doesn't mean you're really contributing shit. I've had to pick up all the slack while you've been going around, trying to become a bass player, running around acting like you were a single man. But now that you've got things on track and you'll finally start earning a little money, you don't reward the one who's done all the work. You reward some Melba who probably just popped up, saw you for what you are this moment, not for what you've been all those years. And now you're gonna try to take my daughter away from me while you play house with this whore?"

And there's this big giant vein in the center of Mama's forehead that's bulging and throbbing. And I'm wondering if it's not going to explode and coat the entire kitchen in a deep, gooey red.

"Faye, go to your room," Daddy says. "And don't worry. We'll figure this out."

"Okay," I say quietly, even though I don't want to go. This was supposed to be about me and Daddy catching up and having some fun. How did it turn so nightmarish? I'm not getting a good feeling about how things are going to end. Even though I shut my door, I can still hear Mama's voice coming harsh and loud. Daddy's is softer-sounding, but just as intense.

"Everything you do in this life has consequences, Jeanne," Daddy says. "Everything. You just remember that. You can't do bad to someone and not expect it to come back around to you."

"Then when will you get yours?" Mama yells. "'Cause I'm not the one who walked out on this. I'm not the one who stepped out with some fast-ass supermarket cashier girl— the first of your many little slipups—six years ago. . . ."

And this goes on, back and forth, until I become aware of only Mama's voice still ranting and raving. I ease out of my room and over into the hallway, before stepping quietly into the kitchen. Mama is standing with her back flat against the broom closet, as if she's been glued to it. Her eyes are all glassy and bulging, her bun has come undone, and with what's left of her red lipstick, she looks like some deranged clown. And she starts breathing really, really hard, like she's going to pass out. She suddenly separates from that closet and starts moving toward me. I just freeze. Too scared to move. Too scared to take in a breath. But Mama doesn't even see me. She just brushes past and walks into her room. The door slams behind her. I hear some things being thrown against the wall, then there's silence.

I start picking up pieces of broken plate and wrapping them in newspaper. Only, I make sure to do it real quietly so as not to disturb her, so I don't cause her to remember that I'm still here. About ten minutes later, she emerges from her room with a coat over her green dress and the big bow pushed up from her shoulder into the side of her face.

"Come on," she says to me. "We're going to the church!"

"But Mama, it's not open now," I say softly.

She stands there for a second. I think my words are registering because she slowly begins to take her coat off. But then she rushes at me and connects with an elbow to my temple.

I fall against the table, knocking over two of the chairs. But it's okay. It doesn't hurt so much. It doesn't hurt because I can see Michael Jackson dancing toward me in his rhinestone suit from the "Rock with You" video. And he's smiling like an angel.

> *Girl, close your eyes, let that rhythm get into you.*
> *Don't try to fight it, there ain't nothing that you*
> *can do.*

17

Easter finally gets here. I say finally because I couldn't
come up with anything to avoid having to spend twelve and
a half hours at Ms. Viola's every day for the four days we
had off for our break. From six-thirty in the morning, when
Mama left for work, to seven in the evening, when she returned, I was forced to perform slave labor. That's a total of
fifty hours of being subjected to whining and crying, and
feeding and burping and cradling babies. Fifty hours of
horse-toothed Gerald cracking corny jokes and snickering.
Fifty hours of my own personal hell. Only break I managed
to get was on Good Friday, when I insisted Ms. Viola respect
my religious yearnings and allow me out for Mass. Once I
got a taste of freedom, I hightailed it over to a McDonald's,
where I treated myself to a Big Mac lunch and considered
taking the F train to Coney Island and flinging myself into
the Atlantic.

Easter Sunday finds me seated next to Mama, trying to
keep my eyes open during the longest Mass ever. There's all

this pomp and circumstance surrounding it—which is not completely horrible at first. The lighting of the Easter candle is kind of cool, and there's a full choir singing, but that gets old quickly enough. First of all, they really need to funk things up, like the choir does at the Baptist church Aunt Nola goes to—although I guess you can only get so funky when you have to sing songs named "The Strife Is O'er, the Battle Done" and *"Regina Coeli Latare."* Secondly, one less reading from the Old Testament wouldn't kill them.

Somewhere around the Gospel according to John, a little gray-haired white woman dressed from head to toe in Easter yellow exits her pew, and my mind runs across the old lady on Parkside Avenue. I start wondering if she's even religious. Does she go to Mass? Maybe she's Jewish. I don't know. I always think of old white people as being Jewish, old Hispanic people as being Catholic, and old black people as being Baptist . . . unless they're from the Caribbean.

Maybe if we hadn't gotten into that fight I would have snuck out from Ms. Viola's and gone back to see her, but she's completely ungrateful. If she's so happy being alone, then good for her.

When that dreadful service is over, Mama and I catch the Flatbush Avenue bus over to Cortelyou Road, then walk the five or so blocks to Aunt Nola and Uncle Paul's, which is where we spend every Easter. I always have a good time there because they're a real family. They're forever telling jokes and laughing and hugging and kissing each other. Well, three quarters of the family is cool. Then there's my cousin Lisa.

I used to get confused when I first started visiting my aunt and uncle by myself. All the houses on their block look the same. They're all two-story attached row houses made with either red or brown brick. Fortunately, Aunt Nola's a bit peculiar, so for half the year, her house really stands out. Her Christmas decorations go up just after Halloween and stay there until Easter.

The doorbell goes *ho, ho, ho* when Mama rings it. Aunt Nola is all smiles and hugs as she greets us. She even says something complimentary about my "sassy new hairstyle" once I take my hat off. I'm pretty sure she's just trying to make me feel better, but I'll take it. Uncle Paul sips his rum and Coke and laughs in the background while my cousin Andre waves from the kitchen. And the house smells like baking bread and roast beef.

Out of the corner of my eye, I spot Lisa sneaking up the stairs, acting as if she doesn't see us.

"Hey, Lisa," I say as I catch up to her. "What's going on?"

There's the loudest sigh before she mumbles "Nothing" through gritted teeth. Lisa's one of those stuck-up beauties, someone I'd get a whole lot of pleasure dishing out a spoonful of misery to. I mean, there's never a blemish on her face or scar on her knee or hair out of its beautiful place. And she's all too aware of this. She's the sun and we're just itty-bitty planets trying to get a little of her glow. My very presence seems to annoy her to no end. I guess it takes her out of her beautiful thoughts and distracts her beautiful mind from whatever it is beautiful people spend their days thinking about—butterflies and unicorns and jelly beans and stuff like that. But this is the thing I don't understand: if you're so pretty, what do you have to be so pissed off about all the time?

She looks at my hair with the slightest bit of interest. I know she wants to say something about it, but doesn't want to risk the possibility of it maybe turning into an actual conversation.

"I need to go upstairs," she grumbles.

"I'll just come and keep you company."

"No. I have my period. I need to be alone."

I find it interesting that since I started getting my period, it only comes once a month. Lisa's seems to show up every time she has to do something she doesn't want to.

As we all get ready to sit for dinner, the bell rings, and Uncle Paul exchanges a weird look with Aunt Nola before he heads for the door. A few seconds later, he's back with . . .

"Jerry Adams, everybody. Jerry, we were just about to have some dinner. You're eating with us, and I'm not going to take no for an answer."

"I guess I have no choice, then," Jerry Adams says. And this is followed by the loudest, cheesiest laugh I've ever heard: "Hey, hey, huh. Hey, hey, huh."

Jerry gets seated right next to Mama and immediately begins stealing glimpses at her from the corner of his eye. I try not to stare, but his name couldn't be more fitting. The man has the wettest, juiciest, drippiest processed curls I've ever seen. It's as if someone dipped his hair in Vaseline, then straightened it all out, then curled it back up, then dipped it in baby oil. I think I'll call him Jheri curl Jerry, or JCJ for short. I'm trying to eat Aunt Nola's lamb, but my eyes keep drifting back to the little beads of liquid just barely hanging on to the very end of each strand of hair. I can't understand how they don't drip down into his food and poison him. I'm waiting and waiting for one to fall, but nothing. They just keep dangling there, like he's put a spell on them and they don't dare defy him.

"So, Jerry, Jeanne is an amazing chef," Uncle Paul says. "Prepares food for very influential people in Manhattan."

"She's a pretty one too," Jheri curl Jerry says. I see my cousin Andre rolling his eyes and giggling.

"I'm a glorified maid is what I am," Mama says nastily before turning to JCJ. "Mr. Adams . . ."

"Oh no. Unless you want to insult me, please call me Jerry."

Mama sips some water, puts Aunt Nola's pretty crystal glass back down on the table, and continues.

"As I was sayin', Mr. Adams, I'm not stupid. Why don't we cut to the chase and call this what it is . . . a setup. But the thing is, I don't need any help getting a man."

"Then why haven't you had one in all these years?" Uncle Paul says under his breath. Mama shoots him a look.

"Because that was my choice. I mean, do you see what's out there? Besides, I've got enough to handle with my job, my daughter, and my God. Don't have time for dating fools."

There's this pause. Then a loud, "Hey, hey, huh. Hey, hey, huh. I love a woman who has a strong mind. I like to call it spice. And spice makes everything better."

Mama rolls her eyes, but Jerry just keeps on going.

"I run a little company that ships barrels to the Caribbean. Barbados, Dominican Republic, Virgin Islands, Dominica even, so I'm more than stable enough to take care of my woman," Jerry says as he winks at Mama. At least, I think it's a wink. Who knows, maybe one of those greasy chemical drops finally made its way into his eye.

Mama's wearing her gray church suit with her black boots. The jacket stops just above her waist, and the skirt is just tight enough to show off her butt. When she gets up to help Aunt Nola clear the table, it's as if her butt is a magnet and Jerry's eyes are beams of iron. He can't seem to look away.

Dinner over, beautiful Lisa disappears into her room to stare at herself in her mirror or brood or do whatever she spends all her time in there doing, while Andre and I sit on the stairs watching the adults, who have moved into the living room. Aunt Nola gathers up her Otis Redding and Sam Cooke records.

"They need to lose that old music and get with some Fat Boys and Run-DMC," Andre mumbles.

Ice starts going into glasses and rum and whiskey begin to flow. The music gets louder, the laughter comes more frequently, and some out-of-date dance moves start taking place between Aunt Nola and Uncle Paul on the brown shag carpet. As they hug and sway and giggle, I notice Mama moving away each time poor Jerry tries to sit closer to her on the couch. He leans in to whisper something, but she sticks a cigarette in her mouth, quickly lights it, and turns so the cigarette creates a barrier between her and Jerry's face. Only, it's coming way too close to his chemically treated hair.

Uncle Paul makes his way over to them and motions for Jerry to go and dance with Aunt Nola. When Jerry does so, Uncle Paul takes Mama by the elbow and walks her into the dining room. I give Andre a look, walk down the hall, and sneak over to the edge of the dining room.

"You got a good man in there and you don't even want to give him a chance," I hear Uncle Paul say. "You sit here screwing up your face and acting all holier-than-thou waiting for God only knows what to come in and steal you away. You're waiting for Charles to come back to you, but you better get over it. It hasn't happened in all these years, and it's definitely not about to happen now that he's found someone else."

"It's just not fair," Mama says. "It's not."

"Jesus, Jeanne. Life's not fair. Things happen. And sometimes there's nothing you can do about it but move on. He was the first man you ever truly loved, and I know that means something. But Charles wasn't perfect. And there are good men out there who are stable, who know that once you have a family, maybe it's time to stop chasing pipe dreams. Jerry's one of those men. And the older you get, the fewer good men you'll find. Time doesn't stop for anybody. One day you're gonna wake up and find you're not so pretty anymore."

That's when Mama looks up and notices me standing there before I have a chance to duck away. But for the moment, she seems more embarrassed than angry. For the moment.

"It's time for me to be heading home," she says. "I've had more to drink than I should have, and I need to get myself prepared for work tomorrow."

I'm hardly able to get my coat on and a couple of good-byes in before she's out the door.

"All right now, Jeanne, I hope to see you again soon!" Jerry yells at her. And Aunt Nola comes hurtling down the stairs after us with a bag of leftovers. Mama takes it with her left hand, thanks Aunt Nola, then grabs hold of my coat sleeve with her right hand and starts pulling me through the gate and down the block, all the while huffing and puffing and hissing.

"You're a real piece of work," she grumbles. "Stealing, lying, eavesdropping on grown folks' conversations. Who knows what else you've been doing. But you mark my words, little girl. What goes around comes around. Keep this up and I promise you that one day soon, you'll come to regret it."

It's as if all the adults in my life are channeling each other. Was everyone sitting in on Devil Nun's lesson about karma? The old lady said practically the same thing, and she and Mama are about as different as two people can be. Then again, maybe they're not so different after all. Mama doesn't really have that many people in her life either. The few friends she had, she's driven off with her moodiness. If it wasn't for Aunt Nola and Uncle Paul, there wouldn't be anyone inviting her to Easter dinner. And I'm pretty sure they only do it because they're related.

18

Just call me a sucker. Because come Monday morning, I show up at the old lady's apartment with some of the lamb and potatoes and green beans we carried home from Aunt Nola's. I planned on never seeing her again, but I guess I don't think anyone should have to spend a major holiday all alone, especially if they're really decrepit and probably only have one or two holidays left anyway.

"Who is it?" she calls out after I ring her doorbell, which is bull, because once again, I saw the light behind the peep-hole change, so I know she looked out and saw it was me.

"It's Faye. From the other day."

"How can I help you?"

She cannot be serious. She's going to cause me to rethink my good deed.

"I brought you something."

It takes more than a minute for the door to finally open.

"Here," I say as I hold the plate out to her.

"Didn't think you'd come back," she says.

"Me neither. . . . So are you gonna take it or not?"

"What is it?" she asks.

I suppose I would have asked the same thing, what with the plate being all wrapped in aluminum foil and super-stuffed into a Ziploc bag so that it's hard to tell what exactly is in there. For all she knows, it could be a big hunk of garbage or a dead baby squirrel or something. But in my defense, I had to go through some *Mission: Impossible*–type maneuvering to get it to her.

While Mama was busy washing up, I transferred some of the food from the leaky tinfoil Aunt Nola had wrapped it in to a Ziploc bag. When I got to Ms. Viola's, it immediately went into her fridge. Only, I had to write myself a note as a reminder to take it out before school. All that trouble for an old woman who is a complete ingrate. All that trouble for an old woman who just looks blankly at me with her peculiar eyes. I really don't think people should have green eyes, only reptiles and cats.

"It's Easter dinner," I say. "I mean, if you didn't have it with anyone."

She just stands there in her doorway sizing up the package, not asking me to come in. I'm hoping she takes it soon, because my arm is starting to tremble from the weight of the food.

"So, did you?" I ask.

"Did I what?"

"Have Easter dinner with anyone?"

"No," she says softly as she finally takes the plate. But in place of some gratitude, the woman straight-up insults me.

"Tell me, are you still being a truant? Still looking for a place to hide from the cops? Hoping I'll let you in?"

"For your information, I have no intention of holing up in your apartment. I'm on my way to school right now."

"You've decided to go back?"

I shake my head. "I don't have much of a choice. Believe me, I gave good thought to not showing up again until sophomore year, but outside of a major disease, I guess it would be kinda hard to explain a two-month absence. As it is, I'm gonna have to get creative in disguising the missed day that's gonna show up on my report card end of semester."

"Then why go through all the trouble of not going in the first place?"

"Well, what would you do if your mother chopped off your hair and left you looking like one of those village girls from *National Geographic*?"

"It can't be that bad."

"Oh, it is, believe me."

She studies my face for a little while. "Let me see it."

"No way."

"I'm guessing you won't be able to keep that hat on in school, so all your classmates will be getting an eyeful of it very soon."

"Most of them already have. You wouldn't believe the humiliation, which is why I had to take that day off. I'd just as soon not have anyone set eyes on it again."

"How about you take the hat off now and show it to me?"

"Didn't you hear what I just said? It's unbelievably ugly."

"Let me see it," she says again.

I sigh, look up and down the hallway, then slide my hat off. The old lady looks at my head for a long time.

"See, you can't even come up with something encouraging."

"Well, it is short. But it's also thick, and it's healthy. Just think, you could have my hair. Maybe there's a little length there"—she bends her neck forward and points to the middle of her head—"but there are so few strands left, I have to spend half the morning arranging them in such a way to make it seem as if I have more."

"Where do you go that you need to care how your hair looks?" I ask.

"I'm old, not dead," she says. "I've allowed enough things to slide. But one thing I'll never neglect is my hair. No woman should ever neglect her hair."

I go to put the hat back on.

"Oh, lose the hat," she says. "If you walk around owning who you are and what you have, people have no choice but to respect you for it. Besides, you shouldn't put so much stock in what your classmates think anyway. It's a given that high school kids can be complete idiots.

"It's your first day back from your holiday break—don't walk into that school already defeated. You go hiding under that hat, those little idiots will definitely sense your discomfort. You go to school owning that hair of yours, they'll have no choice but to get on board. And as for the ones who don't, to hell with them. They'll back down when they see your confidence. Pretty soon, they'll find something else to fixate on."

I allow the old lady's words to sink in as I turn and walk out of her building and down to the bus stop.

* * *

They're still looking and whispering and pointing at me when I get to school, but it's not as mortifying as it was that first day after Mama hacked off all my hair. I don't know if I'm "owning" my new look the way the old lady had in mind, but I keep telling myself to hold my head high and let all their little comments just roll off my back. Whenever I feel my shoulders about to slump or my neck about to hang, I just take a deep breath and allow the air rushing into my lungs to help puff out my chest. It's nearly impossible to stay hunched over when you're inhaling deeply.

By the end of the day, the whispering has died down significantly. And Keisha's friend Nicole even mentions that the style is starting to look okay on me. By the end of the week, no one seems to even notice me anymore. I can't believe I spent so much time obsessing like I did when there's really nothing I can do but go about my business and wait for my hair to grow back. I never would have thought an old white lady with a big attitude and a little bit of hair could make a difference in the way I looked at anything, but she did.

19

For the first time since we mugged the old lady, things are starting to feel normal again—with the exception of the babysitter situation. But all it takes is a week back at school for me to figure a way around that predicament.

"I'm so happy you're coming home with me and Nicole," Keisha says as we come out from the Nevins Street subway station in Fort Greene. "It's been so long since you've been over. We're gonna have a great time. I promise."

"Keisha says your mom is kind of strict," Nicole says to me.

"Yeah, that's an understatement."

"So how'd you manage to get out of having to go home this afternoon?"

"Math study hall."

"What?"

"Exactly!"

Keisha laughs and shakes her head as we pass a corner bodega.

"Think your brother's home yet?" Nicole asks.

"Nic has a crush on that freakazoid," Keisha admits to me. "I don't understand why, but whatever. And Nic, Faye has a crush on Curvy Miller."

"No, I don't," I lie.

"And Faye doesn't lie very well either." Keisha laughs some more. "What are you gonna do if he comes over later? He probably will, you know. I'm not kidding about him being there all the time."

"Whatever," I say quietly. "What Curvy Miller does is none of my business."

The boys who are hanging out in front of the barbershop next to the bodega call out "Yo, baby" as we approach. I kind of want to thank them for not singling any of us out like boys usually do. You know how they'll yell "Yo, baby in the blue jacket," or "What's up, beautiful, with your little pink scarf on." That can get pretty embarrassing, especially when you're never the one wearing the blue jacket or the pink scarf. And I especially want to thank them for not making any comments about my hair. See, Keisha's a cute girl. She looks like a slightly chubbier version of Janet Jackson. And even though Nicole shows miles of gumline when she smiles, she does have a fashion model–type body. With my recent physical alteration, I kind of feel like the third man down on the totem pole.

Fort Greene is a pretty crazy area. It's like the neighborhood has multiple personalities. Keisha's house is eight and a half blocks from the station. We walk down a street lined with trees and the most beautiful old town houses, only to turn a corner and find ourselves in the middle of what looks like Armageddon. Two blocks later, it's back to the tree-lined and elegant again. Unfortunately, Keisha's street happens to be one of those that looks as if it barely survived the final world conflict. It must have been a great street once, but now there are all these gutted homes with boarded-up windows and doors. And half of these abandoned places are covered with graffiti. Keisha's house is one of only a few that seem to have been spared whatever firebombing occurred. She said her mom and stepdad bought it three years before they were even able to move in. It took them that long to fix it up. But her stepdad is banking on the area getting better again. For now, they all live on the first floor and rent out the second and third floors to two other families.

When we arrive at Keisha's brownstone, our first stop is the living room. She yells out her brother's name to make sure he's not home yet, then heads straight for the liquor cabinet, where she grabs a bottle of rum, which she hands off to me, and three glasses, which she hands off to Nicole. She takes another little detour to the kitchen, where she throws a bottle of Schweppes ginger ale into the mix. Once she has all her ingredients, we run down her hallway and hole up in her room. Nicole plops down onto the bed while I curl up on a nearby armchair, and Keisha stands at the dresser and goes to work on her alcoholic concoction.

Her room couldn't be any more girly. Everything is pink or green or flowery, or a combination of the three.

"When will your folks be home?" I ask.

"Not before six, so we have plenty of time," she says as she holds the bottle of rum up to the side of her face, as if she's in an ad for it. "Now, this is a ten-year-old. The good stuff. Ray's friend from Guyana got it for him for special occasions."

It's kind of weird that she calls her stepdad by his first name, but he doesn't seem to mind.

"And today most certainly qualifies as a special occasion," Keisha continues as she goes back to her bartending, mixing a little bit of soda with a whole lotta rum. Since I can't really drink much alcohol without getting sideways, I can already tell that this is going to be an interesting afternoon. But I decide to go for it anyway. The rum doesn't really taste that great, kind of like an all-purpose household cleaner that's been set on fire. After every sip, I feel as if some of the skin on my throat is being peeled off. Keisha definitely didn't add enough soda to it.

Nicole's face is as contorted as mine as she drinks her portion, but Keisha seems to be handling it just fine.

Halfway through the drink, my head starts to spin. And I'm laughing so loud that Keisha has to shush me, but her shushes are almost as loud as my laughing.

"My brother's gonna be home any second now. If he hears us laughing like this, he's gonna know."

"Who cares?" I howl. "But what if Ray notices there's not as much rum in the bottle as there should be?"

"He's not the one who usually drinks it. It's my mom. She probably has to, to put up with him. He's a handful." And we giggle some more.

"What if she notices?"

"She'd probably think it was Kevin. But even if she found out it was me, she'd just sit around and lecture me about drinking and what it can do to my brain cells."

"You're so lucky your mom doesn't hit," I say.

"It's on account of her always reading black history books," Keisha says as she sits down on the bed next to Nicole. "She's convinced that black people beating their kids is a learned behavior from slavery times. She says masters used to beat the slaves, then those same slaves would beat their kids. She says if she beats us, she'll only be perpetuating the slave masters' brutal ways."

Keisha and Nicole both have those "sit down and discuss it" type of civilized families. They met the first day of the school year and have been pretty tight ever since. They have a lot more in common with each other than I have with either of them. Nicole's parents also own a house, nearby in Clinton Hill. And they have no problem paying full tuition for her to go to Bishop Marshall. Sometimes I wonder if Nicole would even talk to me if Keisha wasn't in the picture.

"You're lucky," I say to Keisha.

Nicole closes the *Vogue* magazine she's been flipping through and pops up from the bed.

"I think we should play truth or . . . truth," she says.

"Don't you mean truth or dare?" I ask as I drape my legs over one side of the armchair.

"Nope. In this game, you have to admit something about yourself no one else knows."

"Like what?" I sip some more of my drink.

"Like, for instance . . ." But before she can say anything else, she bursts out laughing. There's a faint door slam and Keisha shushes us. I hear footsteps and voices, then another door slam.

"Yuck. Kevin and his Neanderthal friends are here. Wanna go check and see if your boyfriend is one of them?" Keisha teases me.

"No. I wanna play truth or truth," I say, trying to ignore her. Actually, I don't really want to play, but it's better than Keisha ribbing me about Curvy Miller. "So you go first, Nicole."

"Okay. Lester Johnson from my global studies class—I made out with him."

Keisha gulps half her drink and nearly rolls off the bed. "What? When? Details, details!" she shrieks as she pulls Nicole back down onto the bed next to her.

"It was down in the basement. Music class. I got a pass to go to the bathroom and ran into him. He started telling me how much he liked me—"

"He always tells you how much he likes you," Keisha interrupts.

"Yeah, but usually I ignore him," Nicole continues. "But something about the way he said it this time . . . and he has such nice lips. Next thing I know, we're in the stairwell."

"Oh man, if one of those nuns had caught you . . . ," Keisha whispers.

"I know, but they didn't."

"So how far did you go?"

"Only to second. If I had had more than ten minutes on that hall pass, well, I don't know which base we would have ended up sliding into."

"Okay, wait. I just wanna be clear. When you say second base, what exactly is included in that?" I ask.

Nicole looks around as if she'd forgotten I was sitting in the armchair.

"You know, everything above the waist in front and below the waist in the back."

"Oh," I mumble. "What's first again?"

"You know, Faye, a long, juicy kiss," Keisha answers.

"Then I guess home base would be nothing, then, huh?" I wonder out loud. Based on that explanation, I suppose there might have been one occasion where I happened to trip and fall somewhere between home base and first. Wow! How pathetic is that?

"So what's the deal? Do you really like him?" Keisha asks Nicole.

"Kinda. I mean, your brother's not paying me any attention, so . . . And like I said, Lester has really nice lips. And he wants me to come to his brother's birthday party in a couple of weeks."

"Oh my God. Nic, you have a boyfriend!" Keisha shrieks. And the two of them giggle and flop around on the bed. And I'm left in the armchair feeling like a third wheel.

"Okay, well, what about you?" Nicole asks Keisha. "And make it good."

Keisha is silent for a while. I can't imagine what secret she could possibly have.

"Okay, I'm gonna show you something," she says. "But neither of you can tell anybody." And she bounces off the bed and disappears into her closet. A few seconds later, she comes back out with a couple more magazines.

"Is it the new *Right On!* with the Michael Jackson interview?" I ask.

"Not even." Keisha reveals the cover of one of the magazines. There's a blond woman with the biggest breasts imaginable.

"Hustler!" Keisha says, all giddy. "It's the worst. Ten times worse than *Penthouse.* Fifty times worse than *Playboy.*" She opens it up and I'm bombarded with skin and tongues and body parts.

"Eww. Where'd you get this from?" I ask. And I'm trying to figure out whether I find it disgusting or appealing or both.

"Ray hides them in the basement."

"Look at all the veins in it," I say.

"I think it's kind of cool," Keisha says. "Have either of you ever seen one?"

"Are family members stumbling out of the bath without a towel included?" Nicole asks.

Keisha shakes her head.

"Then, no, I've never seen one up close and personal."

"Me neither," I say.

"I have," Keisha says.

"What?" Nicole and I yell at the same time.

"Jason. You know, the guy I told you guys I like. The one who lives around the corner? Well, he showed me his."

"Just like that?" I ask.

"Well, we'd been talking and I told him I'd never really seen one, so . . . And he's asked me out to the movies."

Nicole lets out this high-pitched, alert-all-dogs squeal, and she and Keisha bounce off the bed and begin dancing around and laughing.

"We both pretty much have boyfriends," I hear one of them say. I kind of watch them for a while, realizing I don't have any good truths. I've got no stories about circling bases, or naked men, or boys kissing me. They'd think I was a loser if I ever divulged the whole babysitter situation. And they'd get depressed if I went into detail about my mom knocking me upside the head. I take another sip of my drink. When I look back up, I notice both Nicole and Keisha gawking at me.

"Well?" Nicole says.

"Yeah, Faye. It's your turn," Keisha joins in.

All I can think of are some of the biggest, baddest things I've ever done. And maybe I'm a little drunk, because my lips start flapping before my brain can catch up.

"Okay, have you guys ever done something that's wrong, that you knew was wrong, but you feel good afterward, like excited good? But then suddenly, you start feeling not so great about it?"

"You mean like drinking Keisha's parents' liquor?" Nicole asks, then bursts out laughing.

"No. Something bigger. Something you could really get in trouble for. Like, for instance, stealing something. In your whole entire life, have you ever taken something that didn't belong to you?"

"Sure I have," Keisha says. And I turn to face her, a little surprised at her answer.

"You? What did you take?"

"A pack of Juicy Fruit. Once. I was gonna buy some potato chips and a Sunkist, then I decided not to, but I forgot to put back the gum."

"Oh," I say, trying not to sound deflated. "That doesn't really count. You have to mean to do it for it to be stealing."

"Oh. I guess I never really stole anything, then."

"I take stuff from my sister," Nicole admits.

"You do?" I realize I sound kind of hopeful.

"All the time. But I always put it back, so I guess that's more like sneaking than stealing. But to really take something that didn't belong to me and never give it back? Nah. 'Cause if somebody did it to me . . . that just wouldn't be right."

"Exactly," Keisha chimes in. "Like when that junkie stole the steering wheel from Ray's car. I mean, he didn't even steal the whole car. What are you gonna do with just a steering wheel? Anyway, I don't like thieves."

"Yeah, me neither." I try to cover for myself.

"But you didn't tell us a truth," Nicole realizes. "What about Curvy Miller?"

"Oh, Faye never has anything good," Keisha blurts out. "She won't even talk to him. What truth could she possibly have there?"

"No. I don't have anything good," I mumble. "I was just

gonna talk about the robber I walked in on, but Keisha knows that story already."

Thank God for the effects of alcohol, because once Keisha gives Nicole the Cliff's Notes version of that incident, they quickly move on to another topic.

20

Bad thing about alcohol, it wreaks havoc on my bladder. Two glasses of rum and I'm running to the bathroom at twenty-minute intervals. So I roll off Keisha's armchair and head for the door.

"Hey, don't let Kevin or any of his friends see you," Keisha calls after me. "You're kind of buzzed, and he'll never let you live that down."

I flash Keisha the okay sign and creep along the hallway, careful not to knock into the walls, which are lined with family photographs that all seem to have been taken in the seventies. I've never seen so many Afros, giant collars, and bell-bottom pants in my life.

It's almost time for me to wrap up "math study hall" and head to Ms. Viola's. But the great thing is, when I get back, there won't be much time for her little baby-tending chores. I'm so happy to have come up with this idea that will give me breathing room at least a few times a week.

After peeing for like three minutes, I stand and am

151

getting ready to flush the toilet when the bathroom door comes flying open. I quickly bend over to pull up my uniform pants, but I make the mistake of looking up at the door as I do this. Bad move. Because my eyes catch sight of my number-two potential husband, Curvy Miller, and I become frozen in my awkward position with my pants around my ankles and my oh-so-unsexy white cotton panties around my knees.

This has just surpassed every disaster I have ever experienced—and there have been plenty—to become the number-one, all-time greatest catastrophe in the history of my being. It's the *Titanic* sinking and the atom bomb exploding and the *Hindenburg* crashing all rolled into one. Everything inside me is boiling and percolating and moving at warp speed, but I can't seem to do a simple thing like pull up my nasty gray polyester uniform pants!

"Sorry about that," Curvy says as he withdraws a puffy Cheez Doodle from a bag and pops it into his mouth. His eyes are focused on my bony legs. "But you didn't lock the door."

I hear something come from my throat, but I'm not so sure it's from the English language. It sounds like a screech.

"You need help with your pants?" he asks as he steps in and closes the door behind him.

What is he doing? Why the hell is he coming toward me? I guess his movement snaps me out of my stupor, because I somehow manage to yank pants and panties up in one swift motion, then quickly flush the toilet.

"I'm sorry," I mumble as I fidget with my vest.

"What for?"

"I don't know."

"So, what's up?" he asks as he crunches on another Cheez Doodle and acts as if we're hanging out someplace normal, like Keisha's kitchen, and not in the bathroom, where he just caught me hunched over half-naked. I mumble something I don't even understand as Curvy extends the bag toward me.

"Oh no. I haven't washed my hands," I say.

I walk over to the sink and he do-si-dos to the other side of me, closer to the toilet. I'm looking at him through the mirror and he's looking back at me. I notice how red his eyes are. It's as if he's part lab mouse.

"So you're friends with Kevin's sister?" he asks.

"Yup."

"That's good."

I quickly dab my hands on a towel, hardly even drying them. I just need to flee.

"Well, I'll get out of here so you can use . . ." But before I can finish the sentence, Curvy has moved back over to the door, quick as lightning, and is leaning against it crunching on his Cheez Doodles. The tips of the fingers on his right hand are all orange. He holds the bag out to me again, but I say no. I never did like the puffy ones, only the crunchy.

"Your hair's different," he says.

"You noticed? Well, it was longer, but . . . Well, it was longer. . . ." I have to tell myself to slow down, to not stumble over my words. "It was longer, but I had to get it cut."

He shakes his head, and all of a sudden, I'm wondering how ugly I must look to him, especially compared to the girls he's always looking at. Girls like Charlene Simpson. And I'm feeling small and skinny and bald and I'm wondering what I'm doing in Keisha's bathroom with him and why he just keeps crunching those snacks and looking at me all weird.

"I didn't even think you knew who I was."

"Of course I do. You're Keisha's friend. So who all's in the room with you and Keisha?"

"Just us. And Nicole."

"What kind of trouble are you guys getting into?"

"Nothing. Talking, you know, flipping through magazines."

"Is that all?" he asks as he steps in closer to me and makes a sniffling noise.

"You can smell it?" I ask. He nods. "I can smell you too." He smiles and watches me some more.

"Well, I should probably get back. . . ." But I stop speaking when I see his face coming toward mine. I'm not sure what's going on here. Maybe there's some schmutz on my nose and he's going to remove it. But before I can even formulate a full thought, his mouth is attaching to mine and swallowing the lower half of my face. And his lips are all soft and wet and Cheez Doodley. And then I feel his tongue. And my eyes open wide and I look up. The ceiling lights above my head seem to be going around in circles.

"Just relax," he says as he backs off a little. "You never been kissed before?"

And I just stare at him, because I have been kissed. In my dreams. By Michael Jackson. But it didn't feel anything like this. Michael never used his tongue. And he didn't taste like a bag of cheese snacks. He just put his soft *Thriller* lips on mine and pressed real hard, then smiled, started pop-locking, and yelled out "Hee-hee!"

Curvy comes for my mouth again. Only, this time, he puts his tongue in even deeper and it feels like a wet, wiggly fish. Maybe like an eel would feel, if I went mad and decided to stuff one into my mouth. And then I feel a hand on the left side of my chest, only, since nothing womanly has really developed there yet, I'm wondering if he's just trying to check my heartbeat.

"I want you to give me your hand," he says as he removes his mouth from mine and steps back.

"What for?"

"Because I want you to feel something."

"What?"

His eyes shift downward. I can't believe this is actually happening. In the space of five minutes, I've gone from being stuck just past home base to rounding first. And now I'm quickly approaching second—or is it third? I'm excited and scared, all at the same time.

Curvy reaches behind his back and clicks the lock on the door.

"Give me your hand," he whispers. I do, and he places it against his chest. Then he starts moving it downward.

"How far are we going with this?" I ask.

"As far as we can."

"Curvy," I say as he adds kissing my neck to the routine.

"Hmm?"

"Are you drunk?"

"Maybe a little."

"Is that the only reason you're doing this?"

"Hmm, nope."

And as I feel my hand being pulled lower and lower, my words start coming out machine-gun-fire fast.

"You know, uh, my aunt Nola had this talk with me when I turned thirteen. And she said that unless you're in love with someone, you shouldn't . . . you know. I mean, if that's what you were thinking about doing . . . with me."

"I don't think your aunt told you the whole story. You know how you fall in love with somebody?"

"You just do."

"If that was the case, everyone would be in love with everyone else. You fall in love when you go all the way with somebody. See, that way, you two become a part of each other forever. That connection, that's what love is about."

I back away a little and look at him. My brain is spinning so fast.

"What about Charlene?"

"Charlene?"

"Yeah, the one you're always hanging all over."

"Just a friend. That's how I am with all my friends. Now, why don't you and me make that connection?" he whispers. He walks over to the toilet, puts the lid down, and sits.

"Why don't you come over here," he says as he pats his leg.

I'm kind of frozen in place as Mama's one-sentence sex talk pops into my brain. Two months after my twelfth birthday, I got this red Hi-C fruit punch stain on my dress. Figured I must have sat in some at Uncle Paul's. Only, I went to the bathroom and there was more Hi-C fruit punch in my panties than there was on my dress, and I couldn't really figure it out, unless there was a tiny little Hi-C gremlin going around pouring juice in people's underwear. Later, when I apologized for sitting in juice, Mama just laughed this weird laugh, lit up a cigarette, and stared at me for like ten minutes.

"You have your period now," she said finally. "Screw around and get pregnant, I'm not taking care of it." And that was that.

A door suddenly slams somewhere in the house, and I snap back to my senses.

"I have to go," I say as I fumble with the lock.

"Wait, you just gonna leave me like this?" Curvy asks as he rushes over to me. His eyes are all squinty, and his Cheez Doodley breath is so warm. "Come on. You know how much I like you. And remember what I told you about how people fall in love. . . . Just a couple of minutes. Maybe I'll end up falling in love with you."

And I want to yell with joy at the top of my lungs. Because he actually likes me. Me with 1984's most unattractive haircut and flat-as-a-board chest region. I go to give him a peck on the lips, only, with all the adrenaline coursing through me, I kind of head-butt him in the chin. But it doesn't even matter.

Once I get the door open, I run out of the bathroom and back toward Keisha's room. I can't wait to tell her and Nicole what happened. To think, I could actually have a boyfriend. Take that, pretty and perfect Charlene.

* * *

"Did he actually tell you that you were his girlfriend? Did he ask you out to the movies or to lunch or to the park?" Keisha asks.

I'm sitting at the edge of her bed, looking at her like she's got three heads. I finally have a truth that pertains to a guy, a truth that could soon put me in boyfriend territory too, but she doesn't seem at all excited about my news. Quite the opposite.

"What does that have to do with anything? He didn't have to. Did you hear what I told you?" I whisper.

"I heard you, but I'm telling you, Faye, I know how my brother and his friends talk, and all that doesn't matter. Half the time they're just horny little toads trying to feel up some girl just because they can or just because they want to get a little something. Sometimes they don't even like her all that much. Sometimes it's just because she's always in their face."

"Not me," I say as I bounce up off the bed. "Besides, he's the one who talked to *me*. He's the one who didn't want to let me leave. And why'd you have to say that, anyway? You don't think he could really like me?"

"That's not what I'm saying."

"Then what is it?"

"I'm just saying, he's always following old tight-sweater-wearing Charlene around like a little puppy dog. He's never once looked your way before. You guys have never even had a real conversation, so why would he just suddenly, you know. . . . "

"Go slumming?" I ask. She's doing a pretty good job of killing my joy. I'm not used to having much joy in the first place, so when I get it, I try to hold on to it for as long as I can.

"Okay," Keisha says. "Tell me what he said again, only this time, word for word."

I sit back down on the bed, and Keisha and Nicole hover over me. I feel as if they're detectives and I'm the criminal they're interrogating.

"I told him I never even thought he knew who I was. And he said he did, that I was your friend."

"At any time did he actually mention your name?" Keisha asks.

"No, but what does that matter? I didn't mention his either."

"Does he even know your name?" Nicole chimes in.

Great, I'm being tag-teamed.

"I've heard stories of people falling in love the moment they set eyes on each other, before they even say a word," I argue.

"Yeah, but once they get the chance to actually talk, usually the first words out of their mouths are 'What's your name?' Besides, it isn't like this is the first time you all have ever seen each other. You've been going to the same school for four months now. And you know everything about him.

You know his first name, last name, nickname. You know where he lives. You probably even know his baseball stats."

"Maybe he just wasn't all that sure how to pronounce it and he didn't want to mess it up," I say.

"Your name is Faye. How's he gonna mess that up—call you Fah?"

I give up trying to explain things, and Keisha and Nicole eventually start giggling and gossiping about their potential boyfriends again. I just shake my head and grab all my stuff in preparation for the train ride back to Ms. Viola's. I don't care what they say. Come tomorrow at school, they'll see just how much Curvy Miller really likes me.

Yahweh. Jehovah. Jah. God. Whoever it is that's up there, would it be so difficult to allow me one little moment of joy? Today was supposed to have been the day I made Keisha and Nicole eat their words. Instead, it's the day I came to realize I can never hang out at Keisha's house ever again! So here I stand, in front of the only other place I could think to go after school, waiting for an eighty-year-old woman to answer her door.

"I've got a proposition for you," I say before the old lady can even get her door halfway open.

"Do I really want to hear this?" she asks.

"Yes, you do. Because it will benefit us both."

"I have a feeling I'm going to regret this, but come in."

She turns, leans on her cane, and starts walking toward the kitchen. I close the door behind me, put my bag down in the hall, and follow her. As she rests her cane against the wall and sits down at the table, I glance at the mound of broken glass, still in the same neat little pile on the floor two weeks after the incident. I try to ignore it, and take a seat across from her.

"After school, I can come by and help you out. Maybe go get your groceries or your medication or your dry cleaning . . . that kinda stuff."

The old lady doesn't say anything at first. She only taps her fingers against the table.

"You said it would benefit us both. I get how it would benefit me, but I can't figure out exactly how it would benefit *you*."

"Your satisfaction would be my benefit."

A loud, high-pitched cackle suddenly bursts from her throat. It scares me nearly half to death.

"Well, what's so funny about that?"

"Once again, little girl, I've lived over eight decades. Now, how much are you expecting to be paid?"

"Not a thing."

"Try again."

"I swear, nothing. So, what's your answer?"

"No."

"What? How can you say no to an offer like that?"

"If you're not going to be straight with me, the answer is no."

"Okay, okay. The truth is, my stupid mother has decided to send me to a babysitter. I'm only a few years away from being twenty—"

"You're fourteen," she interrupts. "You're actually closer to ten than you are to twenty."

"Fine. Whatever. It's still too old to go to a sitter. And the woman wants me to do unspeakable things."

"Unspeakable things?" the old lady asks.

"Yeah. She actually wants me to change diarrhea-filled babies. So I came up with this idea about having to go to study hall three times a week. Never thought my bad math grades would ever come in handy. Anyway, I figured I'd go hang out at my friend Keisha's house most days, but I can never go back there again."

"And why is that?"

"Because of Curvy Miller."

"Keep going," the old lady says as she goes to the china cabinet to grab a couple of teacups and saucers.

"I thought he liked me," I continue as I take my coat off and drape it over the back of my chair. "But there we were at school today, and he acted like he'd never seen me before."

"What did he do to make you think he liked you?"

"He kissed me. And . . . well, he wanted me to . . . you know, be with him and stuff. He wanted me to, you know . . . you know . . ." I look over at her to see if she's looking at me, but she's just pouring hot water from a glass kettle into the cups.

"But I didn't," I add really fast. She already knows I'm a thief; don't need her thinking I'm a hussy too. "I mean, he acted so interested yesterday in Keisha's bathroom, and then today, he totally ignored me. Even when I was right in front of him on the lunch line. Nothing." I have no intention of going into detail about the whole distressing incident, but I can't seem to stop my lips from flapping.

"Guess now I'm wondering if I had done it with him,

whether things would be different. You know, he says that if you do it with somebody, then you and them are a part of each other. And you'll have this love between you forever. Well, I've been really thinking about this. And I believe that some people, like Charlene, this really pretty girl he's always hanging around . . . well, they don't have to do much to have people fall in love with them. I'm not Charlene, or my mother, even. You wouldn't believe how guys act around my mother, even when she treats them like crap. But I'm not like them. I'm not the kinda girl boys are into. The kind that just breathes and all the guys come running after them like puppy dogs. It's not that easy for me. And I wonder if I won't have to do more to make a guy like Curvy like me, a guy who's so popular, who plays on the baseball team. So maybe I have a little bit of regret. See, I didn't do it with him, and now it's like he doesn't even remember I'm alive. I feel like I blew my chance."

I finally catch a breath as the old lady walks back over and hands me one of the cups.

"Anyway," I continue at a slightly slower pace, "now that he's acting like I don't exist, I can't risk running into him at Keisha's again. At least at school I can bob and weave and get lost in a crowd to avoid him. At Keisha's, no such luck."

The old lady sits down, opens a small tin of sugar cookies, then begins stirring honey into her tea.

"That is the biggest crock of shit I've ever heard," she finally says.

My own spoon dangles in midair, and I can feel my eyes

growing to the size of the planet Jupiter. I can't believe the old lady just cursed. I figured she was one of those proper kinds of older folk.

"What has this boy done to show you that he truly likes you?" she goes on.

"I told you already. He kissed me and told me he wanted me to do stuff with him."

"No. That just shows that his oversexed little hormones are jumping around. I mean, has he spent time with you? Has he held your books or walked you home or sat with you at lunch? Has he asked how your day was going or been there when you needed help with something?"

"No . . ."

"And why exactly do you like him again?"

"He's got dimples that just never end. And you should see his smile."

"So you like him because he's good-looking?"

"No. I'm not one of those shallow people who gets stuck on the way someone looks."

"You sure about that?" she asks. "Look, I think you should leave this fellow to that little girl he's chasing around. When you finally meet someone who really cares about you, you'll know it. A bad man is like a bloodhound. He can sense when you have doubts about yourself, when you're overly eager for attention and affection, and he will come in for the kill. And being physical with him, that doesn't win you his love. In fact, it usually makes him respect you even less than he already does. Don't ever let anyone tell you what you have to do in order for him to love you. Just do what you do naturally. If that isn't good enough, then screw them. You just walk away." She sighs deeply.

"You think that fellow is ignoring you now? If you had given in to him, it would have been worse, because he would have been walking around whispering about what went on between you two to all his other little rotten, horny friends."

Once I finish my tea, the old lady leans back against her chair and clasps her hands on the table in front of her.

"So now, instead of helping you avoid school, I'll be helping you avoid the place your mother intended for you to be after school."

"I guess," I say as I look at the pile of broken glass again. Then I ease away from the table. "Where's your dustpan? Just to show I mean business, even though it's not technically an errand, I'll clean all this up for you."

She just points to a narrow door near the entrance to the kitchen.

After grabbing hold of the dustpan and a broom, I go about scooping up all the broken glass and dumping it into the garbage. I notice a few random pieces under the cabinet, so I sweep those up too. Once I'm done, I put the broom and dustpan back where I got them.

"So, what do you say?" I ask again.

She cocks her head a little to the left before focusing on me again.

"The answer is yes," she finally says. "And you can continue what you started."

I'm not sure I like the sound of this. "What do you mean?" I ask.

"Under the sink, there's a can of cleanser and a sponge. If you could get it out for me."

"Most people say please," I say as I try to hand her the cleanser. But she just ignores me.

"Bathroom is over there," she says as she points with her old, crooked finger.

"So?"

"So, you're the one who proposed this little exchange. The bathtub needs cleaning. Then maybe I can soak in it."

"Okay," I mumble. There's no "please," no "I beg of you." Nothing. I just look at her. I know I told her I'd help her out a little, but I thought I was clear in communicating I was thinking more along the lines of running errands. I'm rethinking how I approached this whole thing. I probably should have outlined the chores I was willing to do, because I'm getting the feeling that this old white lady is about to work me like a dog. I mean, scooping up the glass was one thing, but I had nothing to do with her tub getting grimy.

"Perhaps if I hadn't met with an unfortunate incident and hadn't hurt my back as a result, I would be able to bend all the way down to the tub to clean it myself. But as it is, that's not the case," she says.

I just look at the sponge and sigh. This old woman is a lot slicker than I thought. When I look back over at her crinkly face, I start thinking that she really does look old enough to have owned some slaves. Maybe she's all confused in her brain and thinks she's back in Virginia or Alabama or Mississippi and that I'm little black bathtub-cleaning Bertha, only without the pickaninny ribbons and hand-me-down patchwork frock.

"Where you from?" I ask.

"Harlem."

"You're from Harlem?" I ask. I don't even try to hide my surprise. I suppose neighborhoods are always changing. Maybe Harlem was filled with white people back in her day.

"So, after Harlem, you moved down South?"

"I could count on one hand the number of days I've spent in the South."

"They had slaves in New York?"

"Not that I know of," she says. Only, it comes out sorta like a question.

And I'm about to tell her that I'm no slave, but then I see her lying half dead on the floor again and I just roll my eyes, take the sponge and cleanser, and go into the bathroom. Seriously, when the hell did I start getting a conscience? It just plain sucks. So I take off my blazer and I spread the Comet around the tub and start scrubbing. And scrubbing. And scrubbing. I end up tidying all her rooms and doing all her housework while she hovers nearby, watching my every move. Once I'm done, I practically pass out on her bed.

"Do you even remember my name?" I ask as I wipe the sweat from my forehead. "I told you before, but maybe you didn't hear me."

"It's Faye," she says from the little side chair across from her bed.

"So, you do remember it. It *is* Faye. Not Kizzy, or Sally, or Bertha, or . . ." I want to compile a nice long list, but those are the only slave names I can think of. I remember Kizzy from *Roots* and Sally from a story we read in seventh grade about Thomas Jefferson. And Bertha, well, that just sounds like a slave name to me.

"Anyway, what's your first name?"

"Ma'am," she says. I wait for a laugh, as in she just made a joke, but none comes.

"Next to the apartment number on your buzzer out front it says E. Downer," I say, ignoring her. "What does the *E* stand for?"

"It stands for Evelyn. My name is Evelyn Downer. And your Easter food was good, by the way. Thank you."

"Yeah, well, my aunt made it. . . . So how come you didn't have anyone to spend the holiday with? Like maybe that lady in that picture in your kitchen?"

She doesn't answer, but that doesn't stop me.

"Is she a friend? Or maybe a relative. Like your sister. Maybe somebody who used to work with you? Maybe she lives far away now, but you all talk on the phone all the time. Maybe she moved as far as Paris or England and she can only come back every few Christmases—"

I guess she finally has enough of me babbling, because she cuts me off.

"I'm the woman in that picture. Another lifetime ago."

"Then who's the baby?"

"My daughter."

"You have a daughter? I didn't know. Not that I would, I guess. It's not like we're lifelong friends. Are you close to her? You must talk all the time. Not like me and my mom."

"I haven't seen her in forty-two years," she says quietly.

"Whoa! How can you not have seen your own daughter in all that time?" Then I think about it a little. "Wish I didn't have to see my mother for forty-two years."

"No, you don't," she says softly. I look at her and notice her eyes are getting glassy again.

"Well, I have to be going. I used up all my time cleaning your house. And don't worry. I won't hold you to our agreement. I won't bother you anymore. Seems like every time I come over, I end up upsetting you." I turn to leave, but before I can get out of her bedroom, she starts talking.

"You don't upset me. You just stirred up some old memories. I guess I'm simply not used to talking about certain things. Not used to talking much at all these days. It's strange how when you get old, it's almost like you become invisible, too." She kind of says that part more to herself than to me. "But it's nice not always being alone for a change."

She's quiet for a while.

"Your school is in Crown Heights, isn't it? Down there near Eastern Parkway."

"How did you know that?" My words come out really hesitantly, but I can't help it. I'm trying to figure where she's going with this.

"I've seen that uniform you wear before. Go over to the nightstand and hand me that pad and pencil."

This woman is obviously used to making demands. I get her the pad and stand by, waiting as she writes something down.

"Tomorrow. Three-thirty. Meet me at that address," she says as she rips off a sheet of paper and hands it to me.

"Where is this?" I ask as I look down at the address.

"You come tomorrow. You'll see."

I stare at the paper a little longer. I figure I've got nothing to lose. If I get to the place and there are cops or something, I can just take off.

22

It only takes about five minutes for me to walk from school to the address the old lady gave me. The building is just down the way from the Brooklyn Museum and main library. Since it's right off a corner near Eastern Parkway, I'm able to get a closer look by approaching from one of the medians that divide the parkway's eight lanes of traffic. I quickly realize that I have nothing to worry about. It's a medical office.

Once there's a break in the traffic, I hightail it across the street. The first thing I see when I walk into the building is a large, white-faced clock that reads three-fifteen; then I see a gray-haired nurse seated in the reception booth.

"May I help you?" she asks.

"No, just meeting someone here," I say.

"Have a seat in the waiting area, then."

No sign of the old lady, but there are about six people sprinkled across fifteen padded chairs arranged in a U shape against the wall. In the center of the room, there's a long, skinny table with magazines on it. They all seem to deal with being old—only, they use more polished words to describe it. There's *Mature Years, Mature Living,* and *Modern Maturity.* As I walk over to some empty seats in one corner, I realize that the clock is probably the only thing under the age of 150 in that room. I mean, I am surrounded by *maturity.* A couple of the patients actually make Ms. Downer look like a spring chicken. The room even smells old, if that makes any sense. I try not to stare, but I can't help it. One man seems to be asleep or dead—not quite sure which. One woman has plastic tubes going into her nose. I can't figure out what those tubes connect to, being that she's seated in a wheelchair and there are like a million contraptions attached to that. A couple of others seem to be in a daze or a trance. It's kind of depressing, if you ask me. I just wish the old lady would get here.

On the walls are posters with older people smiling and hugging and fishing and eating corn. And these have slogans like "Living a Full and Meaningful Life," "Now Is the Time of Your Life to Do What You've Always Wanted," "Health in Your Retirement," and "Make Your Golden Years Truly Golden."

I pick up one of the few magazines that doesn't have "mature" in its title, *Time,* but I find this pretty ironic, since these people don't seem to have much of that left. I flip through to an article on rising international music stars, but I really don't feel like reading about U2 or Billy Idol or Wham! I don't really want to be looking at all these old people either, but I just can't help staring. I glance over at the clock, which now reads three-thirty, then back at the front door. The only person to come in is a younger woman who goes to sit with the woman in the wheelchair.

Another door opens and a nurse in gray scrubs steps out with a folder in her hand.

"Willows, Brenda Willows," she calls.

The younger woman who just came in gets up and maneuvers the woman in the wheelchair over to the door, and they disappear behind it with the nurse.

It's three-forty, and the whole scene is getting me down in the dumps. I'd rather be somewhere—anywhere—less gloomy. I stand and go to the front door and look up and down the street. No sign of the old lady. I open my schoolbag and wade through it a bit before my fingertips run across a crumpled piece of paper, which I pull out. It's the old lady's phone number. I haven't looked at it since she gave it to me that day. I wonder if the nurse will let me use her phone or if I'll have to go find a phone booth somewhere on the street. Only one way to find out.

I begin my walk toward the reception desk when I hear my name. I turn to find the old lady standing near the door the nurse in the gray scrubs came out from earlier.

"Let's go," she says as she walks over to me.

"Why'd you ask me to come here? I was stuck sitting with those people," I say as I follow her out. "Made me want to fling myself off a bridge. I could have waited for you at the museum."

"It's good to have the ability to remove yourself from this, isn't it?" she asks.

"You could too. Instead of coming to this place, you could just go down to Kings County Hospital, where not everybody is a thousand. Where it's not so glum."

"Yeah, but I'd still be old. What you saw in there, that's my existence every day. And if you're lucky enough to live as long, that will be your existence one day too."

What a thought. It makes me shudder.

"And I go there because it has one of the best geriatric doctors in Brooklyn."

"So what's wrong with you?" I ask.

"I'm old."

"No, I mean, are you sick or something? Are you gonna break some news to me that you only have a week left to live?"

"At this point in my life, I could have just a day. Who knows. I only wanted the doctor to have a look at my back, which is still very stiff."

"So that's it," I say. "You wanted to rub it in a little more. I've already told you I didn't mean for all that to happen to you."

"I know what you told me, but I just wanted you to be aware of what this part of my life is like."

"Depressing?" I say as we near the bus stop at Grand Army Plaza. I'm not so shocked the old lady has a doctor in this area. It's green. It's filled with trees, and the buildings are even ritzier than where she lives. Even the bus stop looks upscale. It's right near the arch that serves as an entrance to Prospect Park and looks like that famous one they have in Paris.

"You haven't been around many old folks, have you?" she says.

"Nah. Mama's mom lives in Dominica, but they don't really get along, so we don't go and visit her anymore. Mama says she's too judgmental and mean. It's funny, *my mother* calling someone else judgmental and mean. Anyway, I knew Mama's dad. She and my uncle Paul moved here with him when they were teenagers, but he died a few years ago. His ticker gave out. My dad's father is still alive, but he lives in Texas. I never really knew Daddy's side of the family too well. So what's it like being old?" I ask as I help her onto a bench.

"It just is."

"What does that mean?"

"It means it just is. What's it like being fourteen?"

"But being fourteen, I don't have much else to compare it to. I mean, I can't compare it to being twenty-one or thirty. But you can."

"That's true. I don't know. I guess being old is different for everyone. People with reasonably good health probably have a better time of it. People with kids and grandkids to look after might not be as lonely. And I would think that people who still work have something to look forward to each morning when they wake up."

"What about you?"

"Well, I have some rheumatism, and sometimes it's a chore to get from point A to point B."

"And you don't have contact with your daughter."

"So it gets lonely."

"And you don't work any."

"No, I don't. I suppose I've become one of the invisible people." She pauses long enough to watch a man bicycle past. "For me, being old is not so good. I always thought that if I lived long enough, I'd be able to sit back and take it easy and enjoy myself . . . that I'd have someone to enjoy myself with. That when I looked back on my life, I'd be happy with what I accomplished and with how I affected other people. I guess that just didn't happen." The old lady stops talking as a bus approaches.

* * *

The old lady is right about being invisible. Here we are on the bus, which is pretty full with kids heading home from school and random people headed to wherever. I don't expect anyone to give up their seat for me. I'm young. But they don't even look in Ms. Downer's direction, and she's using a cane and holding on to my elbow to keep from falling.

The bus lurches ahead before I can get hold of one of the poles or overhead bars, and as I jerk forward, the old lady kind of falls into me. Though I'm standing in front of one of those seats with a sign saying PLEASE GIVE THIS SEAT TO THE ELDERLY OR HANDICAPPED, and the old lady is obviously elderly and, with her cane, darn near handicapped, no one moves. One guy just stares straight ahead, as if Ms. Downer's a ghost and he's looking right through her. And this dude is a pretty solid chunk of man. It wouldn't hurt him any to volunteer his seat. I stare at him for a while, but he continues to look through Ms. Downer. When the driver slams on the brakes on account of a car in front of us braking, Ms. Downer loses her balance once more.

"Why don't you get up and give this lady a seat?" I yell at the guy.

He barely even glances my way.

"You're sitting in one of those seats you're supposed to give up if someone old is standing."

For the first time, he actually looks Ms. Downer in the eye, but then he looks back at me.

"Dis ain't de fifties in Mississippi," he says in a thick West Indian accent. "I don't have to get to de back of de bus 'cause some white lady wants to sit down."

"No, this is the eighties, and she's in her eighties, and you're a big strong man, but you're acting like a little punk whose mama didn't raise him with any manners. . . ."

"Faye," the old lady says softly. I turn to her.

"There's no rule that anyone has to give up those seats for anyone else. It's just a suggestion. Maybe he worked a long day. Maybe he's tired. If he doesn't want to get up, that's his prerogative."

But before I can say anything else, one of the kids two rows back offers up his seat.

As the old lady settles in, I continue to shoot the man the death glare, but then I realize something: I've never given my seat up for any old person either.

"Faye, once you change out of your school uniform, I want you to stew up some chicken. And don't add too much salt the way you usually do. Make some peas and rice along with it, and a nice salad. And if we got any more of those dinner rolls, make those too."

"Yes, Mama."

"Oh, and there should be a box of Duncan Hines yellow cake mix in the cupboard. You bake that up for me, but add about half a cup of rum to the batter. This is grown folks' dessert, okay?"

"Yes, Mama."

"All right. I need it ready for eight-thirty, so you got an hour and a half, which should be plenty. But don't go dillydallying about and cause the food to not be ready. And don't rush through it either and have the food cold, so you manage your time."

"Why does it have to be exactly eight-thirty?" I ask. "When did we start being so precise?"

"Not your job to question me, child. Your job is to do what I tell you."

I just sigh.

"I'm gonna go catch a little catnap. Maybe see what the weekend cliffhanger on *Edge of Night* is. If I'm not out by eight, you make sure to wake me up. You hear?"

"Yes, Mama."

Grown folks' dessert? If I didn't know better, I'd think maybe Daddy was coming over again, but I'm pretty sure that's not the case. If it was, Mama would be cutting and seasoning the chicken herself and making a cake from scratch. And she wouldn't be watching soap operas and napping. She'd probably be going through her closet trying to pick out some ridiculous, overly fussy gown she hasn't worn in a decade. She'd be washing her hair in her special lavender shampoo and sitting under that professional-style dryer Aunt Nola gave her three Christmases ago, worrying about everything being just right. She wouldn't trust me to not oversalt the chicken or undercook the rice.

Since I can't figure out who Mama's mystery guest could be, I'll just have to wait and be surprised.

* * *

At exactly 8:22, the downstairs bell sounds.

"Goddamn it!" I hear Mama shout from the bathroom. "Why can't people get it through their heads that eight-thirty means eight-thirty? Not twenty-five after. Not quarter till."

"I'll get it!" I yell.

"No, let him wait. At least till I get out the bath," she yells back.

So, it's a "him."

The bell sounds again, and again. A couple of minutes later, the bathroom door opens and Mama stomps out.

"Set the table, Faye . . . for three."

"I'm eating with you?"

Mama nods.

"Should I use the good plates?"

"No. Use the everyday plates."

"You want me to change into a dress or something?"

"What for?" The downstairs bell sounds again. "You should probably get that now. Just let him know he's early. Be sure to say that. And that I'm still getting ready. Then seat him in the living room and make him a drink."

As I walk down the hallway, I get an idea of who it could be, but I'm not quite certain. I press the intercom, but there's no answer. Maybe he left, thinking no one was home. I would have. I wait for a moment, then turn to head back down the hall. That's when the front door buzzes. When I open the peephole, all I see is a shock of wet, drippy black hair. Jheri curl Jerry.

Once we're in the living room, I sit Jerry down on Mama's ugly plastic-covered flower couch and offer him a drink. He asks for whiskey. I tell him we only have rum and beer. He says rum with a little soda is fine. Mama has two kinds: Myers's Original Dark, for special people and special occasions—needless to say, it's hardly been touched—and a no-name brand that just has a stalk of sugar cane and the word *RUM* on the label. I don't really know which to give Jerry, but since Mama didn't seem that excited about him, I pour some of the no-name brand into a glass. Then I walk through the wooden beads that hang from the living room archway and into the kitchen, where I fill his glass with ice and Pepsi before bringing it back to him.

"She's still getting ready," I say. "Says you're too early."

"That's 'cause I couldn't wait to see her again."

"Really?" I don't even try to hide my disbelief. "So what exactly is it you like so much about her?"

"What's there not to like? She's sassy. She's strong. She's a good woman. She's beautiful."

And there you have it. He might as well have listed the beautiful part first. I mean, I understand that men are drawn to beauty, but Mama is as mean as a snake. And she was downright awful to Jerry over at Uncle Paul's. But I guess that's the thing with pretty women. When they act up, people just excuse it as them being spirited. I say something not half as harsh as Mama and everyone gets all up in arms.

Mama finally comes out, but there's no gown in sight. She's wearing her blue pantsuit, which isn't as atrocious as it sounds. It's pretty fitted, so it shows off her curves and makes her long legs look even longer.

"Sorry to keep you waiting, Jerry, but you were early."

"My apologies," he says. "I gotta remember you women need your time to get pretty. And boy, did you ever do a good job of it. Guess I was just a little eager to see you. Can't fault a man for that."

"Faye, why don't you make Mama a drink, then join me and Jerry at the table."

"Yes, Mama," I say, and I hang back to make her drink.

"Mmm-hmm, you sure do look nice in that suit," Jerry says as he follows Mama through the wooden beads and into the kitchen, his eyes never once leaving her behind.

I also use the cheap rum for Mama's drink. Once I'm done, I take a big swig, then refill it before heading into the kitchen. When I get to the table, Jerry's looking all anxious and hungry, like a little mutt waiting for feeding time. And he's still telling Mama how pretty she looks and how pretty she smells. Mama just takes the drink from me, gulps it, and keeps this tight-lipped smile on her face.

"Look at this silverware," Jerry says. "I gotta say, Jeanne, you got some beautiful taste. And the plates, whoo-hoo. And I love the way you decorate. I mean, even the place mats are tasteful."

And I'm thinking, is this guy for real? It's our chipped, scratched-up everyday plates. And the place mats are plastic, with pictures of the natural wonders of the world on them. And they say it in big, garish letters—SEVEN NATURAL WONDERS OF THE WORLD. Actually, we're down to five wonders, since two of the place mats have turned up missing.

"Look at this. Grand Canyon, Great Barrier Reef, Victoria Falls. You ever been to any of these places?" he asks Mama. She shakes her head as she lights up and puffs on a cigarette.

"Pretty woman like you. If you were mine, I'd take you around the world in style."

When Mama puts the food on the table, the man acts as if he has never seen chicken before. I don't think he could be any more impressed if Mama roasted up a pterodactyl.

"Ooooooh-weee, Jeanne. Mmm, look at that. You know I like my chicken just the way I like my women. Spicy, hot, and brown. Can't wait to have a taste. Ooooooh-weee."

Same thing with the Pillsbury crescent rolls I popped into the oven.

"Woman, you baked some bread? Smells like a little slice of heaven."

"It's out of a can," Mama says.

"Well then, you opened that can just right, 'cause these the prettiest buns I've ever seen." Then he puts his hand over his mouth as he directs his next few words at Mama. "And I'm not just talking about the ones on the table."

I'm about three seconds from choking on my own very limited supply of saliva. I can't stop staring at him. I've never seen somebody's lips that glued to somebody else's ass before. Not even Sylvester Young in class. And Sylvester compliments Sister Margaret Theresa Patricia Bernadette on how nice she looks every day, which is ridiculous since all she ever wears is the same oversized gray sweater, which makes her look like an enormous possum.

Anyway, Jerry cleans his plate. Every grain of rice is gone. And a chicken leg and wing and thigh and neck bone. He eats all the meat clean off. And the grease around his mouth is now about as thick as the grease surrounding his hairline. It's all pretty disgusting, really. And when Mama gives him the cake, from the box, he acts as if he's being fed manna from God.

I'm figuring all that complimenting and sweet-talking is going to get on Mama's last nerve, but she just sits there twirling her hair and smiling. And she talks to him a little, not mean-like, but kind of civil, almost. She even asks him if he wants something a little smoother to drink. He says yes and they move on into the living room, where she breaks out her good bottle of Myers's Original Dark.

I start cleaning up the dishes, still not able to grasp what's going on before me. When I finally make it back to my room, I close the door and try watching a little TV, but every five minutes, I hear a loud "Hey, hey, huh, hey, hey, huh" come from Jerry. And he's still laughing and carrying on as I climb into bed.

* * *

I wake up really early, probably on account of my brain short-circuiting all through the night as it tried to make sense of all the craziness. I notice the ice bucket and glasses and almost-empty rum bottle as I walk past the living room on my way to the bathroom. Wonder what time Jerry finally removed his lips from Mama's butt and crawled out of here. I'm pretty sure it wasn't of his own accord. Mama probably had to physically remove him.

I reach my hand forward to push at the bathroom door, when it just seems to open by itself, and my eyes catch sight of an image I don't think I'll ever be able to expel from my brain: Jheri curl Jerry, standing there, dressed in Mama's striped robe. And it's not quite closed all the way.

"Oh, hey there, Junior," he says as he fumbles to tighten the belt. "You have pretty good timing. 'Cause Uncle Jerry's all done here. All done."

I'm pretty sure I'm in shock because, despite the bizarre

image on display before me, the only thought going through my mind is, When did Jerry become my uncle?

"Uncle Jerry?" I mumble.

"I'm an only child, so I've never been able to hear those words. But since I'm fixing to be spending a lot more time with your mom now, I think Uncle Jerry will have a real nice flow to it."

"Yeah, well, to be honest, I think I prefer Jerry. Or I could call you Mr. Adams."

"Oh, no need to be that formal. Whatever you feel comfortable with. Guess I'll just have to wait a little longer to hear how Uncle Jerry sounds."

When I finally get into the bathroom, I turn on the cold water and stick my head under it.

It's not until a couple of weeks later, toward the middle of May, that we get our first really nice day of the year—our first day without overcast skies or too much wind or a heavy chill in the air. I've been spending most of my afternoons at the old lady's place, doing chores for her, drinking tea, and talking about random things. Not in a million years would I ever have thought that things would work out like this between us.

Today at school, Keisha goes into stalker mode, trying to get me to go shopping with her and Nicole.

"Seriously, Faye. I mean, I guess I understand you not coming to my house. I understand you not wanting to run into Curvy one on one again, but you can't possibly have anything against shopping," she says, hovering over me as I stand at my locker. "Year-end ceremonies are just around the corner—"

"They're six weeks away. That's not around the corner. That's like through the woods and over the hills in the distance," I interrupt.

"You're such a smart-ass," Keisha says as she shakes her head. "Look, with final exams and the weather getting warm, those six weeks are gonna go really fast. And the last day of school is the only time we get to dress up and wear whatever we want. You don't start looking for an outfit now, it's gonna creep up on you and you'll be panicked that you have nothing to wear. Come on, Faye. It's gonna be great."

"Great how?" I ask. "It's not like there's gonna be some big celebration at Madison Square Garden or down at the Brooklyn Academy of Music, like the seniors have," I continue as I load the books I'll need for homework into my bag. "Middle periods of the day, they're just gonna pile us into the auditorium. The same auditorium we get piled into for every boring assembly. And they're gonna give us certificates saying we completed our freshman year studies. Big deal. It's not like we can get a job for having it. Then they'll say stuff about what we have to look forward to sophomore year. Blah, blah, blah. That's it."

Truth is, I wish we could just wear our uniforms to this event. The great thing about having uniforms is that everyone is equal in the wardrobe department. No one can really show anyone else up fashionwise. And since the uniforms fit so poorly, no one looks that much better than anyone else, with the exception of Charlene Simpson, whose uniforms fit as if they've been tailored to every bend and curve of her body.

With real clothes thrown into the mix, I'm presented with quite a dilemma. See, none of my clothes are all that spectacular to begin with, and with my extra-special stick-figure build, none of them fit particularly well either.

"It's not like it's a black-tie event or anything," Keisha says. "All you need is a nice dress, so why not come to Macy's with us?"

"Look, even if I wanted to, I couldn't. I have an appointment," I say as I grab my jacket from my locker.

"What kind? You've been so secretive lately about what you do, I'm beginning to think you don't like hanging out with us."

"I love hanging out with you, Keisha."

"Then is it Nicole?"

I guess I pause a little too long.

"It is Nicole. What? You don't like her? But she's so cool."

"I never said she wasn't. It's just that you two have a different kinda thing going, with shopping and clothes and jewelry and getting your hair and nails done. And you have boyfriends, and well, that's not really me. So when it's the three of us, sometimes I feel like I don't really fit. When it's just you and me, it's more about stupid things that I can relate to better. You know, music and videos and stuff happening at home and school."

I leave out the part about being embarrassed that I can't afford any of the things they can. See, they get actual allowances—substantial allowances that they can save up and buy some really nice stuff with. Now that I seem to have developed an allergy to ripping people off, the only thing filling my pockets is air. I suppose I could go with them and act like it doesn't bother me to only be able to look while they stock up on new clothes and cassette tapes and posters, but what fun is that?

"I never knew you felt that way," Keisha says.

"It's stupid. It's me. You guys just go have a good time."

"So do you really have an appointment, or are you just saying that to get out of hanging with us?"

"I really do have one. It's with a friend."

"Who?"

"No one you know. It's someone from my neighborhood."

"You mean those girls, Caroline and Gillian?"

"No. Not them. Another friend."

"Well, what's her name?"

"Evelyn. Evelyn Downer. Look, she asked me to come over. Said there's something she wants to share with me and I told her yes, so I can't go back on my word now."

"Fine," Keisha says. I can hear the disappointment in her voice. "If you promised."

"Okay, well, have fun shopping," I say before walking off.

* * *

For the first time since I've been coming to the old lady's apartment, the door opens almost immediately when I knock. But it's not Ms. Downer who's standing there. I'm looking into this white man's face. He's wearing a blue sweater-vest and dark slacks, and he has on these little round glasses. I can't decide whether he's a professor or a cop.

"Ms. Downer is expecting me," I mumble.

"Then you must be Faye?"

"Who are you?" I ask.

"Bill Franklin. Archivist," he says as he opens the door wider. "Come on in."

"Um, I can just go if she has company." But before I can finish, he's pulling me into the apartment, closing the door behind me, and putting his arm around my shoulder like I'm his long-lost friend.

"You're an archaeologist?" I ask as he guides me along.

"No. Archivist. Historian. Film buff. And you're just in time."

"In time for what?" But he doesn't say anything. He just walks me into the living room, which is all dark on account of the thick drapes being closed. He sits me down on the puffy purple couch, next to the old lady, then hits a button on her videocassette recorder and takes a seat in a nearby armchair.

"What's this?" I whisper to her.

"You've been very curious about who I used to be" is all she says.

Before I can even finish taking off my coat, this loud, bold music comes from the television. And the screen is black-and-white with little scratches and dots and glitches shooting across. "RKO Pictures" pops up, then a couple of guys' names, then the name Evelyn Ryder and the title *Lady in the Blue Fedora*. And this woman comes gliding onto the screen, all graceful and regal. When she smiles, there are these wonderful sparkling white teeth. And her hair is swept up under this big hat, with a couple of curls dangling from the sides.

"Is that you?" I ask, because as young as the woman on

the television is, there is something familiar about her. "It said starring Evelyn Ryder. Are you Evelyn Ryder? Because I thought your last name was Downer."

"It is me," the old lady says without taking her eyes off the screen. "Or rather, it was."

So Caroline was right. The old lady really was a movie star. And I'm in complete awe. The woman on the screen is stunning.

"You were so beautiful!" I whisper.

"Yes, hard to believe, isn't it?"

But as I steal a glimpse at the old lady, I can make out some of the same features as the woman on the screen. Only, they're a bit clouded by wrinkles and sun spots and time.

"Not that hard to believe," I say.

And then the film buff starts talking. He's excited and happy and sad and surprised all at the same time. I can't tell whether he's about to laugh, burst into tears, or pee his pants.

"One of the most talented stars of the early years of film."

"If you can say that for someone who only made six pictures," the old lady says.

"Oh, it's not the quantity that counts." The film buff has a really long, skinny head. It's as if it was made of putty and stretched to the maximum. His nose is equally long, and turned up at the end. And his Adam's apple is about as big as I've ever seen one. It's as if he actually swallowed a real apple, whole, and got it stuck there in his throat.

"A star who never got her due," he continues. "But look how brilliantly she shines. Not a twinkle, but full-on combustion." When he says this, he's looking not at the old lady, but at the television screen. And he hardly blinks, as if he's afraid he might miss something. It's as if he's in love with that young image of the old lady on the screen. Weird.

But I'm still focused on the whole name thing.

"I don't get it. If your name's Evelyn Ryder, why does it say Downer on the bell out front?"

"People in Hollywood often change their names," the film buff answers instead of the old lady. "So much of Hollywood is an illusion. It was, and still is, about always looking your best, sounding your best, being the best. Downer's a bit depressing-sounding, don't you think? But Evelyn Ryder . . . magic!"

The old lady's character has two love interests in the movie, and she's running around the whole time trying to juggle them and hide one from the other. Her clothes seem to get fancier in every scene. And her hats get bigger and bigger.

"Did you always wear a hat?" I ask.

"The movie's called *Lady in the Blue Fedora*," the film buff answers again. Only, I wasn't talking to him. And I'm starting to wonder if something's gone wrong with the old lady's tongue.

"It's the very definition of a screwball comedy. Only the third movie Evelyn ever made. The first two, she was little more than a glorified extra. She was twenty-nine at the time, quite long in the tooth in those days for her first starring role, but her beauty couldn't be denied. Wasn't she the most beautiful?" Only, he really isn't asking me this. He's telling me. And he's hypnotized by what's on the screen once again.

I start thinking about how small and lonely the old lady looked when I helped her into her bed that day. I start thinking of her not having anyone to share Easter dinner with. I start thinking of that old-as-dirt picture she keeps framed on her kitchen counter and the fact that she hasn't seen her kid in all that time. What is it, again? Forty-two years. That's three times the number of years I've been alive. I'm thinking of all this and trying to figure out how she went from being the glamorous star I'm watching on television to the lonely old woman sitting next to me.

"The movie opened surprisingly well, so the studios did everything to get as much publicity for it as possible," the old lady finally says. I shoot a glance at the film buff, who I'm expecting to jump in at any moment. But he doesn't. Instead, he gets up and fumbles with the video machine so that the movie is paused. Then he turns back to the old lady and stares, as if he's a little boy admiring his mother.

"They actually told me never to leave the house without a hat," Ms. Downer continues. "They treated me as if I were the same person as my character. It became, 'What kind of hat will Evelyn Ryder turn up in today? How big will it be? Will there be feathers? Will it be satin, silk, plaid?' I got so sick of the whole hat drama. Truth be told, I think I was jealous of my hats. I wanted people to see me for me, for my acting, and I felt they were only seeing me for my wardrobe." She takes a deep breath and lets it out slowly.

"So I refused to wear hats altogether. Then I realized that

as an actor, the worst thing that can happen is that no one is talking about you at all. And I realized that as a woman, you have to find your own style. You have to discover what fits your body, your personality, and make it work for you."

"I never have enough money to get the clothes I want," I blurt out. "I don't get anything in the way of an allowance. Sometimes I see all the neighborhood kids wearing Lee jeans and Gloria Vanderbilt. And Pumas and Adidas sneakers. And I wish I could look just like them. And now we have this school celebration at the end of the year and everybody's dressing up for it. I'm talking clothes from Bloomingdale's with major designer names on the labels. They're all acting like it's the high school Oscars. But Mama doesn't believe in wasting her money on anything that has a brand name. She doesn't believe in wasting her money on clothes for me at all, unless I'm about to burst out of them."

The old lady doesn't say anything. She just nods at the film buff and he restarts the tape. I shake my head. What do Lee jeans and a fourteen-year-old's allowance problems have to do with the style of a big glamorous movie star, anyway? When the movie finally ends, the film buff starts clapping and panting and wringing his hands. Then he takes out a notepad, asks a few questions about the making of the movie, and begins scribbling away. I'm not so sure they even remember I'm there, so I go into my bag and take out my geography book. We have a test in a couple of days. I look down at my watch and realize that since the movie ended, I've been sitting there getting ignored for a whole fifteen minutes, so I start gathering my stuff together.

That's when the film buff jumps out of his chair and gets extra-terrifically excited.

"Oh, would you, Ms. Ryder? Would you?" And he's clapping like a trained seal. The old lady stands slowly and walks into the hallway leading to the bedrooms. She's not using her cane anymore.

"Faye, will you come in here with me?" she asks.

"Sure," I say a little uncertainly, not quite sure what I'm about to get myself involved in.

I'm standing in Ms. Downer's bedroom, just in front of the closet, as she points to the shelf with all the hatboxes she made me restack.

"If you'd grab the top four for me . . . ," she says.

I do as she asks and put them on the bed. Ms. Downer takes the cover off the first box and removes a giant purple hat that looks as if it belongs in *Alice in Wonderland*.

"Is that from a movie?" I ask.

"Sometimes I bribed them into letting me keep some of my wardrobe. Believe it or not, I actually wore this out a few times, away from the movie set. I liked being an original." She turns to me.

"You talked about all the other kids in their jeans and tennis shoes . . . and how you want to be like them. But why? Why look like everyone else? They've all just found a way to blend in. They're afraid to stand out. And part of figuring out who you are is finding that special thing that expresses you, even if it's the craziest thing ever. Even if it's something no one else on the planet will understand."

I check out the old lady in her shapeless brown pants and beige sweater.

"I know what you're thinking," she says. "I guess the more life beat me down, the less energy I had for playing dress-up."

"But you have such nice clothes here."

"Maybe I hold on to them as a reminder of what used to be. Anyway, you're young. You need to find your own unique style."

"I don't really know if there's anything that unique about me," I say. "I'm pretty average."

This strange smile comes across the old lady's lips. "We haven't known each other so long," she says. "But the last word I'd use to describe you is average."

"Well, average-looking. I'll never look like you did."

The old lady gets up and puts that *Alice in Wonderland* hat on my head and turns me in the direction of the mirror on her dresser.

"I had people who picked clothes out for me, people who put on my makeup, styled my hair. I had people who drove me around town, called me in the morning to make sure I was awake. Sometimes all that fussing and fawning makes you lose touch with reality." She closes her eyes for a moment.

"How do you like this one?" she asks once her eyes open up again. I shake my head and shudder a little.

"You're probably right about that," she says with a little laugh.

I follow her back into the living room wearing a green hat with feathers sticking out and what looks like three squirrel tails hanging from the back. She wears a giant black one with a brim wide enough to block out the entire sun.

The archivist lets out a loud gasp, and I turn toward him, wondering if he's choked on his Adam's apple.

"It's like the calendar has been flipped back to the thirties," he says before pointing to the hat I'm wearing. "*Summertime Harvest*. Another RKO picture. Release year 1934."

"That's very impressive, William," the old lady says.

"I told you," he says as he shoots me a look. "I worship this woman, for she is a goddess."

The film buff then points to the old lady's hat. "*Bolero*, also 1934." And he just sits there grinning and staring at the old lady with these wide, excited eyes. He looks as if he's about to burst.

We model another couple of hats before the old lady excuses herself and goes off to the bathroom, leaving the archivist and me alone. I have to will myself not to stare at that lump in his neck as he writes on his notepad.

"How do you know Ms. Ryder?" he asks without looking up.

"Just from the neighborhood."

"You're a lucky little girl. You might be too young to realize it, but you're in the presence of greatness. So much talent and grace and promise. And only six films. Only four starring roles. Personally, I think the world lost out as much as she did when she turned her back on it all."

"Why did she? What happened?"

"Not enough, and at the same time, too much."

"Okaaay." I drag out the word, since I have no idea what he's talking about. "So are you writing a book?"

He nods.

"About her whole life?"

"At first, I was just interested in her career. To be honest, I didn't even know she was still alive when I started this project. And when I found her a year and a half ago, she wouldn't even talk to me. It took almost eight months. But I quickly realized how much her personal life affected every move she made. How it affected her turning her back on a potentially brilliant career so quickly."

"When you say personal life, are you talking about her daughter?"

He closes his notepad and looks directly at me. "You know about that?"

"I know she hasn't seen her in a very long time. And I know how sorry that makes her. But she won't say much else about it."

"It's too painful for her. I think the only reason she finally agreed to talk to me is that she hopes her daughter will pick up this book one day and understand why Evelyn did what she did. Of course, by that time, it will be too late."

"What do you mean?"

"I mean that one of the guidelines I had to comply with to get her to cooperate was that the book would be published only on her death. It's more or less written. I'm just here doing some fact-checking. All the artwork has been completed. But not until she's gone will the public be able to read it."

"Wow . . . Well, do you even know where her daughter is? What her name is?"

"Her name is Delaine Lawson. And the sad part is that she moved back here from Florida a couple of years ago and works at a nursing home right in Manhattan. They're just a train ride apart."

"Does Ms. Downer know that? Does she know how close she is?"

"I offered to tell her, but she doesn't want to know. Her only concern is that Delaine is doing okay, and that Delaine's son, who is grown and living on his own, is also okay."

"But it just doesn't make any sense," I say. "Them living in the same city and not speaking. No matter what's happened between them."

"For some people, it's easier to walk away from difficulties than to confront them."

"Well, maybe you should try talking to the daughter . . . to this Delaine Lawson person."

"I did. I even tried to interview her for the book, but she refused to be a part of it. I think she expelled Evelyn from her life a long time ago and doesn't want to stir up any of those emotions."

"But why? What could have happened between them that was so bad?" I ask.

"I think I'll leave that up to Evelyn to tell you."

"But she won't. And what does it matter if you tell me now, if you're gonna have it in your book anyway?"

"As long as she's still here, it's not within my right to make public what she's confided in me."

The bathroom door creaks open, and he lowers his voice.

"I do think the world needs to know who she is. They need to know she didn't just disappear and turn to dust, and that her life was filled with as much complexity and sorrow as it was with talent and richness. But it all has to be done according to her time line."

As the old lady walks back into the room, I nod at the archivist. I wonder whether one of the stories she'll tell him will involve three girls who forced their way into her apartment to steal 280 bucks out of her *Joy of Cooking* book. And I wonder whether she'll tell him about that one particular girl who almost killed her . . . accidentally.

As the archivist and Ms. Downer resume their conversation, I start thinking about this Delaine Lawson person and wishing there was something I could do to get her and the old lady back together again.

Since Macy's is not really in my price range, I decide to go do a little window-shopping on Flatbush Avenue a few days after my hat-modeling afternoon with Ms. Downer. Maybe Keisha's right about starting early. And I figure the way my hair is, it might take extra time to come up with an outfit that can detract from it. And just in case I come across something, I've decided to bring along thirty of the seventy dollars I keep tucked away in the giant unabridged Merriam-Webster's dictionary in my room, which is one of the few places Mama would never think of snooping around in. The other forty dollars I kind of feel weird spending. It's my share of the money we took from the old lady.

Now that it's finally gotten a little warm, Flatbush Avenue is more alive than ever. It's as if all the people who stayed hidden away in their apartments, huddled around their radiators trying to avoid the cold, have decided to come out and exhale away the winter. And there's a slightly slower pace to everyone. There are even a few smiles on faces, unlike in midwinter, when chins are buried in jacket collars, hands are stuffed in pockets, and eyes are focused front and center. Street vendors are out in full force, with knockoff Chanel purses and Gucci scarves laid out on the sidewalk.

The sound of Grandmaster Flash blaring from a radio captures my attention, and I stop for a second to watch these three boys break-dancing for spare change. Two of them are pretty good, but one is a bit more on the epileptic seizure side than the coordinated side. When he tries to do a handstand and spin on his head, he just sorta tips over. Maybe he's the comic relief.

I finally walk on, avoiding the onslaught of people pouring into the street before turning onto Albemarle Road, where the Dressy Dress Mart is located. But just as I'm about to push open the door to the store, I hear this all-too-familiar voice.

"Well, look who it is," Caroline says as she heads right for me, with Gillian at her usual place by her side.

"I guess we should consider it a privilege to have you grace our presence, O Holy One. Even if it is by accident."

"What are you talking about?" I ask.

"Last time we saw you, you said you'd be hanging out with us more, but we haven't seen you since. You're not on the streets. You're not answering your bell. It's like you disappeared off the face of the earth."

"I have a math thing after school now, and it keeps me pretty busy."

"Caroline's been pretty busy too," Gillian admits. And

suddenly, there's this "You give us twenty-two minutes, we'll give you the world," 1010 WINS–style breaking-news moment. And I have to wonder if my ears are tuned correctly this particular afternoon, 'cause Caroline actually says:

"I need to get one of those miniskirts so I can look sexy for my guy. His birthday's coming up and he keeps asking me to give him a treat." And she rocks her hips back and forth. She really could have spared me the image. But what's probably even more shocking, disturbing, and nauseating than her giving some boy a "treat" is her actually having a boy who's interested in her.

"You. Have. A. Boyfriend?"

"Yeah, I got a guy," Caroline snaps defensively. "What of it?"

"Nothing," I say as she reaches across me to push the door open. I walk ahead of her into the store and look back at Gillian, who seems just as much in disbelief as I am. Gillian shakes her head and shrugs, as if to say that she's been dealing with this shock for a while now. I just can't figure out what's in the air. First Mama and now Caroline. I mean, Caroline Johns having a boyfriend is like Jabba the Hutt winning a beauty contest—it doesn't make any sense. I've seen some pretty unattractive people who've had boyfriends, but I just assumed they had nice personalities. I mean, there must have been something to attract another person to them. But Caroline has no redeeming qualities whatsoever. Okay, she has massive boobs, but the way I see it, that's like a pig having a potbelly. She's overweight, so it just comes with the territory. It doesn't make her any more attractive. Anyway, I'm pretty sure this guy doesn't stay of his own free will.

"You want to leave me, I'll bust you in the lip," she probably says. "You looking at another girl when you have me, I'll poke your good eye out." "You better say I'm pretty. Say it or I'll strangle you." And that keeps him there. That, or he's severely brain-damaged and doesn't know any better.

The Dressy Dress Mart is a medium-sized store that only carries clothes for women. The minute we walk in, Caroline starts breezing down the aisles.

"The miniskirts are over there," I say. But she just waves me off and starts taking these little glimpses at the cashier, who's ringing a couple of people up and not paying any attention to us. Then she starts glancing over at the uninterested salesgirl, who's standing near the front door looking pretty bored. She looks like she belongs in the *Flashdance* movie, with her fluorescent-green off-the-shoulder T-shirt and black leggings and ankle boots. She has her left hand up in front of her face and she's staring at her too-long, too-pink Lee-Press-On-looking nails. I've been in the Dressy Dress Mart before and that salesgirl always looks as if she's more concerned with what's going on under her fingernails than with her customers. And she's always chewing the biggest wad of gum. She never asks if you need help. You have to call out to her if you need anything. And when she finally acknowledges you, she's usually sighing deeply and rolling her eyes like you're disturbing her from something really important.

There's also a security guard there, this old Haitian man. He talks with the thickest accent I've ever heard. No one ever knows what he's saying. Pretty much if he says something, you just nod and move on. One of his legs is shorter than the other, so he kind of walks with a limp. Kind of like a peg-legged pirate. And he doesn't even carry a gun. I don't understand how he got his job. I mean, if somebody was to steal something, all he can do is hop after them and throw his billy club. But who knows. Maybe he has really good aim.

So the salesgirl is at the door, and the guard is standing near the back of the store joking with the cashier, who's ringing up a customer. Suddenly, Caroline swings around to where the miniskirts are. With her left hand, she holds one up and studies it. With her right hand, she's stuffing another into the front of her pants. She does this in about five seconds. She does the same with a matching top, then turns to stare at Gillian, who just starts giggling. Caroline's mouthing, "Grab something," but Gillian's mouthing back, "I don't know what I want," as she runs her hands across every item on the rack.

"Whatchu doing?" Caroline growls. "We're surrounded by cool stuff. Just take something. And Faye, what are you waiting for?"

"I didn't say I wanted anything."

"What the hell's wrong with you these days? We're in this store with all this cool stuff. Bored salesgirl over there isn't paying us any attention, and you mean to tell me there's not one thing you wouldn't mind getting your hands on?"

I quickly study the clothes near me. There are the usual leggings and T-shirts and pants and a rack filled with Gloria Vanderbilt jeans. A little farther off, I notice a couple of nice dresses. And then I spot a stylish white blouse and poufy black skirt that would not only work for our year-end ceremony, it would probably also give me the illusion of a shape.

I have to admit, it's pretty tempting. But here's the thing. I haven't done anything like this since our episode with the old lady, and I'm feeling a little hesitant. Maybe I'm actually still traumatized by what happened. Then again, maybe thieving is like riding a horse—once you fall off, you gotta get right back on. I know I made all those promises after everything went down with the old lady, but now that this opportunity has presented itself, I'm kind of curious to see whether I still have it in me. I feel my heart beating a little, but I don't know if that's from excitement or apprehension. I guess there's only one way to find out.

I swipe the blouse first, then look over at Caroline, who seems to be salivating. She gives me a big grin and loud whispers, "I knew you could do it. You're still one of us."

I move over to the skirts next and find a size small, which I begin stuffing into my bag as well. But then I kind of freeze, midstuff. Something just doesn't feel right. Even though I'm going to be the one wearing the outfit, I'm not salivating the way Caroline is. I just don't feel the same level of excitement I used to when I knew I was getting one over on someone. It's like the whole activity has completely lost its appeal. And then something starts creeping into my stomach. There's this stabbing pain that might possibly be . . . guilt. And I suddenly start pulling the clothes back out of my bag.

I turn to look behind me, surprised that Caroline isn't acting the fool and carrying on. But there's no sign of her, or of Gillian. I look toward the door. No salesgirl. But I catch sight of Caroline bolting through it with Gillian on her heels. I'm trying to figure out what's gotten into them, when I sense someone behind me. And I turn to find the security guard looking straight into my eyes.

For someone with only one good leg, he sure is nimble . . . and stealthy. I don't know, maybe the good leg is like a rocket-powered pogo stick he uses to launch himself into the air. Maybe one of his leaps is like ten of a normal man's steps.

"W-wait, this isn't what it looks like," I stammer out. But I can sense that he is not about to believe anything that comes out of my mouth, so I decide to make a run for it. But the guard latches on to my wrist. Let me tell you, this old man might have a bad leg, but there's nothing wrong with his hands. And I start thinking of something I heard before. When one of the senses isn't so good, like eyesight or hearing, the other senses become sharper to make up for it. So maybe it's the same with bad legs. They make your hands stronger. The man has a vise grip on my arm and the salesgirl is walking over to us, sucking her teeth and rolling her neck.

"What she do, Reggie? What she do?" she yells with the thickest Brooklyn accent ever.

"Sim clothes. Dey in her bag. She a t'ief."

The cashier stops ringing up merchandise and starts craning her neck to see what's going on. Caroline and Gillian are probably halfway to Clarkson Avenue by now. And I'm wondering how my luck can be so bad. But I figure old Reggie the security guard can't hold on to me forever, and if I can get a running start, I can get away. The salesgirl wouldn't dare risk losing one of her press-on nails by trying to grab at me, so I have a chance.

The guard nudges me along while trying to pull my bag off my shoulder. Only, I'm trying to hold on to it. Then I figure if I let go, maybe he'll let go of my arm and I can make a run for it. . . . Though he'll have my school ID, so he'll know who I am. But I'll worry about that later.

The salesgirl has returned to studying her nails, so I let go of the bag. And I just start running. But the guard starts pogoing after me. *Boing, boing, boing.* He can really move with that one jet-propelled leg of his. And the salesgirl is no longer focusing on her nails. She's now yelling, "Reggie, don't you let her get away!"

Oh, but I see the door. And it's getting closer and closer. As I reach for it, I can taste freedom. But then, just like those stupid teenagers in those scary movies when the axe murderer is chasing them through the woods, I slip and go down three feet short of the finish line. And that gimpy guard goes down right on top of me. I try to wriggle free, but I can't seem to budge him an inch. I'm yelling and screaming and cussing and struggling. But there's not a peep coming out of him, no movement at all . . . just dead, gimpy weight.

27

The guard is laid out on a stretcher as the paramedics carry him out the store's front door. If they hadn't told me the opposite, I would have sworn he was dead. I've never seen any live person so still before.

I'm now seated in the back of the store, in the manager's office. I guess it's an office. There are all these boxes and clothes wrapped in plastic and other inventory and stuff. But in the very back corner is a desk with a phone and calendar and calculator and adding machine and pens and things like that. This cop is grilling me about where I live, but I tell him no one's home. Then he starts telling me he can only release me to an adult. I can't possibly call Mama. If she has to leave work to come pick me up from police custody, there's no way I'll make it to my fifteenth birthday. And forget about Ms. Viola. She'll have Mama on the phone quick, fast, and in a hurry. I think about calling Aunt Nola, but I don't want to let her in on my sordid dealings.

"You're going to have to give me a name and number, or

you're going with us to the station," the cop says to me. And it suddenly just spills from my mouth. Ms. Downer's phone number. But I regret it the moment I say it. The old lady's going to be pissed or disappointed or both. She's gonna think I haven't changed at all since that day we forced ourselves into her apartment. I wish my words were on a cassette tape I could just rewind. But they aren't. And then I think, What if she's so angry she doesn't even show up? Then I will have wrecked it with her and I'll have to call someone else anyway.

But she does show up. And as she stands at the front of the office/inventory room talking to the cop, I feel my heart sinking. They're talking in these low voices, so I can't really hear what they're saying, although I can imagine. She looks over at me a couple of times. Her eyes are completely still, with no expression registering on her face. And I'm feeling really guilty. Had Mama shown up, I would have probably felt embarrassment and anger, since all she would have done is carry on like a lunatic. But when somebody just remains calm and stares at you, it's strange. You can't help but imagine all the thoughts that might be going through their mind.

The old lady finally walks over with the cop trailing behind her.

"They're releasing you to me," she says. "I have a taxi waiting outside."

* * *

I can count the number of times I've been in a taxi—four. Those other times it made me feel all snooty and upscale having someone drive me around. Today, the ride is not such a good one. After the old lady tells the cabbie to drive us back to where he picked her up from, she doesn't say a single word to me. I just sit there staring out the window. I see these two little kids laughing as they skip on home with their parents. They look so happy. I'm pretty sure they've never had a day where some old, gimpy security guard's heart gave out while he was chasing them.

The old lady still doesn't say anything to me as we walk down the hallway of her building. She doesn't say anything as we walk into her apartment. She doesn't even say anything as she makes the tea and toast. There's only the sound of the plates rattling and the faucet running and her shoes on the tile floor. She doesn't even really say anything when I ask to use her phone to call the sitter. I take that to mean she's okay with it, so I go into the living room and talk real low once Ms. Viola picks up. Don't really need Ms. Downer overhearing this little fib about me having to stay for an extra tutoring session.

When I return to the kitchen, she hands me a tray with the tea and toast and butter and jam on it. I carry it into the living room and watch as she slowly maneuvers herself into the armchair next to the couch.

"What time does your mother get home?" she asks.

"I don't know. Around seven, I guess. Why?" But she doesn't answer me.

"You're not gonna ask me what really happened?" I ask.

"Would that change the outcome of things?"

"But I wasn't stealing the stuff. I mean, I was, because

Caroline egged me on. But then I felt bad about it and changed my mind. I was actually trying to put the stuff back. And it wasn't even my idea to begin with."

"It never is, is it?" And she fixes this heavy stare on me.

"But I never meant for that man to get hurt. I mean, who has a heart attack while they're chasing somebody? He wasn't in any shape to be a security guard. Probably had a bad heart to begin with. It wasn't my fault."

"Wasn't it?"

"No. And I was only there in the first place because I wanted to get some new clothes for our year-end ceremony. You were the one who said I shouldn't be satisfied dressing like everyone else."

"So now it's my fault too? Faye, you need to understand how your actions affect other people. It might not have been your intention, but you were still in there stealing, taking from people who were just trying to earn an honest living, from people who were only looking forward to finishing out their day at work and then going home to their families. That man won't be making it back home to his family tonight. He won't be hugging and kissing his loved ones. Now, maybe he wasn't in any shape to be a security guard. But does that make what you did any less wrong?"

"I know!" I yell. "I know. I'm horrible. Horrible! No redeeming qualities whatsoever. You think I don't know that? I steal and I lie and I hurt people, and as much as I've been trying, I just can't seem to do any good. I hurt that security guard just like I hurt you before. And I'll probably hurt someone else in the future."

I shoot up out of the chair and go into the kitchen to grab my jacket and knapsack.

"Where are you going?" the old lady asks.

"I don't know. Just away from here."

"I told those officers I'd look after you. And I meant that. At least until your mother gets home. If you step one foot out that door, I will call them back and have them explain to her what happened today."

I walk back into the living room and slam my knapsack on the floor. Only, since the floor is carpeted, it doesn't have much of a dramatic effect. "I don't get it. Why do you even care?"

"Because when I look at you, I think of my daughter. I think of how her life might have been if I had done things differently. I think of how mine might have been. I think of the confusion and insecurities she must have had because I wasn't there to answer all the questions a mother should have been there to answer.

"Faye, you think you are this terrible person, and you're not. You are a sweet, funny, imaginative young lady. And you act as though you don't, but you care. If you didn't, you would never have come back here to see if I was okay. But it's as if you see weakness in caring. Maybe because you think your mom doesn't care, although I'm certain she does. She simply doesn't know how to show it. But just because she doesn't treat you the way you should be treated doesn't mean you have to treat the world the way you do. You're better than that. You're so smart. The world is there for your taking. I don't want to see you throw that away. *I* care about you too much."

And then, all of a sudden, I feel my cheeks getting hot. And I feel my eyes blur with water. I swear, I can have somebody call me the worst names—stupid, ugly, not worth a damn—and I just roll my eyes and shrug. It's like I'm Superman: bad words bounce off me. But I'm not used to anyone saying anything kind to me. I don't know how to react. But I refuse to cry. So I tighten the muscles in my face and open my eyes real wide. I'm not about to make any noise. Not a moan or a wail or even a sniffle. But then I see the old lady stand and move over to me, and I feel her hands against my back, all bony and skeletonlike. I don't want her to touch me, so I try to shrug away from her. But she takes a seat on the couch and leans in to hug me. And I feel how frail she is. And it's becoming harder and harder for me to control the muscles in my face, no matter how much I scrunch it up.

When she moves off into her room, I lie on the couch and replay the events of the afternoon. They're going around and around in my head but I somehow manage to drift off for a while, because the next thing I'm aware of is her saying, "Faye, it's nearly seven o'clock. Isn't your mother home by now?"

I spring up off the couch and quickly get myself together. Shoot. I meant to get back to the sitter's before Mama got home.

"One moment," the old lady says. Then she shuffles off to her bedroom again. I want to go, but I wait for her to come back. When she gets to me, she's wearing a beige sweater over her brown pants and shirt. She's also put on a little beige hat. With her white skin, she sort of blends in with all that beige and looks like a Band-Aid.

"You're going out?" I ask.

"I'm going with you."

"Where to?"

"Your home."

"Why?"

"Because you're a fourteen-year-old girl who's had a very traumatic incident, and you need to tell your mother. And if I don't go with you, you won't tell her."

"Nah, I'll tell her. I was gonna tell her."

"Tell her what?"

"That . . . well . . . I don't know. Tell her what happened."

"If that's the case, then why did I hear you leaving a message that you were still at school?"

And all of a sudden, my head starts spinning, and I'm feeling dizzy and outside my own body. And my stomach is starting to do backflips, like there's an acrobat in there. Or maybe it's Nadia Comaneci dismounting from the balance beam to a perfect ten. Whatever it is, I don't feel that well. And I think about just pushing the old lady down and running.

"Why do I have to tell her?" I ask.

"She's your mother."

"Easy for you to say. You don't know her. She's not gonna understand."

"That you witnessed a man go into cardiac arrest and almost die? I don't care how difficult she might be. You're her daughter and she needs to know. Besides, the police might need to get in touch with you again, and then what?"

"Then *you* can come with me."

But she's obviously not about to listen. I try everything to change her mind, but it doesn't work. And so I labor down Parkside Avenue like I'm heading off to my execution. If this old woman whispers a word to Mama about what took place at the Dressy Dress Mart, I'm no longer of this world.

It's staying lighter a lot later now, and as I look off into the sky, I catch sight of the most brilliant oranges and purples and pinks as the sun gets ready to set. I try to think of a thousand ways of getting out of this situation. I'm a pretty fast runner, so if I took off down Flatbush Avenue like the Flash, the old lady would just have to let me go. I mean, look at how slowly she moves. I could make a break for it, stay away for a few weeks, and when I came back, she'd probably have gotten over it. My brain tells my feet to go, but I look over at her and how she's concentrating so hard on each step she takes. And I think about how her hug felt and I think about how I never really had a grandma. I think about the nice words she said to me. I think about how we met and I just sigh. I want to make my big escape, but I just can't seem to.

28

The thing about my apartment building is, it pretty much blends in with the others on my street. It has six floors, like most of the other buildings, and it's made of the same reddish-brown brick. It has fire escapes zigzagging across some of the front windows, and a fairly long walkway from the street to the lobby. But as I round the corner from Bedford Avenue, it suddenly seems so prominent. It's as if someone has replaced it with the Empire State Building. And as we get closer and closer, my entire body starts to get cold. I'm thinking this is how people about to face a firing squad must feel.

"This is my building," I say as we turn down the walkway. Moments later, I'm standing in the lobby looking at the call box and at the apartment number, E11, but I just can't press it.

"Go on," the old lady says softly.

I swallow, but my throat closes up a little. Finally, I take a breath and push the number. We wait a while and there's nothing. And I'm thinking, Maybe Mama isn't home yet. Maybe there was a fire in the subway and they had to evacuate her train. I get ready to let out a sigh of relief when there's this crackling sound followed by the words, "Faye, is that you?"

"Hi, Mama," I say. Before I can finish, there's this loud buzz. I push the front door open and hold it for the old lady to walk through. As the elevator climbs from floor to floor, I start feeling a little faint. At least, I'm feeling the way I think people probably feel when they're about to faint, considering I've never passed out in my life.

I don't say anything when Mama first opens the door. I just swallow really hard. But her piercing look toward Ms. Downer prompts me to speak.

"Mama, this is Ms. Evelyn Downer."

Ms. Downer nods and smiles a little, but Mama just keeps standing in the doorway, puffing away at a cigarette and staring at her. Then she sighs this big "Woe is me" sigh and shakes her head.

"What the hell did you do now, Faye?"

"I didn't do anything."

"Then who the hell is this woman with you and why is she here?"

"There was an incident today," the old lady begins. "Go on, Faye, tell her."

So, there I am, standing at the end of the long lonely hall with Ms. Downer, who Mama doesn't seem to want to let in. I'm figuring that after Mama hears my story, she probably won't want to let me into the apartment either.

"All of a sudden, you can't talk," Mama says. "What did you do now? Go on."

"I didn't do anything. I was in a store. And there was this security guard. And he ended up having a heart attack. The next thing I know, he's lying on top of me like he's dead. And the cops called Ms. Downer, so she came and took me back to her place."

Mama stands there staring at me, her right hand still holding on to the door, her left hand now making its way from the cigarette up to her forehead. Her eyes get real narrow and her face gets all weird and contorted. But then her face suddenly becomes still.

"Wait a minute. Wait a minute. I thought Viola said something about extra tutoring since your finals are coming up." Mama looks over at Ms. Downer. "And why did the cops contact *you*?" But before the old lady can speak, Mama continues.

"And nobody's answered me yet. Who exactly is this woman?"

"She's my friend," I say.

"Your friend? You're fourteen. This woman is . . . she's . . . I really don't know how old she is, but she probably has seventy years on you. What fourteen-year-old is friends with a senior citizen? And *once again,* why did the cops contact her? Come to think of it, why were cops involved in the first place? And why were you even in that store? Were you stealing shit again?"

JCJ suddenly comes walking out from the elevator, whistling cheerfully.

"Hey hey. Looks like a party in the hallway. What's going on out here?" he asks.

Mama blurts out something about me causing trouble again, so JCJ tells her to invite everyone in so we can sit and talk about what happened without the whole fifth floor knowing our business.

So now we're all in the living room. Me and the old lady are sitting on Mama's ugly beige couch with the blooming flower print. I hate this couch. Why Mama won't remove the annoying plastic that makes a crunchy noise and sticks to the back of my legs in the summer is beyond me. Anyway, Jerry's sitting on one of the matching armchairs, which is also covered in plastic, and Mama just hovers there with a newly lit Virginia Slim between the middle and pointer fingers of her left hand.

"So paint this picture for me. How the hell did you two meet?"

I just shake my head and look down at the brown carpet, because it's all about to hit the fan.

"I was having trouble with some groceries and Faye helped me out," the old lady says. And my eyes shoot over to her. I'm so thankful she left out that tiny little part about me ripping her off and almost killing her. I think Mama must have caught my look of shock and surprise, because she then takes a puff of her cigarette and focuses on me.

"That what happened, Faye?"

"Yes, Mama."

"Hmm. Okay," she says after another puff. "So how did

this helping with the groceries turn into you two becoming bosom buddies?"

"I made her a snack. We talked about school. I'm old. I'm not that well. I don't really have anyone to talk to. I asked if your daughter could maybe pop in from time to time. She has."

"We're still talking about Faye here?"

"Yes."

Mama shakes her head and arches her eyebrows, then takes a really long drag.

"Uh-huh," she says. I can't tell if she believes any of this. But it's not a lie. It's just a very carefully constructed and edited retelling of the truth.

"So at this store today, tell me what happened. Only, I'd appreciate a little more detail this time."

The old lady starts saying something, but Mama cuts her off.

"I'm speaking to my daughter, Ms. Downer."

"I apologize," the old lady says.

"I was in there with a couple of kids walking around looking at stuff. And the old security guard who works there, well, he just up and had a heart attack. And he sorta fell on me."

"And you didn't provoke him any?"

"No, ma'am."

"Lots of incredible things happening here. Let me ask you this: If it was just a heart attack, what were the cops doing there?"

"Maybe they happened to be outside walking their beat," I say.

"And again, you called"—but Mama doesn't say her name, she just points—"this person because . . . ?"

"She lives nearby, and I knew she'd be home. And I know you don't like me disturbing you when you're at work."

Mama turns to Ms. Downer.

"Is this what happened?" she asks.

"I only got there at the very end," the old lady answers.

Mama doesn't offer Ms. Downer any tea or even some water, which I think is pretty awful. She's old. Old people need to drink lots of liquids. But JCJ has some manners, and he brings her some orange juice. Ms. Downer is in the middle of saying something when Mama suddenly mashes her unfinished cigarette into an ashtray and claps her hands together.

"Thank you, Ms. Downer. It was very enlightening meeting one of Faye's . . . friends. Jerry, please show Faye's guest out. It's getting late."

I continue sitting on that couch, listening to the wooden beads as they knock together, listening to the two sets of footsteps as they recede down the hallway. I try not to look up because I can feel Mama's electric glare. I hear the front door shut behind the old lady, and as if that triggers her, Mama starts going off.

"You call some old random white lady instead of your own mother," she hisses at me. She's standing over me all tall and strong and threatening.

"Come on, Jeanne," Jerry says as he walks back through the wooden beads, causing them to sway and clack together some more. "She's a kid. She was scared. Probably didn't want to worry you."

"You don't know how sneaky she can be, Jerry!"

"Jeanne—" Jerry starts to say.

"You're. Not. Her. Father. She doesn't have one. Maybe if she did, she wouldn't be acting like this. Maybe if that father cared enough to keep the family intact, none of this would be happening."

"Yeah, I guess you're right. I'm not her father," Jerry says quietly.

"And maybe you should go on home tonight," Mama says. "I need to have some time with my daughter."

If eyeballs were able to make sounds, mine would be screaming. I'm shooting Jerry the most pleading of looks, but he doesn't seem to pick up on it.

"Not my place to get in the middle of family," he says. "So I guess I'll see ya, Faye. Good night, Jeanne."

Jerry walks back through the wooden beads. His footsteps get quieter as he makes it farther down the hall. Then there's an opening and closing of the front door. I keep staring at the beads as they move slower and slower and then come close to knocking into one another. I want to run my hands across them and have them make noise again, because with Jerry gone and Mama staring at me with fire in her eyes, everything feels so ominous and still.

I try to look up at Mama, but it's like looking directly into the sun. Her eyes are just too intense. I try to move past her, but she doesn't give any ground. She doesn't move back or forward or step out of the way. I try to step around her, and that's when I see it. But it happens so lightning fast, I have no time to react. Mama uses her left elbow to connect with my jaw. And suddenly, there's this ringing sound in my ear.

* * *

I know how to make sure it doesn't hurt as much. I just close my eyes and stand real still. The thing is, if you move around a lot, she has to move around a lot. And the extension cord might slip out of her hand. And as she quickly grabs it back up, she might catch it at the wrong end, and you risk getting the part with the plug on it across your face. And if you keep your eyes open, it makes your heart skip a beat every time you see it coming at you. So I stand there real still and hold my breath. And I make my brain drift somewhere far away. And soon, I'm not even in my bedroom anymore. I'm not naked. I don't even really feel the lashes across my back. I feel like a jet plane, flying against the wind. The wind is hard and it beats at my back, but it's not so bad. And I fly above the birds. And pretty soon, the wind becomes just a breeze. And if I keep holding my breath, I start feeling so light. Now I'm no longer a jet plane. I am one of the birds, flying in V formation. The breeze ruffles my feathers, but only a little. I've almost reached where I'm going. And soon, I'll be able to land in a meadow full of flowers. I'll be warm again, and I'll be free.

29

It's ten degrees cooler today than it was yesterday. I think on Eyewitness News two nights ago, Storm Field said it was going to be around sixty-two, but it feels even lower than that to me. I'm glad the park bench the old lady and I are sitting on is out in the open, with no trees shading it. That way, I can soak up as much of the sun as possible. Its warmth feels so comforting against my face.

We're down at the edge of the lake, near this little gazebo.

"I just want to apologize," I say. "For what I did at that store. It was stupid. It was just me not really thinking again. And I also want to apologize for Mama."

"Were you punished?"

"Not really Mama's nature to punish. She's more of a 'deal with the situation right then and there' kinda person."

Ms. Downer doesn't say anything for a while. "Well, you don't have to apologize to me for her. You can't control what other people do or how they act. Besides, I think it's understandable that she was upset."

"What about my apology?" I ask. "Do you accept that?"

Instead of answering, Ms. Downer stands slowly and starts walking toward the lake.

"Ms. Downer," I call out after her. But she keeps walking. I stay on the bench and watch her for a moment.

She finally stops once she reaches the water's edge. I pick up her purse, which she left where she was sitting—I mean, we are in Brooklyn—and walk over to her. A group of ducks floats by a few feet away. I stand there listening to them quack. From behind us I can hear voices get louder, then trail off.

"Faye, I know I haven't always been as forthcoming as I could have when you've asked me questions about certain things in my life. But it's because I'm ashamed of some of the things I've done." She lets out a big breath of air.

"You know, my mother thought I was foolish saying I was going to Hollywood to be in pictures. She said I'd just be hurt and ridiculed, and that my soul would be beaten down. And then there was the fact that I was married, with a young child. But there was something so strong inside me that was driving me.

"Nowadays, all the films seem to have big explosions and special effects that leave you speechless. When I was a little girl, there wasn't even sound. Just a little music to accompany the action. I would save all my money and go to those silent pictures. And once the lights went down and the music started . . . I can't explain what it did to me. Then one day, I saw this movie called *The Homesteader*. There was the most exquisite woman with this wealth of energy carrying that picture. She had beautiful light brown skin, which really stood out to me. I mean, the only people you saw with brown skin in pictures those days, well, they were cleaning the white man's house or shining his shoes. And she moved as gracefully as the wind. She completely mesmerized me."

I hear a rustling sound behind us and turn to see a fat jogger stuffed into a silver sweat suit. He looks like an over-sized Jiffy Pop popcorn container. As he huffs and puffs on by, I start wondering where the nearest pay phone is, in case there's going to be a need to dial 911.

"I always knew there was something else for me in life. Something bigger. Something better. Now, I had taken theater classes, and I could sing," Ms. Downer continues. "I could dance. That's where I met my husband, doing a show up in Harlem where I was the lead performer. But I always felt there was a ceiling . . . a limit to what I could do and how far I would be able to go. But then through fate, or divine intervention, I had a talent agent approach me right at the corner of Thirty-Third Street and Seventh Avenue one day and tell me I was pretty enough to be in front of the camera. I took a chance, with my husband's blessing, and I went to Hollywood. We figured that within the year, we would take stock of things, and if I was working and making good money, he would quit his job and relocate with our daughter. But things happened so quickly for me, in a way I never planned; in a way it only ever happens in the movies. I was a bit of a novelty. 'The Bolivian Bombshell' was the term they were using."

"I didn't know you were from Bolivia," I say.

"Never been there in my life. But I was just exotic-looking enough to have them intrigued. There was a fine line then. Too exotic, and you could scare off the masses. Just a little exotic, and they went crazy over you. Someone said I had a Bolivian mother and an American father, and everyone believed it. And I didn't say anything different. Anyway, there was an instant buzz, and people started to invest in me. They believed I could become something very big. I believed it too. And I got a taste of a fairy-tale life. It was all my dreams coming true, from when I used to sit in the back of those theaters wishing I could be up on the screen. Within the first year, I had small parts in two movies. And they started talking about a starring vehicle for me. Something else happened within that first year. I fell in love with someone—a man who was not my husband. A producer named Sam, who was helping shape my career.

"It's amazing how quickly I became consumed by my own ambition. How I became caught up in my own hype. Suddenly, my life in New York drifted further and further into the past, so much so that I no longer seemed to be able to associate with it. I got my husband to give me a divorce. I sent money back, loads of it, and swore him to secrecy about our relationship.

"He was a good man, my husband. Loyal and caring. I was never greatly in love with him, but I knew he could give me a nice, trouble-free life. I knew I would never go hungry being with him. When I became pregnant, he gave up all his dreams of being a performer and fell back on his electrical skills. Just so he could feed his new family.

"Anyway, once I was free to date who I wanted, I started spending more and more time with that producer, and I became as much a part of his being as he was of mine. He started confiding in me, telling me things he had never told anyone before. He said he wanted to marry me and that he needed to lay everything out on the table. No secrets. And some of the things he had done to get to where he was were terrible. Beyond terrible, but he admitted them to me. And I think I loved him more because of it."

"Things like what?" I ask.

"That part I'll keep hidden," she says, with a sad smile on her face. "I figured his opening up was his way of saying he really did love me. I guess I didn't realize he had so much inner turmoil. He just needed someone to be his sounding board. Anyone. But I decided that if he could be so open, I had no choice but to be the same with him—since our love was so great." She lets out this strange little laugh. "And I had a secret that was boring a hole through me. A very big one. And so one night, as we were relaxing in front of the fire, I got up and went to my suitcase. I took out some pictures I had hidden in the lining and I put them on the sofa."

She motions for her purse and I give it to her. She pulls out her wallet and fishes through one of the compartments for a couple of old black-and-white pictures enclosed in plastic. She hands the first one to me.

"My husband and me on our wedding day."

I try not to look shocked, but I'm pretty sure I don't succeed. I think back to the picture on Ms. Downer's counter, and I realize there wasn't a shadow at all over that baby's face. That baby was black. And now I understand why. The old lady's husband is as dark as me—dark hair, dark eyes, dark skin.

"I thought people couldn't get married back then if they were . . . you know. If they were different," I say. "Wasn't that a crime?"

"Edgar and I weren't as different as you might think," she says. But I'm not following her. And then she hands me another picture.

"My parents," she says. "The picture is so old you might not be able to tell, but both my mother and father were what people used to call half-caste or mulatto."

"Whoa" is about all I can come up with.

"That night when I showed Sam this picture, I felt lighter for getting such a heavy secret off my chest. I felt that it would bring us even closer. I thought that because he cared for me, my parents both being part black would have little effect on him. But after I shared my burning secret, he reacted with so much hatred and animosity, it was as if he became a different person. He told me to leave Hollywood, to just disappear without a trace, as if I had never existed. He told me he would do anything to prevent the shame this bit of information would cause him, his studio, and his family if the truth ever got out. He told me he'd have me killed if I didn't leave. And the funny thing was, he represented himself as a man who believed in equality for everyone.

"I never meant to deceive anyone. I went to California knowing exactly who and what I was, hoping I could change things. I thought I would work in classy black films, like the ones Oscar Micheaux made. But fate intervened. Someone who just assumed I was South American found me, and I simply didn't say anything to make him aware of the truth. There were lovely actresses like Nina Mae McKinney, like Fredericka Washington, and because they were black, their careers were so limited. Fredericka could pass for white, but she chose not to. I guess I could have made this choice too . . . but then wonderful things started happening so quickly, and before I knew it, there was no way to dig out of the hole I found myself in. My life was now a thousand times better than I could ever have imagined. I just decided I would go along with it. But unfortunately, with 'passing' came some monumental sacrifices. There was no way I could be seen with my half-black parents, with a black husband, with my daughter . . . so I made a decision I've lived to regret.

"In the end, I really did disappear. I went to France for a while, started a whole new life there. But I missed the adoration. I missed the life I had gotten accustomed to. I was so confused and unhappy. For a while, I just spiraled down. Went through a depression I thought I would never climb out from."

I don't know what to say, so I just stand there quietly, stealing these little glances at Ms. Downer. I can't believe she's black like me. Well, maybe not completely like me, but partly. And I can't believe how crazy her life has been.

"Faye, I'm telling you this now for a reason. I know I'm always talking about regrets and how one bad decision can affect so many other things in your life. I just want you to see that this doesn't come from an empty place. This isn't just about an old woman wanting to hear herself talk and pointing her finger and saying 'Do as I say.' It really does come from me not wanting your precious, young, promising life to end up in the sadness mine has. So when you ask if I accept your apology, of course I do. But I want to make sure it's not a hollow one. I want to make sure you're not just saying it because you think it's what you're supposed to say or because you think it's what I want to hear. I want to make sure you'll do your best to really think before you act, because sometimes what's done can never be undone."

30

I am completely freaking out. I just felt something tickle my right leg, and I'm quite certain it wasn't a feather. I'm sure of this because I'm not outside on a field trip to the Botanic Garden, or in the yard at school, or even in Prospect Park. I'm in my kitchen, under the table, kneeling on the cold linoleum floor. And my nightie stops just below my knees, leaving the lower part of my legs very bare and very available to any of the nighttime critters that inhabit our apartment. If I wasn't trying to be secretive, I would let out a scream that would wake the dead. See, I know it's a cockroach. I can feel its nasty little legs brushing against my skin. I squirm and jerk my feet this way and that, but I have to be careful not to kick the metal legs of any of the dining chairs and wake Mama. If she comes out and finds me under the table with the telephone off its wall mount, along with a flashlight, a pen, and pages from a phone book, she will surely pop a blood vessel. I mean, I'm pretty sure I look as if I'm in the middle of some supersecret spy mission.

After one more backward kick, I no longer feel any creepy-crawlies on my body. I want to shine the flashlight behind me and make sure whatever was violating my person is really gone, but I decide it's probably best not to. No telling what else I might find back there.

Though it might seem like it, I'm not losing my mind, camping out under my kitchen table in the dead of night. It's been three weeks since I got that morsel of information about Ms. Downer's daughter from that archivist, but I've finally figured out what to do with it. I'm going to try to undo the old lady's greatest regret by finding her daughter and talking to her myself. I'm going to march right up to her and tell her just how much Ms. Downer loves her and still thinks of her every moment of every day of her life, and wants to be her mother again. I can't stop imagining their first moments together after nearly half a century. I can't stop imagining the joy and the tears and the laughter. The thought of that gives me the courage to remain on the cold kitchen floor despite the threat of an insect encounter and the sudden appearance of what would surely be a thoroughly aggravated Mama.

I came up with the idea in, of all places, Sister Margaret Theresa Patricia Bernadette's class, then hoped and prayed the film buff would show up at Ms. Downer's again during one of my visits. I figured I could somehow get him to give me the daughter's address. But he never did turn up. And then the old lady started looking at me funny, telling me I was acting suspicious, so I just cracked and asked her when she was expecting another visit from him.

"William has gotten about as much information as he can from me. The book is more or less completed, so no more scheduled visits. I suppose if any other questions come up, I'll get a call from him. Or maybe he'll drop by if he feels like wasting an afternoon on a casual visit with an old woman."

It's not like I could have just come out and asked her for the film buff's number, so I had to really put on my thinking cap. Anyway, there I was lying in bed a couple of nights ago being grossed out by the thought of what Mama and JCJ were doing in the bedroom right next to mine, when it dawned on me that I had enough information to find this Delaine Lawson person myself. I just needed to do some *Charlie's Angels*–type investigating.

I couldn't remember whether the film buff had said Delaine Lawson worked at a hospital, a clinic, or a nursing home. I just knew it was something medical and in Manhattan, which led me to the main library's reference section for the first step of my mission. See, they have phone listings for every borough in New York City there. A fistful of change later, I had a Xeroxed copy of the Yellow Pages listings for all Manhattan health facilities.

So, back to me under the table, which is where I've been for the past hour or so, and also where I've been for several hours the past couple of nights. This is step two. And I swear, as I dial each number, my fingers shake so much it's as if I'm coming down with a sudden case of palsy. Trying to maneuver a rotary dial quietly is just about impossible, and since Mama is too cheap to get a push-button phone, I'm forced to suffer. Jerry's not here tonight, which is shocking in itself, considering he camps out here most every night now. But that means Mama's got no diversion, so I'm forced to be ghostly quiet. The only way to cut down on the loud clicking noise the dial makes is to keep my pointer finger in the finger hole and slowly crank the dial around and back to its resting position. Now, this isn't too bad if a phone number has a lot of ones and twos in it—those are closest to the finger stop—but when it's a bunch of eights, nines, and ze-roes, forget it. It ends up taking forever for those numbers to make a full rotation. So here I am, going down the listing of medical establishments. But between my slow-motion dialing, being put on hold, and being transferred, it takes like ten minutes to complete each call. Anyway, I might not have mastered my dialing technique, but I have mastered my conversation:

"Such-and-such hospital/clinic/nursing home," the person on the other end will say.

"Hi, I'm trying to reach Delaine Lawson," I respond.

"What department, please?"

"Uh, nursing?"

"Sure, hold while I transfer." Then there's a pause, followed by more ringing.

"Nurses' station."

"Hi, I'm trying to reach Delaine Lawson."

"Is she a patient?"

"No. A nurse."

"I'm sorry, we don't have a Nurse Lawson."

"Oh, could you transfer me back to the operator, please?"

"No problem. Please hold." Pause. Ring.

"Operator."

"Yeah, I was calling for Delaine Lawson. I thought she was a nurse, but I guess she's not. See, my brother took a message saying I got a call from her. This was earlier in the day, but seeing that the call came from a _____"—I fill in the blank with *hospital, clinic,* or *nursing home*—"I thought it might be important. But he didn't write down what the call was for. Can you just check if there's a Delaine Lawson in another department?"

Okay, that last part I came up with in today's religious studies class. I had to think of something, because a couple of places got snotty with me after I got snotty with them for insisting that I had to tell them what department she was in. I wanted to say, "I don't even know who this person is. I'm on a wild-goose chase here, trying to do a good deed for once in my depraved life. Can you just give me a break and help me out?" But that little speech I came up with has been working wonders.

The thing is, over the past two nights, and a couple of times during the days when I was able to scrounge up enough change and stake out a pay phone, I've gone through every clinic listed. And every hospital. Thank goodness there are only so many of those. Now I'm almost through with the nursing homes, and I still haven't found her. I've been dealing with charley horses, finger cramps, nasty roaches, my feet going numb, lack of sleep, and the possibility of my perpetually irate mother busting me, and I still haven't come across Delaine Lawson. I'm doing everything to try not to lose hope.

"Ridgeway Nursing Home," a lady's voice says.

And so I whisper the opening line of my monologue. I try not to fall asleep as the phone rings and rings and rings in the nurses' station. I'm really praying here, because I only have four more listings left after this one.

"Nurses' station," this Spanish-accented voice says.

"Hi, I'm trying to reach Delaine Lawson," I whisper.

"Delaine Lawson?"

"Yes," I say. I know what the next line will be, so I beat them to the punch. "She is not a patient."

"I hope not," the lady on the other end says. "But she's not here. She was on an earlier shift today."

Hearing those words makes my tired, cramped muscles spring to life again. I straighten up a little too quickly and bang my head against the top of the table. I hold real still, making sure Mama didn't hear anything, making sure she hasn't started shuffling around.

"She works there?" I whisper before I realize how ridiculous I sound. After all, I did call for her. "I mean, earlier. She worked there earlier?"

"Yes," the person says.

"Okay, thank you," I say, and I hang up the phone.

I point the flashlight at the Xerox of the phone book page, circle the address for Ridgeway Nursing Home, then let out a deep breath. I'm feeling incredibly nervous all of a sudden. This could actually happen.

31

Well, I already know this is going to be a bad night. I guess I didn't think it would take me so long to get into the city. The thing is, I don't go into Manhattan that often, so I'm not all that familiar with train lines or that convoluted subway map with all the color-coded connections. I thought I had it all down, but did I ever make a mess of it. Right after school, I hopped on the number 2 at Franklin Avenue, then transferred to the number 1 local at Times Square/ Forty-Second Street, which took me to West Seventy-Ninth Street. Seemed to make sense to me, since the nursing home is on Seventy-Seventh Street. Problem is, it's on *East* Seventy-Seventh. Doesn't sound like that much of an issue—just walk a couple of streets over. Unfortunately for me, there's a slight obstacle in getting from West to East Seventy-Ninth: Central Park. The last thing I wanted was to get lost in there and become one of those statistics you read about—attacked by some homicidal maniac or beaten up by some deranged homeless guy. Anyway, I ended up having to get really creative to link up with the East Side local train, which finally let me off near where I needed to be.

I'm usually only in Manhattan for some school function, like when they take us to a Broadway show or to the Met or Guggenheim Museums to broaden our cultural horizons. And it's pretty corny to admit, but I'm kind of in awe of the place. I can't look up at those skyscrapers without wondering how they were able to build them that high. And everyone always seems so important and in such a hurry, especially those businesswomen in their skirt suits and Reebok tennis shoes. There'll be three hot dog vendors on the same street corner fighting for the same customers, and cars and cabs zoom by, all trying to out-honk each other. It's fast and wild and noisy and wonderful. Only, today, it barely has any impact on me. I'm so nervous and hopeful that everything will go well with the old lady's daughter, I walk the four blocks from the subway station to the nursing home hardly noticing a thing.

When I get to the address I scribbled down, I just stand there staring at the building. It's not exactly how I pictured a nursing home. I guess I thought it would look more like an old manor, like what Batman lives in, with a nice green, tree-filled yard out front where all the people being nursed could sit out and garden, or take in nature, or inhale from their oxygen tanks. I'm aware it's in the middle of the city, but still. This place reminds me of the apartment building the Jeffersons live in, not much different from any of the other high-rises on the street.

I walk into the lobby and some extra-plump, overly

happy lady seated behind a desk greets me. And I'm wondering how she can have a job at a health-care facility when she could be a poster child for hypertension and diabetes.

"Oh, aren't you a little cherub? Look at you. Look at you," she says as I walk up. She keeps wiggling her nose like Samantha on *Bewitched* and talking in this odd baby voice. I actually have to look behind me to check to see if there's a toddler in the vicinity. But it's just me. Once again, I know I might be a bit smaller than average, but seriously!

"Are you here to see your grandma or grandpa?" she asks.

"My grandparents are long dead," I say. I guess I'm harsher with my words than I intended, because her eyebrows shoot up to the top of her forehead. The good thing is, she begins speaking to me in a normal-person voice.

"I came to see Delaine Lawson," I continue. "She's a nurse here."

"Let me call the nurses' station. Is she expecting you?"

"Not exactly."

"Maggie," she says into the phone, "is Delaine there? Uh-huh . . . uh-huh . . . Oh, I see."

I'm not so sure I like the way she said "Oh, I see."

"Honey, what's your name?" the woman asks me.

"It's Faye Andrews."

"Well, she has a guest," she says back into the phone. "A little girl named Faye Andrews. Uh-huh. She's here in the lobby. Okay." She hangs up the phone and wrinkles her nose again.

"She's on her rounds."

"What does that mean?"

"She's looking in on patients. Once she's done, she'll come down."

"Once she's done?" Doesn't this woman know I don't have all day? "Well, when will that be?"

"Shouldn't be too long," she says. The phone rings and she goes to pick it up, but looks over at me again before she starts speaking to the person on the other end. "Just make yourself comfortable."

I really have no choice, so I go and sit down in this waiting area that has the hardest padded chairs ever. The backs slope a little, so I'm forced to sit at this weird angle. I look around at the large framed photographs hanging on the walls. Pictures of mountains and rivers and forests and streams. I wonder if they hung them to counter all the concrete and asphalt and brick the patients are forced to look out at every day.

Two male nurses wheel out these two people who are Moses-coming-down-from-the-mountain old. I'm really not all that certain they're still alive. The nurses maneuver them over to the front windows and just leave them there—I guess so they can look out onto the street, or at least the small outdoor patio area. I watch them for a while, wondering if they're about to have a conversation and talk about, oh, I don't know, whatever it is people who are too old to walk and eat by themselves and pee by themselves talk about. But they don't say a thing. They just sit there staring straight ahead. This place reminds me of that clinic Ms. Downer had me meet her in, only it's about ten times more depressing. I swear, over the past couple of months, I've been around more old people than I've been around the whole rest of my life put together.

When a couple of female nurses round a corner, I start to stand up. One is younger, but the other, well, she looks like she could be in her fifties. She's a little dumpy, with tan skin, frizzy gray hair, and greenish eyes like the old lady's. I'm pretty certain it's her daughter, so I straighten out my jacket and take a few deep breaths. I'm so excited even my palms are starting to get sweaty. I cross my fingers, because I want this to go as well as I dreamed it would.

I smile and step forward. Only, the lady with the frizzy hair doesn't walk over to meet me. She just laughs real loud at whatever her friend is saying and walks through the front door without ever looking in my direction.

I sit back down, realizing I have no idea what this woman is going to look like. Maybe she'll look like the old lady. But maybe she'll look more like the old lady's husband. Maybe she'll be lighter. Maybe she'll be darker. Maybe her hair will be straight. Maybe curly. I just have to be patient. But when I look down at my watch, I see it's almost twenty minutes after five. It's going to take me at least an hour to get back to Brooklyn. I guess it really doesn't matter much at this point. I'm doomed.

About twenty-five minutes later, I see this other lady walk into the lobby with purpose. She glances my way, then walks over to the information desk and talks to *Bewitched*. Then she looks over at me again. She just stands there for a while before she starts coming forward. I'm getting a bad feeling. This woman definitely shops at the big-and-tall store, and she's tough-looking to boot. I'm thinking Delaine's supervisor is about to throw me out of the nursing home.

"You're Faye Andrews?" she asks once she's standing in front of me.

I nod slowly. "Should I know you?" I ask.

"I don't know. You asked for me."

"I asked for Delaine Lawson."

"I am Delaine Lawson."

Okay, so maybe I could have played off my surprise a little better, but I'd need to have taken some serious acting lessons. See, I'm figuring I got the wrong Delaine Lawson because this woman does not look like she could be any relation to the old lady. Everything on her is just kind of in-your-face: big ol' eyes, a wide nose, round lips. Even her voice is big, and deep, and intimidating.

"I'm looking for the Delaine Lawson who is the daughter of a woman named Evelyn Downer, who also has another name, Evelyn Ryder."

And just like that, the puzzled smile that was on her face completely disappears. It's as if a set of imaginary fingers latches on to the corners of her lips and tugs them downward.

I give her a second to process. But that second turns into about a minute, and she still hasn't responded, and I'm realizing that maybe this isn't the wrong Delaine Lawson after all. Finally, her eyes shift a little, and I see the muscles in her face tighten.

"What's going on here?" she asks.

I'm suddenly getting the feeling that if this Delaine Lawson person could have taken my words and stuffed them back into my throat, she would have. And she wouldn't even use her nursing skills on me as I stood there choking.

"Your mother is dying," I blurt out. Can't help it. It's the only thing I can think of to keep her from walking away. And the way I see it, it's not really a lie. I mean, the old lady is like a thousand, so she's closer to dying than she is to anything else. Besides, Uncle Paul once said that after you're born, you spend every single day afterward inching closer to death. So you're going downhill from the moment of birth. If you think of it that way, I'm totally telling the truth.

"How do you know my . . . How do you know her?" she asks. I can't tell if she's softening a little or if she's just in shock.

"She's my friend."

"Your friend? What are you, twelve?"

"Fourteen, thank you," I say with just enough attitude to let her know I don't appreciate her incorrect estimate. And personally, I don't think it's that weird—a teenager and an eighty-year-old person being friends.

"So . . . she knows where I am?"

"I don't think so."

"What do you mean, you don't think so? Didn't she send you here to relay this story about her dying? To try to clear her conscience?"

"She didn't send me anywhere." After I say that, the

daughter kind of looks me up and down, then pushes her plum-painted bottom lip out a little. I'm sensing that she doesn't believe me.

"Where are your parents?" she asks.

"In their skin, right where they're supposed to be," I answer. But then it hits me that I shouldn't piss her off, 'cause then she'll just leave and never go see the old lady, so I backtrack.

"My mother's at work."

She pulls me over to the waiting area, puts her hand on my left shoulder, and presses down so that I'm forced to sit. Then she sits. She even angles her chair a little so she's turned toward me.

"How do you even know who I am? How did you find me?"

"This man's writing a book about her."

"Oh, that," she says, easing back in her chair. I watch her every move, and I start thinking about how slight the old lady is, especially compared to this Delaine woman, who's not fat big, but big-boned big. Like she's been working in a field somewhere lifting haystacks and rolling giant logs. But I guess her size works for her, being that she's a nurse and probably has to move half-dead patients around all day.

"You talked to him?" I ask.

"By phone. And only long enough to say I didn't want to talk to him."

"How come?" When she doesn't answer me, I ask again. "How come you didn't want to talk to him?"

"Because if he's writing a book about her life, I'm the last person who'd know anything about it. She left when I was still a baby."

"She must have had her reasons."

"She did. Money, fame, and greed. A career meant more than her family." She lets out a deep breath, then does something really weird. She pats my head, like you would your cocker spaniel.

"This doesn't concern you," she says as she starts to stand.

"It does, 'cause she's gonna die and all. She really doesn't have very long." Again, not a lie, considering how many days she's already spent on this earth. "And she feels guilty about things with you and, well, she doesn't know I'm here, but I don't want her to die with regrets. And you should want to see her before she goes, even if it's only for a little while. Even if it's only to hear her side of things. 'Cause you probably are curious. I know I would be."

The daughter shakes her head, and before she can move off, I dig through my bag and find the piece of paper I wrote the old lady's address and phone number on when I was stuck on the train. When I extend it to her, she just stares at it like it's been dipped in poison. But I don't give in. I don't pull my hand away.

"It's her information," I say. "I won't know what you do with it once I'm gone, but you can take it and think about everything, and then you can do what you feel."

She looks at the paper a bit longer, then goes to take it, but hesitates a little. I keep my arm really strong, and she finally caves. She just folds it up without looking at what's written on it, tucks it in the pocket of her white nurse's pants, and walks off.

I look down at my watch. It's six o'clock exactly, and I'm nowhere near Flatbush. As I said before, despite my good deed, this is definitely not going to be a good night for me.

32

When I get back to my building, Gerald is standing outside looking up and down the street. The moment he spots me, he starts waving his arms wildly.

"My mom had me come look for you. She's real worried. Real worried. I'm pretty sure you're gonna be in trouble," he says once I reach him.

"Whatever," I say. "Did my mother ring for me already?"

"Nah."

My watch reads seven-fifteen. I thought for sure Mama would have been home by now. But I guess I lucked out. And it's only because my journey back home was nowhere as complicated as my journey into the city, and my connections were sitting there waiting for me as I got into the stations.

"Maybe I can help," Gerald says as he gallops behind me into the building. I stop and look at him.

"Maybe I can say that I saw these boys roughing you up. That they were practically holding you hostage and you couldn't even breathe, and I had to run over and save you."

"What?" is about all I can say to him. I wait till he opens the lobby door, and I walk on ahead.

Ms. Viola carries on and fusses when I get there. She's all "Blah-blah-blah. After seven in the evening." And I'm thinking, Yeah, yeah, whatever. And she's like, "Blah-blah-blah. Should have been home from study hall by five-thirty." And I'm thinking, Okay, okay, whatever, once again. And then it's "Blah-blah-blah. When your mother called to say she was going to be late, I told her you weren't even here yet." Oh boy. That's not so good.

Gerald is standing next to me with all his giant teeth exposed. And he's whispering, "Want me to tell her about the hostage situation?" And I'm trying to elbow him real hard so he'll shut up. Since Ms. Viola already spoke to Mama, the half-assed excuse I came up with on the train doesn't even matter. I just take my seat in the dining room and try to drown out the crying of the lone remaining baby. Actually, *creaking* is probably a better word for what he's doing, since he sounds like an old door in a haunted mansion. So between the creaking and the thought of the special brand of torment I will be receiving from Mama for my latest stunt, my head starts to pulsate. And when I can't take it anymore, I try thinking about Michael Jackson. I think about those pictures of California I've seen in *Ebony*—the ones with the never-ending mountains and the clear blue skies. And I think about how it will be once we're married. I won't ever have to worry about what time is showing on the clock. I won't ever have to worry about devil nuns or hurtful mothers. And I won't ever have to worry about babysitters, unless it's one I hire to take care of our ten pop-locking, hit-song-singing, shiny brown children.

Gosh, I just want everyone to go away: Ms. Viola, her horsey son, that little creak monster. If they knew what made me late, maybe they'd all shut up. But I'm not about to tell them. Let them continue to think I'm a sneaky, rotten delinquent.

An hour and a half of me fending off Gerald passes before the doorbell sounds. I'm pretty sure it's Mama, who's decided to make a special trip to collect me. Probably couldn't wait for me to get upstairs to knock me upside the head. I take a few breaths and prepare for my fate. I'm not about to tell her the real reason I was late, so I'm pretty sure I'm in for more than a few rounds of torture.

I hear Ms. Viola walk to the door, but when she opens it, it's not Mama's voice that greets her.

"Hey, how you doing? I'm picking Faye up for Jeanne," I hear Jerry say as I start walking.

"I'm not sure what's going on with her," Ms. Viola says. "You know, maybe you all can talk to her. If anything happens, I don't want Jeanne holding me responsible. Because these young teenagers these days, I just don't know."

I want to yell out that if something happened to me, Mama would probably get down on her knees and thank the good Lord in heaven.

As Jerry and I walk down the hall, I wait for him to say something. You know, like "Faye, your mother sets up these boundaries for a reason," or "Seven o'clock? What could you possibly have been doing out until then, when you were supposed to be in by five-thirty?" But he doesn't say any of that. He doesn't say anything at all until we reach the stairs that will take us the one flight up to our floor.

"Faye, sit here with me for a second," he says as he settles onto one of the steps.

"You're about to nag me about being late to the sitter, aren't you?" I ask with an "I don't care either way" attitude.

"Seeing that you're home and okay's all I really care about. Besides, it must be tough being a teenager and having to go to a babysitter. You're ten times better than me. I'd be late every night. Still, you should call, just so everybody doesn't worry. Anyway, in answer to your question, no, I'm not gonna be nagging you. What I did want to talk to you about, though, is that your mama had a little accident."

Now, I know I should be scared or concerned or something, but the only emotion I feel from Jerry's news is hope— hope that Mama might be laid up in the hospital and unable to manhandle me for being so late.

"She took a tumble while she was running up the stairs to transfer trains at Atlantic Avenue," he says. "Banged her knee pretty good. But don't you worry, Faye. She's all right. Just a few aches and pains and a little swelling. I went and picked her up and we popped into Kings County, where the doctors checked her out. She didn't want to, of course, but I insisted. Even after all her fussing, I'm sure she's happy I did. Anyway, that's why we're a little late getting you."

"Oh" is all I manage to say.

"And, uh, Faye. Couple more things. You sure you don't want to sit down next to me?"

"No, I'm fine, thank you. I'm okay where I am." Although, standing over him does force me to look down at the oil slick he calls a hairstyle.

"You know I care about your mom, right?"

"Uh-huh," I say.

"I know she's a little rough around the edges, but I really believe she's a good woman. And, well, I'm tired of being all by my lonesome. Tired of coming home to no one there. And after this incident tonight, I think she's seeing that it's better for a woman to have a man around. Especially a woman who has a kid to support." He stops for a moment.

"What are you trying to say, Jerry?" Now, I'm not trying to hurry things along so I can be confronted by Mama, but I'm all too aware that this little talk is turning into an episode of *As the World Turns*.

"What I'm trying to say, Faye, is . . . Well, I'm gonna be moving in with you and your mama."

"You're gonna be marrying her?" I ask.

"Well, for her, this'll be a pretty big move, so we'll go one step at a time. But between you and me, I'd love to marry her, so I'm looking at this as a stepping-stone. And she's told me she's finally signed those papers from your father, so I think it's only a matter of time."

"You're already certain you want to marry her when you all just met at Easter? It's only been like a month and a half."

"Guess this is one of those things you just can't put a time frame on."

I honestly don't get it. I'm sure that if Mama wasn't as pretty as she is, Jerry would never have stuck around as long as he has. Once again, pretty trumps mean.

"Look, Faye. I understand your concern. I know it's been just you two ladies for a while now. I want to make sure you don't feel like I'm taking over your territory."

Taking over my territory? I want to tell Jerry how fine I am with this turn of events. I want to tell him that never has a head full of drippy curls ever looked so good to me. With a third person in the apartment on a full-time basis, a lot of pressure will be taken off my shoulders. For a split second I consider hugging him, but, well, I suppose hugs just don't come that easily for me.

"Well, you're there a few nights a week now," I say. "Guess this just makes it more official. Maybe now Mama will be happy. Congratulations, Jerry."

"Thanks, kid. That means a lot to me." Then he reaches into the inside pocket of his jean jacket and hands me an envelope.

"What's this?" I ask.

"Don't know. But it came for you."

No one ever sends me letters. I look at the front of the envelope and see that there's no name where the return address is, only a street number in Fort Lauderdale, Florida, and a zip code.

"Where'd you get it from?"

"Your mama didn't want to have to climb the stairs to the

mailboxes, so she asked me to get the mail for her. I figure it's from your daddy. I know he's living down in Florida now. And since it's addressed to you, I also figured it's for your eyes only. Besides, I've seen how worked up your mama gets anytime his name is mentioned."

I get ready to rip the thing open, but Jerry stops me.

"She's gonna be wondering if I got lost coming to get ya. Why don't you read it when you're back in your room?"

I put the letter in my knapsack.

"I don't know what's in there," Jerry says. "But maybe it's best if you don't tell your mom about that letter. She's already blowing hot air about you coming up missing. This might be a double whammy for her tonight."

When we get up to the apartment, Jerry pushes the door open and yells to Mama. "Here she is, Jeanne. She's all good and in one piece. Anyway, I gotta shove off for a bit and finish up at the shop. I'll be back in a couple of hours." Then he turns to me, winks, and smiles. Only, I wish he wasn't leaving, because now I feel like I'm heading into a raging storm without any kind of protection.

As I take those thirteen steps down our apartment's narrow hallway, I just keep reminding myself to breathe. I know Mama's in an extra-special mood, especially since she had to waste time, and money, probably, at the hospital. When I get to the kitchen, I see her seated there with her left pant leg hiked up above her knee, which has an ice pack on it.

"Hello, Mama," I say quietly.

"Well, hello, Ms. Andrews. Mmm-hmm. I'm calling you

Ms. Andrews because obviously you think you're grown. You think we're on the same level. That you don't have to follow any rules, and that you can come and go whenever you please." She gets really quiet, which is never a good sign. And then she stands slowly and starts hobbling toward me.

33

I'm not so broken up about having to go straight to bed. Locked away in my room, I can be alone and at peace. I clutch Daddy's letter, waiting for Mama to go to bed before I turn on a flashlight and begin reading it. There's a police siren wailing somewhere out there in the night. First it sounds really faint and far away, but then it gets louder and louder, like the car's become airborne and will soon be driving through my window and crushing me in my bed. But just as the sound reaches a crescendo, it begins to trail off. The people who live in the upstairs apartment are moving some furniture around, and squeaky, scraping sounds filter down from the ceiling. Then it stops and all is quiet.

I stare at the clock as the numbers tick on by. I hear the buzz of Jerry's robust voice when he returns. Soon, the shuffling around and muffled conversations taking place outside my door are silenced. And I hear Mama's door slam shut.

I grab the flashlight from my nightstand and get ready

to open the letter. But then the phone rings. A few seconds later, I hear Mama's voice coming from the kitchen. She's obviously trying to be quiet as she speaks in whispers. She says something, then there's a long pause, then she says something again. I figure she decided not to take the call in the bedroom because she didn't want to wake Jerry, so I go back to my own thoughts. But then her voice suddenly begins to come in loud bursts. I get out of bed and walk over to my door, careful to open it slowly so it doesn't squeak and alert her to my presence. And that's where I stand listening.

"She's acting the fool," I hear her say. "Not coming home when she's supposed to, not having answers for where she's been." Long pause.

"What I'm saying is, your daughter needs a father figure around. . . ." Suddenly, I notice Jerry inching over to the doorway of the kitchen. Only, he doesn't go in. He just stands off to the side listening, like I'm doing from my own doorway.

"You didn't think of that when you decided to go chase your latest piece of tail, did you? Well, you need to start thinking of what your not being around is doing to her." There's a long pause. When Mama speaks again, she lowers her voice so much I have to wedge my ear right into the crack of my door to hear anything at all.

"Damn it, Charlie, it's time to stop playing around. I got me somebody in my life now . . . and pretty soon . . . Well, by the time you come to your senses, it might be too late. I'm not gonna be available forever. In fact, I might not be available for very much longer, so this could be your last chance to step up to the plate."

I see Jerry's face as he turns to go back into the bedroom. It's so sad and defeated. And his eyes are red-rimmed and shiny. I feel really bad for the guy. He's most definitely loud and annoying, but he's been good to Mama . . . and to me.

I close my door, get back into bed, and pick up Daddy's letter. It's thicker than an envelope usually is when it just has a sheet of paper in it. When I open it, the first thing I see is the Kodak stamp that's always on the back of photographs. There are three pictures in there. The first one is of Daddy standing on the beach. The next is of this tiny little otherworldly baby with a big old cranium and not a tooth in its head. It's really light, almost pee-yellow in color. And its weird little arms are all spastic-looking, even in the picture. And I notice that it's so fat it doesn't really have wrists—just hands that are jammed into arms. The last picture is of this short lady holding on to the alien baby and Daddy holding on to her. And then I open the letter up and start reading.

Dear Baby Girl,

    Now I have a little baby boy too. Just came into this world. Isn't he wonderful? Your little brother is named George, after your granddad. I know I didn't mention this part to you before, but I thought it would be too much to drop all at once—me moving away, getting married, and a baby too. But he reminds me a little of you when you were first born. Just the biggest smile and all the light of the world in those eyes. I wish you

*could be here to see him and hold him like I can. I
think you'd be in love. But I don't want you to worry. I
want you to know that you haven't been replaced in my
heart. I've had fourteen years to know you, while I'm
just discovering this funny-looking little fellow. I know I
haven't been the best dad, that I've been gone more than
I've been around, but it's mainly because I was always
trying to find a better life for myself so I could give you
a better life. Things haven't exactly gone as planned,
but I feel good about the future. I'm still working on
getting you down here for the summer. If all goes well,
before you know it you'll be meeting your baby brother
and hanging out with your old man again.*

Love, Daddy

I have to lean on my forearms and lie on my stomach, on
account of my back being so sore. I refold the letter, put it
back into the envelope along with the pictures, and tuck it
under the pillow next to me.

Daddy is really starting a new life. Now that there's a
baby, there's no turning back. I'm not sure how to feel about
this little brother. I mean, I never wanted to be an only
child, but when I thought about having a sibling before, I
figured he or she would be living in the same house as me.
And I wanted to have one when I was still little so we could
grow up together and be close. I wanted to have somebody
to giggle and roll my eyes with whenever Mama went on
one of her crazy binges. But this is a baby. And I've made it
quite clear how I feel about babies. The only solution would

be if we could maybe stick that kid into a time machine or body-altering contraption and just push a switch and—*poof!*—have him instantly grow up. Besides, this kid'll be living in Florida and I'll be in New York.

And then something occurs to me. The last time Daddy was away and sent me a letter, I came to find the envelope all torn open and jagged. Mama didn't even try to play it off by taping it up or pasting it back together.

"It's my letter," I said to her. "It's addressed to me."

"Yeah, but this is my house. The lease is in my name, so the way I see it, whatever goes on under this roof is in my jurisdiction, and I can do whatever I want with it."

"Well, what about my privacy?"

"Go get a job and get your own place. That's what about your privacy."

I'm figuring Mama doesn't know a thing about this baby, and I don't want to be the one she finds out from, so I remove the letter and pictures from under the pillow and stuff them into my geography textbook. This letter is going to be living in my locker for the two and a half weeks left until the end of school. After that, I'll have to figure out somewhere else to hide it. The way I see it, Jerry is right. If Daddy wants Mama to know about this baby, it's up to him. I'm not going to be the one to light a match to this powder keg.

34

After all I've been through, there's no way I'm about to go the whole day without finding out if Ms. Downer's daughter has gotten in touch with her. So first thing in the morning, I'm standing in front of the old lady's apartment ringing her bell. I'm so excited I can hardly stand still. I can see her opening her door, eyes filled with tears. I can almost feel her grabbing on to me and hugging me and thanking me for changing her life. And as I hear her footsteps shuffling against the wood floor, followed by the click of the locks, I can't stop the smile from spreading across my face. I take a deep breath and brace myself.

She opens the door and I stare at her expectantly. And I stare at her some more. But I can't really tell by the look on her face whether something life-changing has happened over the last fourteen hours of her life.

"Back to truancy?" she finally says.

"What?"

"Shouldn't you be on your way to school?"

"Oh, that. There's some teachers' conference or something this morning, so we don't have to be there until later."

Thieving isn't coming as easily for me these days, but the lying might have actually improved. I'm not so sure whether that's good or bad.

"Why don't you come in, then," she says, heading back down the hallway.

"Okay . . ." Well, she was an actress, I'm thinking. She's probably just a wiz at controlling her emotions.

Twenty minutes into my visit, I'm sipping tea with her and eating shortbread cookies. I'm about to have another tardy on my report card for nothing.

"So, how was your evening?" I ask.

"Fine," she says as she squeezes lemon into her tea.

"What did you do?"

"Same as usual."

"Which is?"

"Which is read, listen to some music, make a little food. Why are you so curious?"

"Oh, I don't know." I shrug. "You didn't get any phone calls or visitors or anything?"

She doesn't answer. She just keeps staring at me.

"Maybe it's just too early," I mumble.

"Faye, what are you up to?"

"Nothing. Guess I'll just see you after school," I say as I stuff what's left of my cookie into my mouth and get up from the table.

What a letdown. I don't even wait for her to respond before I make my exit.

But after school, the results are not much different. No phone calls, no visitors. And what's worse, she doesn't want to stay inside. Now that the weather has gotten so nice, she feels the need to get as much fresh air as possible. Thing is, I'm afraid if we leave the apartment, Delaine Lawson might stop by or call. And if they miss each other, maybe the daughter will get cold feet and never show up again. But there's no talking her out of it. So outside of tying her to the radiator, I have no choice.

We walk across the street to the park and down near the edge of the lake. The good thing is, I can see her building from where we sit on a bench just past the walking and jogging path. I look into the sky as the sun plays hide-and-seek with some puffy white clouds. The moment it peeks out, Ms. Downer closes her eyes and angles her head a little upward.

"So how long do you plan on staying out here?" I ask.

"Are you on some kind of schedule?"

Actually, I am. I have to get back to Ms. Viola's by five-thirty. Even a minute later, and she's supposed to get the hotline going to Mama.

"I was just looking forward to sitting around your cozy apartment having tea and cookies," I say instead.

"You're the most peculiar child," Ms. Downer says without shifting her head away from the sun.

"Well, you're probably out here all the time, being that you live so close."

"Not as much as you might think. When it's too cold, my bones start to ache, so I just stay inside. And when the heat really comes on in July, I get a little overwhelmed.

Then there are other times when I simply don't have the incentive."

"You know, you can hire people. Like a maid or a companion or someone like that."

"Hiring people costs money."

"So what? You're rich."

"I'm not rich. I'm good at maintaining."

"What does that even mean?"

"It means that the apartment I live in and what I have in it is about all I possess in this world, but I make it work for me."

"But you were a movie star. And weren't you the one who told me about all those people you had doing stuff for you . . . dressing you, doing your hair, and fetching your food?"

"That was fifty years ago."

"What about that book that archivist is writing? Didn't they break you off more than a few Ben Franklins for that?"

But the old lady just shakes her head. "It's a biography. He was going to write it with or without my help. When most people thought I was long dead, somehow he found me, so I figured, might as well make sure his facts are also my facts so that if certain people read it, they'll have my truth. I've not asked to be compensated in any way. . . ." Her voice trails off a little.

"By 'certain people,' do you mean your daughter?"

She nods and lets out a quiet sigh. And I'm realizing just how important it is that I get the old lady and her daughter together now, since it will be too late by the time the book comes out.

"Have you thought recently of trying to see her again?"
I ask.

"Think about it all the time."

"And?"

"You sure have a lot of questions today."

"I guess. So . . . why not try one more time?"

"Because the last time there was any contact, she made it very clear to me that she'd rather I didn't. That she had completely cut me out of her life and her thoughts."

"And when was this?"

"Before you were born."

"Maybe how she feels about you has changed."

"I doubt it."

"Then she's a pretty heartless person, if you ask me."

"No. No," Ms. Downer says quietly. "I was the one without a heart."

"Because you gave her up? Sometimes it's better to let something go if you can't take care of it properly. You could have been like my mother. She doesn't love me. She doesn't even really want me."

Ms. Downer turns her head slowly and looks at me for a while.

"How do you know that?" she asks.

"This last Christmas, I heard her talking to my uncle Paul. She said that without me, she would have had a better life. And if you could see the way she looks at me sometimes . . ."

"What people say isn't always how things really are. Maybe your mother sees your father in you. Maybe that hurts too much. Your mother's behavior probably has nothing to do with you. Faye, when people have personal demons, they take it out on the ones closest to them. Believe me, I know all too much about this. Unfortunately, you can't fix other people's problems. That's up to them. You can just keep being you."

"But most of the time I wish I wasn't me. You know, I thought that when she got her new boyfriend she wouldn't be as mean to me. But she still is. Or she completely ignores me. I just wish I had another mother. Somebody who'd make me toast. Somebody I could go to the park with."

The old lady's really quiet for a while. I turn my head a little to peek up at her face. She's looking out at the ripples in the lake.

"I'm a lot more than what you see before you," she says. "I'm old. That's true. But I've had quite an eventful life. I've had my moments where I wasn't the easiest to get along with either. If you had met me all those years ago instead of now, you would understand."

She sighs a little and continues looking out at the lake. I can tell her mind is a thousand miles away. I kind of want to hug her, but I don't know how, so I just start looking out at the lake too, at the ducks that continue to float back and forth.

"Either way, I'm really glad I met you," I say quietly.

"Me too." But then she quickly adds, "Maybe not quite under the particular circumstances . . ."

I laugh a little.

"I guess things happen for a reason," she continues.

"Although, I was recently thinking about your two partners in crime."

"I don't see them so much anymore. I guess I'm figuring out they're not my real friends. You know, they never even checked to see if I was okay after everything that happened in that store and with the security guard. They were those two *possibles* I told you about before. But now, they're not even that."

We sit there quietly for a while.

"I don't want you to steal anymore," she says. "If you really need something and you can't ask your mother, you can ask me. Okay?"

"Yes, ma'am," I say. I want to tell her that it wasn't all about needing things. It was also about having control over something. About showing those who think they're better that you have some power too, that you're good at something too. But I don't know how I could ever explain this to her, so I just let it go.

"Do those girls know you come over here?"

"Oh no. They would never understand that."

"I'm not so sure *I* understand. You're young, and there's so much out there you could be doing with kids your own age. Why do you choose to waste your time with me?"

"Guess I feel better about things when I'm around you."

"You mean you don't feel as guilty about what you did to me?"

"Maybe at first. But the real, honest to goodness truth is, now I come because I like it. When I'm with you, it's easy. I can just be myself. You know the bad stuff I've done, so I don't have to pretend that doesn't exist. But also, when I'm with you, I don't *want* to do the bad stuff. It's like I have something good to look forward to. You know, sometimes when I'd go to sleep, I would really pray the Lord my soul to keep. I would pray that I just wouldn't wake up the next morning. Things would be simpler that way, and Mama would be happier."

The old lady clamps her bony fingers down onto my hand and squeezes really tight.

"You have no idea how good a person you really are and how you're able to affect other people. If you weren't here, this world would be different somehow. Don't ever underestimate your value. And don't ever let me hear anything like that come out of your mouth again. Do you understand me?"

"Yes, ma'am."

She finally lets go of my hand, but she doesn't turn away.

"Now, I also remember you mentioning one definite friend. Why don't you tell me about her?"

"Keisha? She's great. She's smart and she's nice."

"So why don't you spend more time with her?"

"She doesn't know about you, or a lot of the stuff I've done. Sometimes I feel she's too good for me."

"A woman will always have her secrets. Not everyone needs to know all you've done. But you should never feel someone is better than you, because if you do, they'll sense it and feel that way too, or worse, feel sorry for you. Faye, the fact that we have any sort of relationship is testament to how amazing you are. But I do think I've been selfish. I've come to rely on you to not feel as lonely. But it's unfair to you. You've got, what, a little over two weeks left in the school year?"

"Yeah."

"That will go by in the blink of an eye. Then you'll have summer break, when you should be going to movies and to Coney Island with friends. You shouldn't be cooped up with an old woman all the time. You've got to spend some time with kids your own age. Besides, I won't be here forever, and then what?"

"What are you trying to say? That you don't want me coming around anymore?"

"That's not what I mean. I'm just saying you should also spend time with friends you have more in common with."

"I kinda feel like I have more in common with you than with anyone else," I say quietly. I reach my arm around her waist and allow my head to fall against her shoulder. She feels so slight and so frail, but she feels like love.

35

"He's the cutest thing I've ever seen," Keisha coos in this high-pitched voice.

"Keisha, these pictures have been hanging here a week now, and every time I open my locker, you act like it's the first time you're seeing them."

"I know. I'm just so excited for you. Even though my brother's a freak of nature, it's good having him around sometimes. And it's gonna be even better having a baby brother, because you won't have to put up with any lip from him." After a long giggle, Keisha lets out a sigh. "But it's funny how I'm more excited about it than you are."

"What's there to be so excited about? I've never even met him," I say as I study the picture that has only my little brother in it. It's taped to the inside of the door to my locker, next to the other two pictures Daddy sent. Finally, some of the empty space is filled. I always felt like such a loser since the only picture I ever had in there was one Keisha and I took at a portable photo booth in downtown

Brooklyn. You walk by other kids' lockers, and it's like collage central.

"You know, that's your problem, Faye. You just don't enjoy the great moments in life," Keisha says.

"Maybe if I had any, I would."

"Well, you will today. We'll go look in a couple stores. It'll be cool," she says as I close my locker.

"What about Nicole?"

"She can come next time."

I think about this for a little while.

"No, Nicole's cool," I say. "I've just been all screwed up. I wouldn't mind if she came along."

"Really?" Keisha says. "I'm glad you feel that way. And I'm happy we're hanging out again. How about this? Nicole can come next time. Today, it'll just be us."

I give Keisha a smile as we head out of the school.

"You think your mom will be able to make it to the ceremony?" Keisha asks once we're walking down Eastern Parkway.

"She probably won't be able to get off work."

"So who's gonna come see you?"

I shrug. "I don't know. I've told my aunt Nola and my uncle Paul. Maybe my mom's boyfriend. Maybe a friend of mine from the neighborhood. Who knows?"

"Well, I'm sure you'll find somebody. Seven more days and then we're no longer freshmen. And after the weekend, only five. No one will be able to call us newbies anymore! It's crazy even thinking about it."

I think about the other countdown I have going on. Or

maybe in this case, I should say count-*up*. It's been more than a week since my trip to see Delaine Lawson. Eight days, and nothing. Now, I'm not head-in-the-clouds hopeful and stupid about stuff, but I really thought she would have called by now, or popped in to see the old lady. After all, it *is* her mother. Then again, sometimes I wish for a train to jump the tracks and take out *my* mother, so I guess I can understand how she can be mad. I can understand that after forty or fifty years of not talking to somebody, you might not be able to think of a thing to say, even if you got the chance.

Then again, maybe she lost the old lady's contact information. Maybe when she took off her uniform pants, she forgot she had put the piece of paper in the pocket, and she threw them into the washer by mistake. Only, by the time she figured this out, it was too late and the water and All-Temperature Cheer had faded the ink on the paper and made it impossible to read. Or maybe she accidentally spilled some medicine on the paper. Maybe she wants to go, but after all the time that has passed, she can't seem to will herself to take that first step. I'm going to have to figure something else out.

"You're quiet," Keisha says as she fishes a couple of those individual packets of saltines out of her pocket. I think she swiped them from the cafeteria. She rips open the plastic, crumples up the crackers, and scatters them along the sidewalk for the nasty little gray and white rat-birds gathered there. I watch as they run, hop, and fly over to peck at the food.

"No, I'm fine. But why do you feed the pigeons? They're pretty disgusting."

"No they're not," she says. "They're the city's special pets. They can adapt to anything, and they're tough and can survive the streets of Brooklyn . . . kinda like you."

I elbow her and she elbows me back.

Some of the stores in this part of Brooklyn—Park Slope— are kind of chichi-froufrou. Clothes aren't so overstuffed on racks that you risk breaking a finger trying to sift through them. There aren't boxes stacked up right there in the showroom. These boutiques have a lot of light and space, and they feel clean and smell sweet. They're quite different from the stores farther down on Flatbush—the stores near where I live.

Keisha points to a candy-cane-striped poodle-style skirt, and I just giggle.

"I would never wear that," I say.

"That's exactly why you should try it on. I'm gonna go for this polka-dotted jumpsuit. We'll see which outfit looks worse."

It's definitely a draw. As we step out of the fitting room, I realize that not only do we look equally bad in our outfits, we look as if we belong on a Disneyland float. Once we finally stop laughing, I grab the price tag.

"Oh my God. This thing is a hundred bucks," I say.

Keisha tugs at the price tag on her jumpsuit. "I got you beat. One-twenty."

"Are they serious?" Once Keisha nods her head, I continue. "I only have thirty bucks. I could never afford the stuff in here. I mean, I wouldn't want to afford this particular skirt thing, but even if I did . . ."

"So what? We're not about to buy any of this."

"We're not?"

"No."

"Then why are we here?"

"Just to look around, get ideas, have fun."

"Don't you and Nicole shop in these places all the time?"

"No."

"You go to Macy's on Thirty-Fourth Street. That's not cheap."

"No. But they have sales sometimes. And it's not like we come out with bags full of stuff. Lots of times, we hit up the thrift stores. Ten bucks for some Sergio Valente jeans. Three bucks for a blouse."

"Really? We don't have thrift stores around my way."

"Well, let's go to one now. See what we might find."

"All this time when you and Nicole would be talking about Macy's and Bloomingdale's, I thought that was where you guys bought all your clothes. And I knew I couldn't afford that, so . . . "

"So you'd act like you couldn't come or you couldn't hang out that day?"

"Yeah."

"Faye, you don't have to be embarrassed with me. And so what if window-shopping is all you can afford to do? That's half the fun. Then you can take those ideas and try to find similar clothes at a place where the prices are more your speed. And don't worry about it if we don't find anything at that thrift store. We'll just try another. I'm not giving up until we get you an outfit."

"I like the sound of that," I say.

Keisha smiles. "Good. Now let's get out of these ugly outfits. And quick, before we run into someone we know."

36

The last day of school finally rolls around. The seniors will be graduating tomorrow at the Brooklyn Academy of Music, but today it's the underclassmen's turn to shine. The freshman ceremony will take place first in the school assembly hall, followed by the sophomore ceremony and then the one for the juniors.

We spend the first couple of hours in our usual Friday classes, but everyone already has summer fever, so no one's paying much attention to anything our teachers are saying. There's just this nervous/excited buzz about the two months we're about to have off. I can't say I'm looking forward to this as much as everyone else. For one, I'm still not sure whether Mama will allow me to go visit Daddy down in Florida. I'm thinking no is the likelier answer. And if I remain in Brooklyn, chances are I'll be at the sitter's every day reliving the days of slavery, when black people worked but didn't get a cent of pay. Since there will be no school, I won't be able to use the whole "math tutoring" ruse. Maybe

I'll come up with a summer-school scenario, although once Mama sees that despite all the so-called tutoring, my math grades never really did improve, it might be a harder sell.

By a quarter past ten, all of us freshmen begin filing into the auditorium. We're to be seated according to homeroom classes, and even though I'm in a different homeroom from Keisha and Nicole, I manage to finagle a seat next to them. That way we'll have each other to joke around with through all the boring speeches and the handing out of certificates.

The students are in the center section, while the two outside sections contain families and friends. I look around at all the unfamiliar faces. Uncle Paul couldn't get off from work and neither could Mama. But I spot Aunt Nola almost immediately. Impossible not to, with the oversized emerald-green hat she's sporting. My eyes drift down to the matching dress, and I'm thinking she's confused my freshman year-end ceremony with the St. Patty's Day parade. When she notices me, she throws her white handkerchief into the air and begins waving it furiously.

A few of the last kids to file in decide to spice up their walk by humming Herbie Hancock's "Rockit" and adding some dance moves to it. I look up at the stage, with the giant glittered-out banner that reads CONGRATULATIONS FRESHMAN CLASS OF 1984. My eyes drift down from there to the two rows of chairs arranged on either side of the lectern near the center of the stage. I can see Sister Margaret Theresa Patricia Bernadette seated there. She doesn't look too happy about the *Soul Train* line that has developed. Father Benjamin, the head of the school, probably doesn't even notice, since he appears to be midnap. But a couple of the teachers are actually smiling.

I turn my attention back to the crowd and continue scanning the rows when I notice this tiny figure tucked into the back corner seat on the opposite side of the auditorium from Aunt Nola. And even though I can only see the very top of her outfit—a white frilly neckline peeping out over a maroon sweater—I can tell that Ms. Downer has dressed up for the occasion. And she's wearing one of her hats, a little black pillbox. I wave, and she smiles.

Once everyone is seated, Father Benjamin gets up and starts talking about living righteously according to the teachings of the Bible and the Lord. Then comes a long, drawn-out speech about practicing the virtues of chastity, temperance, charity, diligence, patience, kindness, and humility during our time off and throughout our lives. Only, he keeps drifting away from the microphone, and I can only make out every other sentence. At one point, he just stops talking for like a minute, but it's obvious he's not done with his speech. The teachers all whisper to one another, and Keisha and I start laughing. I'm pretty sure he's fallen into one of those sudden old-people naps. You know how they'll be sitting at the dinner table talking to you, asking about school and your exams, then all of a sudden, they're out like a light, and you're not sure whether they're asleep or dead. So there's Father Benjamin, not speaking, not moving, just leaning up against the lectern. And then, just as suddenly as he stopped speaking, he starts up again, as if he's been given a jolt. And the mike makes this loud whistling sound, which is followed by boos, claps, and catcalls from the middle section of the auditorium.

A couple of teachers speak, including Devil Nun. Only, all I hear from her is "wah, wah, wah," like the adults in the *Peanuts* cartoons.

Since they go alphabetically, my name is one of the first to be called for the freshman year completion certificate. And I'm shocked because someone is hooting and hollering and whoo-hooing all over the place for me.

Once I'm on the stage, Father Benjamin hands me a piece of paper that has my name written on it in calligraphy, then shakes my hand. And I can't help but think how funny it is that they're making such a big deal out of this.

"That's right, Faye. You a sophomore now, baby. You a sophomore." Jerry's voice rings out above the polite applause as I make it down off the stage. He's standing at the back of the auditorium cheering like the Yankees just won the World Series.

I thought I'd be a little embarrassed if he showed up, on account of his hair. But it's nice having a cheering section. It's nice having my three guest spots filled, especially since I didn't think there would be anyone there to support me at all.

I wave my certificate at Jerry, who yells the entire time I'm on my feet and doesn't stop until I'm back next to Keisha. He's really an okay guy. I just hope Mama doesn't screw things up with him.

"Let me see it," Keisha says excitedly before I can even get my butt back into my seat.

"It's just a stupid piece of paper," I say.

"Yeah, but it's the last thing we'll ever get as freshmen in high school."

"And after this, we only have one more year where the pressure is off," Nicole adds. "Once we're juniors, we'll have to start thinking about colleges and maybe even about moving away from home."

"Moving away from home," I echo. What wonderful words.

After the ceremony, everyone pours out into the atrium. There are hugs and more congratulations before Aunt Nola leaves with Jerry, who has agreed to drop her off at home on his way back to work.

I walk around looking for Ms. Downer, but she seems to have disappeared into the sea of people. Charlene manages to stand out, though. And as usual, Curvy Miller is circling around her, even though he's a sophomore and should be with his own class, getting ready for their ceremony. I just shake my head. Guess Ms. Downer was right and I did get a little caught up in the whole looks thing myself. Why else would I have liked a guy who never really showed me an ounce of interest?

Once I rejoin Keisha and Nicole, they let me in on their plan to go to a nearby Italian restaurant for lunch with some of the other kids. But when Keisha stops talking mid-sentence and gestures over my shoulder, I turn to find Ms. Downer standing there.

"I'm so happy you came," I say as I give her a hug. "I want you to meet my friends Keisha and Nicole. And Keisha and Nicole, I want you to meet my friend Ms. Downer."

"It's good to meet you girls. Keisha, I've heard a lot about you," Ms. Downer says. "Faye, can I borrow you for one moment? I won't keep you away from your friends for very long."

"It's okay, Faye," Keisha says. "I need to go talk to my folks. We'll just meet back near the door."

I walk with the old lady back into the auditorium, which is a lot calmer and less congested than where we had been standing.

"You sure look fancy today," I say.

"Well, I suppose a good occasion calls for good clothes." She goes into her handbag and pulls out an envelope, which she hands to me. I open it to find one of those "You're a Graduate Now" cards inside.

"Well, I didn't actually graduate yet. . . ."

"I know, but try finding a freshman year-end ceremony card . . . not so easy."

I laugh as I flip the card open. Inside are all these crisp, clean bills. I count them—with my eyes, not my fingers, because I don't want her to know I'm doing it. That seems a bit rude and tasteless. And there's like four hundred dollars. But the weird thing is, I'm nowhere near as happy about this as I should be.

"In the short time I've known you, you've come such a long way," she says. "And I know there are probably a few things you'll be needing when it comes time to start school again. Maybe school supplies. New clothes, shoes . . ."

But I don't really say anything. I just stand there looking at all that money, feeling guilty about accepting it.

"Is it not enough?" she asks.

"It's the most money I've ever had," I say.

"I would have gotten you an actual present, but I don't know what you like, and I figured you might enjoy it a little more if you were able to shop for it yourself."

"But I can't keep it," I say. And I pull 280 dollars out of the total amount and hand it back to her. "Well, not all of it."

"What's this?" she asks.

"It's what I owe you. I've owed it to you for a long time now. Just wouldn't feel right having it. I really do like your present. And I still have a hundred and twenty of it, and that's more than enough for me to get some cool stuff with."

Ms. Downer looks at the money for a while, then smiles, nods slowly, and tucks the cash away in her purse.

The Saturday after the last day of school is all rainy and grim. It's Jerry's birthday, and he's having his assistant manager open up the store for him since Mama has decided to make him breakfast to celebrate. I'm thinking this is a really good sign for Jerry, because she never makes breakfast. It's always every man for himself, with toast or cereal or a random piece of fruit.

When Mama realizes she's out of eggs, she dispatches me to go and pick some up from Waldbaum's. I don't really want to, since the thunder is rumbling something awful outside. And I'm pretty comfortable watching the Saturday-morning cartoons. But it's not like I can say no without risking death, so I grab an umbrella and head out.

There's hardly a soul in the supermarket, probably on account of the weather. Then again, I'm not usually trolling through the aisles at eight-thirty on a Saturday morning. But just as I grab a crate of extra-large eggs, I see Caroline racing a grocery cart toward the refrigerated section.

Gillian is right behind her. They haven't seen me, and my first impulse is to make a beeline for the cashier, pay for the eggs, and hurry on out. But that impulse is pretty quickly trumped by anger.

You would think that in the five or so weeks that have passed since the whole Dressy Dress Mart incident, they would have popped up at some point to make sure I was okay. Maybe left a note under my door. But there hasn't been any sign of them at all. They haven't been ringing my doorbell or waiting outside my building for me. They haven't even been hanging out in front of their own building. It's almost like they've been lying low. I guess recently I haven't exactly been running around trying to make time with them either, but considering the seriousness of what happened, you would think they would have been curious enough to check on me. They must have noticed I didn't come sprinting through the doors of that store. For all they know, I could have been caught and thrown into juvie hall, or worse yet, killed. Shot point-blank by a trigger-happy NYPD cop.

I'm not so mad at Gillian, since she's more or less mentally impaired and doesn't know any better. She might even have told Caroline they should check on me. But if Caroline said no, that would have been the end of that. It's not like Gillian would ever do anything on her own.

Caroline almost bites it as she tries to pop a wheelie. I move right into her path, planting myself in front of the dairy items. I watch as she and Gillian horse around and giggle. I watch as they get closer and closer to me. I watch as Gillian finally notices me, and the smile leaves her face.

"Ooh, she's not dead," Gillian almost yells out in shock.

Caroline brings the cart to a sudden stop and just stares at me. "Ooh, girl, there you are. Where you been?" she asks. But there's more surprise than excitement or relief in her voice.

"Haven't heard from you all," I say.

"That's 'cause we thought you was dead," Gillian says.

"Shut up," Caroline barks at her before turning to me. "How'd you get out of there?"

"I walked."

"Well, we waited for you. I swear on my grandmother. But so much was happening. . . . Then the cops came, and the ambulance, so we just figured we better get out of there. We thought that wobbly old security guard had shot you or something."

"Shot me with what? His bad leg? No. But he had a heart attack. Right there on top of me. I couldn't move. I was just stuck there, and you guys didn't even come back to see if I needed help. And you were the ones who really wanted to steal those clothes."

"So? Nobody forced you to put that stuff in your bag. And we had nothing to do with old peg leg's heart stopping, so why are you acting all mad as a hatter like we owe you something? We don't owe you diddly-squat. If anything, you owe us. You owe me. You didn't have an ounce of courage when you first moved around here. And you might think you're big and bold now, but you're not shit. I'm the one who's always carrying you. Without me, you can't do shit. You look like shit and you ain't worth shit. And that's why your mama treats you like shit."

Heat spreads over my face, and I feel as if I'm about to step out of my own body. From the corner of my eye, I make out the quart-sized glass bottles sitting there on the milk shelf. And I know that if I just latch on to one, I could wield it with all my might and bring it down against Caroline's bloated head. And maybe that would put her out of her misery and put me out of mine at the same time. I'm trying to breathe. I'm trying to tell myself she's not worth it. But I feel myself shaking. I close my eyes and try to think of what I'm about to do. I think of that gimpy-legged security guard and the old lady. I think about that word *karma* and about making better choices.

When I open my eyes, I feel this calm come over me. Caroline and Gillian both look as if they're bracing themselves for whatever storm is about to come, but I just shake my head, force a smile, and say, "You know what I've realized? Hardly anything good has happened to me since I met you guys. So don't worry about having to 'carry' me anymore, Caroline, because I wouldn't want to hold you back any. So this is me releasing you. Good-bye forever. And that goes for you too, Gillian."

"Forever?" Caroline yells as I start walking away. "Yeah, we'll see how long that lasts. 'Cause we're the only friends you got. We're the only ones willing to deal with your stupid ass. Summer's here. What you gonna do with all your free time? Have some nice mommy-daughter get-togethers? We know that'll never happen. Or maybe sit around talking to yourself, wishing you had a friend. Forever? Yeah, right. We'll see you when you come crawling back, ringing our bell, begging for someone to hang out with."

I don't let her words affect me. She'll see just how long forever is to me. Once I pay for the eggs and walk out into the warm rain, I find myself shaking again. But it's not from anxiety or fear. It's on account of this excitement that's come over me for standing up for myself. I can't believe how good I feel.

* * *

There's a little bounce in my step as I get off the elevator and walk down the hall. But when Jerry opens the door to our apartment, it all changes. It's as if he has been waiting there for me to get back. I swear, I don't even have the chance to pull my finger away from the buzzer before there's the click of the lock being undone. And I hear Mama ranting and raving in the background.

"I've not even been gone a half hour," I say. "What could possibly have happened in that short amount of time?"

"Maybe you should go back out," Jerry says to me.

"It's raining. Hard. Besides, I don't have anywhere to go."

"Is that her?" I hear Mama yell out. And Jerry's shoulders fall a bit.

"Yes, Jeanne," he says as he ushers me in. See, the thing is, Mama has had her moody spells since Jerry's moved in, but she hasn't had one of her "lock her away in Bellevue" shrieking spells till now.

"What happened?" I ask again as I follow Jerry down the hallway.

"She found the pictures."

"What pictures?"

"The ones your father sent. And the letter too."

I just shake my head. When I packed up my locker, I stuffed the pictures into the inside pocket of my loose-leaf notebook. The notebook is still in my knapsack, which I shoved under my bed.

"What was she doing in my bag?"

"Awww, man, little Faye, it was all my fault. I decided to go over some figures as I was having my coffee. I'd been adding things up in my head, you know. And your mother says why don't I just use a calculator. But I don't have one. Well, I do at the shop, but . . . And she says you use one for school, so she goes to your room. But a good amount of time passes, so I tell her it's no problem if she can't find it. That's when she comes out holding the envelope with the pictures and the letter, looking like she's just seen a ghost."

We get to the end of the hall, and Mama rushes up to me, stopping only about an inch from my face. And her eyes are huge, and there's this superhuman vein throbbing away in the center of her forehead.

"How long have you had these?" she asks. Only, she's not yelling anymore. Her voice has become calm and measured, which makes me more uneasy than when she's ranting and raving.

"N-n-not so long," I stutter.

"Then why is this envelope postmarked two and a half weeks ago? Unless they had a hurricane down in Florida, one I didn't hear about . . . and unless that hurricane picked this letter up and out of the mailbox and blew it all around the state, there's no way it took that long to get here. Why didn't you tell me about this, Faye?"

"I don't know. I guess I just figured it wasn't my place. That Daddy would have told you."

"Well, he didn't. He didn't." And she's shaking a little. And part of her hair falls out of the loose bun she had it up in and settles on her shoulder. And her eyes are glowing red. She looks like how I picture that crazy lady in *Jane Eyre,* the one who was locked away in Mr. Rochester's attic.

"Jeanne, why you getting mad at Faye? She didn't do nothing. It's not that big a deal," Jerry pleads with her. But it makes no difference.

"Not that big a deal? Not that big a deal? How would you feel if the person you've been married to for fourteen years just up and has some babies with someone else and you're the last one to know?"

"I wouldn't care. If I wasn't married to that person anymore."

"Well, technically, that's not the case."

"What you talking 'bout, Jeanne?"

"I didn't sign those papers yet, so technically, we are still married. We're still married!"

"Wait, but I thought you said you signed them. And what should it matter if he's marrying someone else? Truth is, I want to marry you, Jeanne. I want to make you my wife. So there. He's not the only one marrying someone else now." But Mama doesn't answer. She just keeps looking at those pictures.

"So what you think of that, huh, Jeanne? About becoming my wife? Mrs. Jerry Adams?"

But Mama doesn't even seem to hear him. She's just pacing and poking at that giant vein in her forehead with her left pointer finger.

"So he's off having bastard babies. It's not just some fling. It's not just some fling."

"It doesn't matter, Jeanne. You're with me now. And I love you. This is your time to move on. This is our time to move on . . . together."

"It's not fair. I gave him all I had. I gave him his daughter. Shouldn't that be enough? But he just . . . he just makes someone else more important. He has a child with someone else."

And I look over at Jerry. He's standing in his undershirt, which is tucked into his high-waisted, stonewashed jeans. And he has these little man-breasts that are pushing up against the fabric. But that doesn't even gross me out as much as it probably should. His face is like I've never seen it before. He looks as defeated as any of those wrestlers who've ever had to step into the ring against Superfly Snuka. And as Mama continues to pace and ignore him, Jerry grabs his pullover from the back of one of the kitchen chairs, pats my left shoulder, and starts to leave. And it reminds me of how Daddy looked that night I last saw him.

"I'll see you later, right, Jerry?" I say.

"Yeah, Faye," he says. But his words are not so convincing.

38

Thank God for the rain, because without it, our apartment would be shrouded in silence. I want to turn on the radio, but with the mood Mama is in, I decide it's best to have things remain as quiet as possible. She shut herself away in her room right after Jerry left, and I haven't seen her in the two hours since. It might be a little late for it, but I decide to make breakfast anyway. I scramble up some eggs and warm some of the precooked sausage patties in the oven. After the bread pops out of the toaster all warm and brown, I arrange everything on a plate and walk over to Mama's door. I put my ear against it, but the only thing I hear is the rumbling sky. Finally, I knock.

"Mama," I say. Only, she doesn't answer. "Mama, I made some breakfast. I'll bring it to you if you want." But she still doesn't answer. I try the door and it opens, with a rush of smoke coming at me. I try to stifle my coughs.

"Thought you might be hungry, so I brought you some food," I say. But I don't advance any closer at first, in case she's about to have one of her throwing fits and is deliberating whether to launch an ashtray or a phone at me.

She's lying on her bed in her black slip, propped up against two pillows. There's a cigarette in her mouth. And since there's more of her mascara staining her cheeks than coating her eyelashes, she kind of resembles a giant raccoon. But despite all this, she still somehow manages to look beautiful.

"I brought you some food," I say again as I finally start moving forward. I do it at a very deliberate pace. I'm pretty sure I look like one of those animal-control specialists dispatched to capture an escaped beast. You know how they always approach so gingerly, as if they're preparing to be attacked.

I reach her nightstand without incident and put the plate down. Then I shoot a quick glance at her. Something about the way she looks is making me uneasy. Well, that's not really a news flash. But today is different because she has a look to her I've never seen before. Defeat.

"Mama, are you all right?" I ask.

She shakes her head slowly.

"Why does Dad's new baby make you so upset?" As soon as the words come out of my mouth, I regret it. I'm sure they're exactly what she needs to hear to snap her out of her funk and make her go off the deep end on me. I don't usually bother her when she's in one of her moods, but here I am in her territory, butting into her business. Her eyes shift a little and she finally looks at me. But she doesn't really seem angry. And she actually responds.

"I don't know why," she says softly. "Listen, Faye, I think maybe you should pack your suitcase with some stuff. And you should call your aunt Nola and tell her and Paul that I need for you to stay there a little while."

Usually, I'd be doing backflips after hearing this. And it's not like I don't want to go, but I know in my gut that something's really wrong here. Guess I got so used to Mama always being irate, I don't know how to react when she's anything but. Weird, huh?

"Well, how long should I pack for?"

"A week, maybe two. Maybe longer. Once you're all done, you go on over there. This afternoon. You understand?"

"No. Not really. I mean, are you going somewhere? You and Jerry, maybe?"

"I just need a little time. That's all. I'm just so tired, and I need a little time."

"Time away from me?"

When she doesn't say anything else, I walk out of her room, closing the door behind me.

I eat by myself and look off at the rain as it smacks against the kitchen window. I especially focus on the little drops that cling to the bars of the fire escape.

Once I'm done, I pull my travel case out of the hall closet and start packing some clothes. Then I dial Aunt Nola, who is confused as to why I'm the one calling to ask about staying with her, and not Mama. But she reassures me that I'm always welcome there.

I don't leave that afternoon. I just go to my room and look out at the rain and think about all that's happened over the last few months. And I wait. I wait for Jerry to come back. I wait for Mama to come out of her room. I wait for the phone to ring. But none of these things happen. I never thought I'd say so, but right about now, I wouldn't even mind hearing one of Jerry's boring stories about some barrel he had to ship to Antigua that ended up in Anguilla instead. I wouldn't mind hearing that weird laugh of his. But Jerry doesn't come back that afternoon or even that night. I stay up until one, but I never hear the front door open. I never hear footsteps in the hallway. No voices, no noises, no "hey, hey, huh." There is only the trickle of raindrops against my window.

Mama doesn't leave her room at all. Not even to go to the bathroom. The next morning when I knock on the door, she doesn't answer. But when I try the knob, the door opens again.

"Girl, didn't I tell you to get going to your aunt and uncle's?" Mama asks. She's still in her black slip. Still lying in the same position as the day before when I brought her breakfast. I look around for the plate. It's on the floor near her bed. There's still food on it, but I can tell she ate a little.

"I just wanted to make sure you were okay."

"I was here taking care of myself a long time before you ever came around," she says. That sounds a little bit more like the Mama I'm used to.

"Go on, now, Faye. Go on to your aunt and uncle's."

"Okay, I will. But only if you answer this one question: What is it about me that makes it so hard for you to love me?"

Mama suddenly looks confused.

"You've never once told me you loved me. So I just want to know, why am I so hard to love?" I ask again.

Mama's eyes soften a little. She reaches for the box of Virginia Slims on her nightstand and takes out a cigarette, but she doesn't put it into her mouth or light it.

"What are you talking about?" she asks. "Of course I love you. You're my child."

"Then maybe it's that you don't like me."

She shakes her head slowly. "It's not you. It was never you. It's me. I can't seem to figure out what I'm feeling inside. I can't figure out why things make me as angry as they do. Life shouldn't make me as angry as it does. Running out of milk shouldn't make me as angry as it does. . . ." Her voice trails off and she lets out a long sigh.

"No, it's not you, Faye." Those are the last words she says to me. I stand around a while longer, but Mama seems to have zoned out.

I return to my room only long enough to grab my suitcase. I suppose I didn't realize exactly how heavy it was before, because it takes way too much energy to get it down the hall and out of the apartment. I guess when you're not really used to going anywhere, it's hard to gauge exactly how much to pack.

It's pretty warm outside, and it seems like there are a million people on the street. Four girls jump double dutch a couple of buildings away. One has her long hair in cornrows, and there are all these beads hanging from the end of each braid. I stand by for a few seconds, watching her hop around furiously, trying to figure out how she doesn't knock herself out from the force of her hair adornments. When she trips over the ropes and messes up, she turns to look questioningly at me and the suitcase resting near my leg. I take this as my cue to continue to the bus stop, so I grasp the handle of the suitcase and go back to hauling it down the street. But I only make it a few steps before another hand latches on to the handle. I look over to find Gerald standing next to me.

"What are you doing?" I ask.

"I saw you from my window. Where ya going?"

"To catch the bus to my aunt and uncle's house."

"For how long?"

"Don't know."

"Well, this is way too heavy for you to be dragging around. I'll carry it for you." He shakes my hand away. "Hey, if you're around at all this summer, maybe I could take you for an Italian ice or something," he says once we start walking.

"I don't know," I say.

"It's cool. I understand. Pretty girls always go for those good-looking guys."

I stop right there in my tracks. "You think *I'm* pretty?"

"Of course. Anyway, it's okay. You don't have to hang out with me if you don't want to."

I sneak a look at Gerald. All of a sudden, his teeth don't seem as horselike as they did before. And he wouldn't look lanky if he was sitting.

"It seems like it's gonna get pretty hot this summer," I say. "So, if I don't go visit my dad in Florida, I'm probably really gonna be wanting an Italian ice."

* * *

Uncle Paul's got his britches in a bunch when I get there. He's carrying on and screaming about me lugging a suitcase that's almost as big as me through the streets of Brooklyn; about why I didn't call so he could come and pick me up; about why my mother didn't help me. But I relay all that's happened over the past couple days, and he gets really quiet. I catch the look he shoots Aunt Nola's way before he goes storming out the door.

A few hours later, he's back. But he's not alone. Jerry is right there next to him. And he's asking to talk to me alone in the kitchen.

"I have something for you," he says as we walk in. And in his hand is an envelope with the American Airlines symbol on it. "It's a plane ticket to Florida."

"Did you buy this?" I ask.

"Nope. Your dad sent it last week."

"And you held on to it?"

"Negative there too. Your mama had it. Couldn't decide whether or not she was gonna have you go down there. But now, well, I guess she sees it might be a good thing for you."

"When?"

"End of the week."

"So you went over there with Uncle Paul? You saw her too?"

Jerry nods.

"She's acting strange, even for Mama," I say. "What do you think?"

"I think she's had a lot of things not go the way she's

wanted them to. I think she's had a lot of disappointments, and she's feeling real tired and beaten down. I don't think you know this, Faye, but she recently got let go from her job. I didn't even know it. Not until we just went over there. Anyway, she barely has enough energy to take care of herself right now, and she knows she has to be able to take care of herself before she can take care of you or anyone else, me included. So she's just gonna need some time. She's gonna have to figure out a way to get back her confidence and herself."

"Sounds to me like she's having some kinda breakdown," I say.

"What do you know about those kinda things?" Jerry asks. "I don't know if I'd call it that, Faye. Think right now I'd call it a life transition."

"How long will she be transitioning? How long will I be away?"

"Wish I could say maybe a few days or a week. But truth is, I don't know right yet. I don't think she knows right yet."

"So you still gonna be living there with her?"

"No. No. I don't think she needs any extra pressure from me right now. And I'm not a stupid man. I understand that I'm not her first choice. But I'll be there for her whenever she needs a friend. Whenever she needs some help. You can count on that."

I can tell that Jerry's sad, but he's trying to put up a strong front for me.

"Will I see you again?" I ask.

"Well, first of all, it's not like I'm dying. And I'm always popping in to see Paul here. But same thing goes for you as goes for your mama. Whenever you feel the need, just give old Jerry here a call."

Despite all the wetness and greasiness, I hug Jerry. And it's not nearly as bad as I thought it would be. Well, I make sure I avoid any face-to-hair contact by angling my head away. And I have to hold my breath a little to block out the burnt-chemical smell, but his hug is bearlike and firm. And I can feel how much he really cares.

39

"Faye, the money I gave you is to spend on things you need, not on me," Ms. Downer says as the lights in the number 6 train dim for a few seconds, then come back on full blast. "And if you wanted to take me out to eat, we could have done it in Brooklyn. There are plenty of fine restaurants there."

"Right, but the finest restaurants are in Manhattan. Besides, I'm gonna be gone the whole summer, so you should enjoy the time you get to spend with me now, even if we'll be spending it in Manhattan. And when was the last time you were here in the city, anyway?"

"I don't know. Maybe a couple of years. But there's really no need for me to come here anymore."

"I disagree," I say as I check my watch. It's two-fifteen and we're only a couple of stops from Seventy-Ninth Street, which means we're right on schedule.

"And why do you keep looking at your watch?"

"Because I don't want us to be late for our reservation."

"Will you tell me exactly where we're going, at least?"

"Upper East Side."

"Which is where we are now. But what kind of food? Which restaurant?"

"You never come here. You wouldn't know anyway," I say. "You're just gonna have to wait till we get there."

Once we get off the train, I hear the old lady calling for me to slow down. I didn't realize I was walking so fast. But when I stop and turn, I notice she's about six feet behind me. And this happens like three more times, and the place we're heading is only about four blocks from the station. I have to force my legs to go slower to stay at the old lady's pace. I'm so excited, it's as if I've lost all control of my muscles. I steer her toward a familiar-looking building. Since it's such a warm day, there are a lot more patients in the courtyard than the last time I was there.

"Faye, this doesn't look like a restaurant," Ms. Downer says as we slow down.

"It's not. But I need to make one small stop."

"What, you're checking me into a nursing home?"

"No," I say with a chuckle. "It's so much better than anything you could ever imagine."

I spot an empty table in the farthest corner of the courtyard and lead her over. She's pretty hesitant about it all, but she follows me. Once that's done, I run into the building.

After talking to the really large woman at reception, I sit down next to a couple of those crazy-looking old people who seem to be able to look in only one direction—straight ahead—and who smell as if they've been bathed in Vicks

VapoRub. I sit there waiting and waiting. Every couple of minutes, I go over to the front door and stick my head out to make sure the old lady hasn't taken off. It's killing me having to wait. And even though only ten minutes pass before Delaine shows up, it seems like a lifetime.

But Delaine doesn't come alone. There's some big sumo-wrestler-like security guard tagging along. Like any of the five feet and ninety-five pounds of me would be able to harm Delaine in any way. But before she can say anything or ask her goony sidekick to remove me, I start flapping my lips.

"This will only take a minute," I say. "And you can have this man follow you. But there's something out in the courtyard I think you should have a look at."

She shoots a glance at the guard, then looks at me again. "Please . . ."

"Let's make it fast," she says. "Scotty, just stay close by."

I walk through the door first, followed by Delaine and then Scotty.

"It's just over here," I say as I head to the table at the corner of the courtyard where the old lady is seated.

The closer Delaine gets, the faster she begins to walk. And then she clicks into supernurse mode.

"What's wrong with her?" she asks.

Ms. Downer turns toward us and begins to stand slowly. At first there's not any recognition on her face.

"Are you all right?" Delaine asks her. "It might be better if you sit back down."

But Ms. Downer doesn't say anything. She just keeps

staring and staring. And then I see this lightbulb go on in her eyes.

"She doesn't live here with us," Delaine says to me.

"No. She doesn't."

"Well, we can't just accept people off the street. We go through a whole admittance process."

"She's not trying to move in. She has her own home. In Brooklyn." But this doesn't seem to trigger anything in Ms. Downer's daughter.

"Her name is Evelyn," I say. I don't say anything more. I don't need to. Delaine just freezes. Her body straightens completely and her head snaps back.

As I look from one to the other, I suck in my breath. This is electrifying. I want to set off fireworks Fourth of July–style and moonwalk like Michael Jackson did on that Motown twenty-fifth anniversary special.

"Delaine?" The old lady's voice comes out all crackly and hoarse as she says those two syllables.

They just look at each other for a while. The daughter opens her mouth as if she's about to say something, but nothing comes out. Then the old lady does the same. I'm thinking a hug is going to come, a holding of hands even, but there's only a shake of the head by the younger woman, who then kind of waves the guard off. Once he turns to go back into the nursing home, she sits. The old lady does the same. So now they're sitting next to each other and they're both kind of staring out into the distance, not saying or doing anything much at all.

"What are you doing here?" Delaine finally asks.

"I don't know," the old lady says as she looks my way.

I start backing off. I move all the way to the other side of the courtyard, but I never take my eyes off them. I understand they might need a little time to build up to a big show of emotion.

Finally, a steady rhythm comes to the movement of their lips, and there seems to be some sort of conversation. But I can't hear what's being said. I can't even guess what it could be. Neither one ever moves to sit across from the other. Neither one ever embraces the other. Then, after about fifteen minutes, Delaine gets up and quickly walks off into the nursing home, while Ms. Downer just continues sitting there.

I stay put, thinking maybe the daughter is about to come back out; that maybe she's just gone to tell her supervisor she has to take the rest of the afternoon off to be with her recently rediscovered mother. But after a couple of minutes pass and she still hasn't returned, the suspense gets the best of me. I run over to Ms. Downer and flop down across from her.

"What happened? What did she say?" I'm practically yelling, I'm so excited. "Is she gonna come visit you in Brooklyn? Maybe have you over to her house for dinner? Is she coming back out? When are you two gonna really sit down together and catch up?"

Ms. Downer is very quiet, and I begin to sense that the tears bunched up in the corners of her eyes aren't from joy.

"I don't suppose there will be any dinners, Faye. She's in shock, I think. It took her a long time to get to a place where she was able to move on from her feelings of abandonment and hurt. Years, really. And she thinks it's manipulative of me to try to get to her with the use of a child."

I feel as if I've been punched in the stomach, forcing all the air out of me. It wasn't supposed to turn out this way. Delaine Lawson was supposed to have gotten all emotional and sad-happy. She was supposed to have been full of forgiveness.

"But it wasn't your fault," I say. "You didn't even know. I was the one who did everything. And the past is the past, right? Why can't she just get over it?"

"If only things were that easy. If only life were like a movie. But it's not. I can't tell you how many times I was supposed to go and see her, and I just never showed up. That was when there was still the chance of a relationship. The few times I did go, I made sure I had had more than a few drinks, to try to deal with my guilt. But the drinking made me say and do some horrible things. When she was about fifteen, I decided that I was stable enough to take care of her again. But she told me I had lost my chance. That she'd rather stay in the situation she was in, living with her grandparents. I was so hurt, I went off and did what I did best. Got drunk. But then I showed up again. And the things I said to her, you shouldn't even say to your worst enemy. They were vile and filthy and horrible. And I did it in front of her friends." One of the tears escapes and rolls down her cheek. She wipes it away quickly. "How did you even find her?" she asks.

"I got the film man to tell me her name. And he said she

was working at a nursing home in Manhattan, so I called all the clinics and places like that till I found the one she worked in."

"You never cease to surprise me, little girl."

"I'm sorry, ma'am. I didn't mean to cause you any trouble. I was just trying to help. I figured if she could know you like I do, then she'd be your daughter again. And you'd have a family and wouldn't have to be alone. Don't be mad at me."

"Mad? How could I be?" the old lady says. "You were trying to do something good. But things aren't so simple. The feelings she has for me have been built up over so many years. Can't just expect her to lose them and say all is forgiven in a matter of a few minutes. Still, at least I got to see her."

"Maybe after some time, she'll think things over and reach out to you," I say hopefully.

"Maybe," Ms. Downer says, though from the tone of her voice, I'm not so sure she really believes this.

* * *

The day before I leave for Florida, the old lady invites me to spend the afternoon with her. The entire bus ride to her place, I keep hoping that maybe she won't be the only one there to greet me when I show up. That maybe her daughter will be right by her side. But once I walk into her apartment, it doesn't take long for me to realize that we're alone. Ms. Downer seems to have made whatever peace she's needed to with how things turned out. I guess I'll have to make mine . . . but I'm still going to hope.

40

I look straight up at the small coconuts in the tree that's shading me. Daddy put a hammock up between two of these little midget palms. I'm not so sure how good an idea that is, considering how much it would smart if one of those coconuts got loose and came barreling down. I'm thinking concussion territory. But they're the only two trees in the backyard that are sturdy enough to hold someone's weight and spaced out the right distance, and I've been bouncing around for a month and a half and haven't ended up in the hospital yet. Besides, the trees are so short, the coconuts wouldn't have a very long distance to travel, so I'm sure that would cut down on the amount of cranial damage.

I like the way I feel when I'm laid out here, just swinging free and staring up at the sky. When the clouds shift a certain way, a little bit of the sunlight sneaks in through the spaces in the palm leaves and roasts whichever part of my body it happens to hit.

I can hear my baby brother crying from inside the house.

He's pretty whiny and annoying, so I'm glad I'm outside. Sometimes when I'm nearby, Melba will try to get me to pick him up and rock him back and forth, and I end up having flashbacks of my time at Ms. Viola's. I'll do it every once in a while, but it's pretty unsettling, because he'll just keep crying and shaking and wheezing and convulsing. And I become convinced he's about to explode in my arms like a human grenade. But he never does.

I hear Melba's voice all calm and lilting as she sings him a little song. She has a strong Caribbean accent. When Boy George or Simon Le Bon or George Michael sing, you can't even tell they're British. I figured it would be the same for everybody. But when Melba sings her little lullabies or her mop-the-floor songs, there's no mistaking that Trinidadian accent.

Daddy's fiancée is a bit ditzy, but she's nice enough. She's always making coconut buns and cakes and trying to ply me with them. She's pretty skinny herself, so I don't know why she's got this "fatten up Faye" obsession going on. But she's convinced that, given time, she will have me as plump as a peach.

When I first got down here, I tried not to think about Mama. I just tried to focus on getting to know Daddy again, and his soon-to-be-wife. But I did find out Mama's been going into Kings County every day for some retuning. Not my word. It's what Daddy and Aunt Nola and Uncle Paul called it. "Retuning." Makes it sound like she's a guitar that needs its strings tightened. Anyway, she hasn't been happy and is hoping these sessions will show her how to be.

I feel sorry that we've never had the kind of relationship other mothers and daughters have. It's funny how I used to dream about a hurricane coming to New York and blowing her away, or a pterodactyl flying overhead and grabbing her in its talons and taking her off to the Land of the Lost. I should be shouting from rooftops now that I don't have to be around her all the time, now that I don't have to deal with her madness and her meanness. But I'm not. There's not really happiness or sadness about this. I don't know. It sort of feels like I've become one of those kids like Diane Jackson or Sheila Gray from school. One of those kids without a mother. Anytime someone would ask them about their moms, they would say she wasn't around anymore, and it would always get all tense and awkward. Diane's mom died, but everyone knew Sheila's mom just got up one day, decided she didn't want to have to deal with kids or a husband, or any responsibility at all, really, and just plumb took off. So everyone would try to avoid talking about parents and moms and Mother's Day and stuff like that around them. Now I feel kind of like Diane and Sheila. Well, maybe not like Diane, since there's no chance her mom will ever come back.

I'm relieved to be staying in a place where people talk and laugh at the dinner table and ask how my day was and really care to hear my answer. But the weird thing is, I feel a little guilty about being relieved. Still, it's been so nice seeing my dad every day. When he was living with me and Mama, it would only be once or maybe twice a week that we'd all be able to have dinner together, since he was always traveling around trying to make money playing his bass. Here I feel like I'm part of a real family. I feel like if I were to walk out into the street and get hit by a car, there are people who wouldn't tell me it was my fault for causing the accident; people who would come running to the hospital to make sure I was okay, and maybe even bring me *Right On!* magazines and chocolates. It's nice to know there's someone out there who doesn't blame me for the world being bad, or for the Son of Sam killing all those people, or for John Paul I dying after only a month as pope, or for all those folks in India being poor. It's nice to not be blamed for someone having a bad day. It's nice to not have to try to be invisible because I'm afraid if I make any noise it will remind that person I'm there and only make them angrier. It's nice to not feel I have to whisper to myself to make sure my voice is still intact. It's nice to feel that me being me, and me being alive, can actually make someone happy.

What all this means for me right now is that I have to decide whether to go back to New York in two weeks and move back in with Aunt Nola and Uncle Paul and keep going to Bishop Marshall, or stay here in Fort Lauderdale and attend the local high school. Daddy wants me to stay, of course. Part of me wants to, but I'd miss Keisha and the old lady. And this would be my third school in two years. Daddy's already enrolled me, just in case, and I only have a few more days before I have to give him my decision.

As I watch a little blue-and-green hummingbird whiz about, I try to think of what the old lady said about forgiveness. Gosh, I haven't spoken to her since I first got down here. I'm going to have to ask Daddy if I can call her over the weekend. Anyway, it's not that I can't forgive Mama for being so mean to me. It's just that I can't forget how it felt to live with all that meanness. And I don't ever want to know that feeling again.

I allow my eyelids to close for a few seconds. When I open them, Melba is standing over me holding my brother in one arm and a rectangular white box in the other.

"What's in the box?" I ask.

"Don't know. It's not addressed to me. Came for you express mail," she says.

"I've never gotten anything express mail. Hardly ever even get anything regular mail."

"Want to open it together?" she asks.

"I'm good," I say. That's the other thing about Melba. She doesn't really understand boundaries. I wait for her to head back to the house before swinging my legs over the side of the hammock and studying the box. It's from a "W. Franklin," but I have no idea who that is.

Once I get the sealed flap open, I notice a book. The front cover is made up of shades of gray, except for this one bright stroke of blue, the hat on a woman's head. And even though it's a sketch, I know who it's supposed to be. *Lady in the Blue Fedora* is in black cursive letters at the top, with the words *The Disappearance of What Would Have Been a Hollywood Legend* at the bottom.

There is a sheet of typing paper folded over a white business envelope that has my name on it. I unfold the paper first. It's a note from the archivist that reads:

This is called an advance reader's copy. Evelyn
wanted you to see the book even before it was released.
And make sure you have a look at the dedication pages.

But I'm totally confused, because I remember what the archivist had said about when the book would be made public. But if it's an advance copy, does that mean it hasn't been made public yet? Does that mean the old lady is still alive? I quickly flip to the first of two dedication pages.

There are only five words written on it: *Thank you, Evelyn. Bill Franklin.* But the next page contains a dedication from Ms. Downer.

To my daughter, whom, through no one's fault but
my own, I never got the chance to know. And to young
Faye. I will always be grateful for the company you
gave in some of my loneliest hours.

I close the book and just stare at the envelope that has my name written on it. And even though it's like a thousand and fifty degrees with swamp-like humidity, my hand starts to shake. So I take a really deep breath, lift the flap, and pull the letter out. And my eyes focus on this flowery cursive with big rounded letters.

I once met a little girl who had lost her way. I didn't
think there was any hope for her. She was just one of
the many children in this sometimes harsh city who
lacked the guidance and the discipline to be able to just

be young. And she would end up as another statistic. I was convinced of this. I never thought I'd see her again. Not so sure I wanted to see her again. At the time, I was just focused on seeing another day. But she came back. And I couldn't figure out whether she was the boldest kid I'd ever seen or was just stupid. There was a part of me that wanted to hold her in my arms and squeeze her until she saw the error of her ways. And there was another part that didn't want to have a thing to do with her. I figured if I kept her at arm's length, I'd never see her again. But here she came, back again. And again. And as I got to know her, I got to know the heart of a confused little girl. And I wondered, Is that how my little girl felt? Is that how she felt, knowing her mother had left her for something she thought was better? Did my actions ever cause my own little girl to engage in such destructive behaviors? Did she ever feel like turning her back on the world?

Why didn't I call the police once I realized exactly who you were? Because of that guilt I felt. I thought, maybe if I did a good deed for you, I'd in some way be forgiven for the bad deeds I had done to my own child. But as I got to know you, I began to think of you as my grandchild.

If your eyes are seeing these words, Faye, it means we will not have any more afternoons together sipping tea or strolling in the park. But as you become a young woman, I hope you take with you the few lessons you might have learned from me. Remember to always

be you, and not the you someone else wants you to
be. Don't be the you you think you ought to be to win
someone's acceptance.

Don't waste your time craving the love of those who
don't love you. You cannot make someone feel a certain
way for you. If the person you are isn't good enough for
them, know that you will eventually attract someone it
is good enough for.

And find it in your heart to forgive your mother,
for there are so many things about her life you will
never understand because you will not have ever
lived it as she has. She has to go through her trials
and tribulations. Not everything she does is right or
good, but if you hold on to feelings of anger over her
behavior, it might end up affecting the treatment of
your own children later in life.

If, as the years creep by, you can remember only
one thing about this old woman, I hope it's these words
I've written for you today. You are a very special young
woman, and I call myself fortunate to have had you in
my life, no matter how short that period has been.

I refold the letter and look up at the sky again. I don't try
to control the tears as they begin to fall. I don't understand
why things happen in life the way they do. Maybe it's not for
me to understand. But I feel as if I've lost the grandmother
I've only begun to know. And not even thinking of Michael
Jackson doing the moonwalk can make me feel any better
about this.

The colorful hummingbird flutters back over and hovers just above my head. And suddenly, the decision I have to make about going to school comes to me as clear as day. I'm going to go back to Brooklyn and move in with Aunt Nola and Uncle Paul to finish up my schooling at Bishop Marshall. That way, Mama can come visit me, and maybe we can get to know each other all over again. Maybe we can be friends. If it doesn't work out, at least I gave it a try. But if it does work out, maybe I'll finally have a real mother.

I can't seem to stop looking at that hummingbird, and I find myself thinking back to some of the lessons we learned in religious studies class. If there really is such a thing as resurrection, I wonder if the old lady is somewhere in another dimension looking down at me. And if there is such a thing as reincarnation, I wonder whether she's watching from a place even closer by.

"Ms. Downer?" I call out to the hummingbird. Its wings seem to flap even faster, and it shoots up into one of the palm trees.

I'd like to think that she's as close as that little bird. And why not? I'm starting to think that life can hold a whole lot of possibilities.

Acknowledgments

Thank you, Katie Shea, for having enough faith in my blind query letter to want to read more of my work, and then for taking me on as a client. I am also very grateful to Rebecca Short for her belief in my main character's voice, and for tirelessly going over my manuscript and giving valuable notes that helped to make that voice even stronger. My family and great friends keep me happy and sane when I'm not writing. I especially want to single out Courtney Byrd and Anthony Palmer, who enthusiastically read the manuscript in its early stages and gave honest opinions and much-appreciated suggestions.

About the Author

CAROLITA BLYTHE was born in Kingston, Jamaica, and raised in New York City. A graduate of Syracuse University, she lives in Los Angeles, where, when not writing novels, she works behind the scenes on television shows. Her debut novel was *The Cricket's Serenade*. She has also published travel articles and short stories. An avid traveler, Carolita is a New Yorker at heart and enjoys spending summers worshiping the Yankees and autumns pulling for the Jets.